THE PLEASURE OF HER COMPANY

MRS DASHWOOD'S STORY

SALLIANNE HINES

A GRASSLANDS PRESS publication

www.salliannehines.com

Cover design by Sallianne Hines and Rachael Ritchey

Interior design/formatting by Sallianne Hines

- ISBN 978-1-7333844-4-5 (paperback)
- ISBN 979-8-9862078-5-8 (hardcover)
- ISBN 978-1-7333844-7-6 (large print)
- ISBN 978-1-7333844-5-2 (ebook)

ABOUT THE REGENCY ERA

OR — WHY DO THEY CARE SO MUCH ABOUT GETTING MARRIED?

In the Regency Era, a *gentleman* was a man who had/needed no profession other than managing his estate or wealth, and the title *gentleman* might also apply to a clergyman or anyone in trade who had enough wealth to be deemed "respectable."

A *gentleman's daughter* could not, for the most part, inherit an estate, own land, or have money of her own. Under the early nineteenth century British legal system, "primogeniture" determined that inheritances went from father to eldest son, in whole—estates were not divided amongst the children, even the sons, because that would lessen the wealth and power of the estate. If there were no sons, the estate was often entailed to the nearest-related male relative. This left a widow and daughters with little to nothing and wholly dependent on the kindness and generosity of the male who did inherit.

Lacking kindness from the inheriting male, the widow and daughters would depend on other relations—as Mrs Dashwood did in *Sense & Sensibility* when her cousin Sir John Middleton rented her a cottage. Some money might be left for a girl's dowry if the estate was not heavily encumbered (mortgaged); but when a woman married, all her wealth was usually assigned to her husband to use wisely or to gamble away, as he chose.

Women in this economic/social class of "the landed gentry" were not allowed to work. If they did not "marry well," their lives could be unpleasant indeed.

CHARACTERS FROM Austen's *Sense & Sensibility*

Mrs (Francine) Dashwood—*widow of Henry, formerly of Norland Park, now resident at Barton Cottage*

Elinor Dashwood Ferrars—*married to Edward Ferrars, disinherited clergyman on Colonel Brandon's estate*

Marianne Dashwood Brandon—*married to Colonel Christopher Brandon, retired miliary man and owner of Delaford estate*

Margaret Dashwood—*youngest of three sisters, still at Barton Cottage with her mother Francine*

Sir John Middleton—*owns Barton Park, leases Barton Cottage to his cousin Francine*

Lady Middleton—*insipid wife of Sir John, talks only of her children*

Mrs (Lucretia) Jennings—*widowed mother of Lady Middleton, has two married daughters, a large jointure, and nothing to do but marry off other young ladies*

ADDITIONAL CHARACTERS CREATED FOR THIS BOOK

Mrs (Emmeline) Harrington—*widowed sister of Francine Dashwood, visiting from the midlands, will soon have the dower house at Hawthorn Hall*

Mrs (Cecelia) Whittaker—*older married neighbor and friend of Mrs Jennings*

Mr Charles Creighton—*recently widowed brother-in-law of Colonel Brandon, owns Whitwell estate, has a son (James)*

Mr Cecil Walford—*widower, owner of Southleigh estate*

Rees Newbury—*young man who has caught Margaret's eye but leaves for the Navy*

Rose Carey—*good friend of Margaret's, granddaughter of the Whittakers*

Admiral Marcus Tennant—*a dashing widower, retired from the Navy, lives at Bellevue at Sidmouth, has a daughter Florentina (Florrie)*

Mr Geoffrey Manning—*owner of cliffside dwelling Atlas Hall, loves hawking*

Mr Michael Wheeler—*friend of Mr Manning, also lives at Atlas Hall*

CHAPTER ONE

*T*hank goodness for Margaret. The boisterous spirit —and unwed status—of Francine Dashwood's youngest daughter obliged such a devoted mother to refrain from dwelling on her own situation. Widowed some four years, Francine had begun to question her life's purpose. She was no one's wife. No one's daughter. She was still a sister—as Emmeline's temporary installation at Barton Cottage reminded her daily—but Francine's older sister required nothing from her. Emmeline had always been self-sufficient; at a young age, she became mistress of their childhood home when their dear mother passed away unexpectedly. With Francine's parental duties now waning, she concluded she would soon be needed by no one.

Both older daughters had married well, and Francine now found herself with an abundance of empty hours. Her daughters' homes *were* an easy distance—if one could call carriage travel easy. And the journey might be accomplished in half a day or less with good weather, sparing one the worry about questionable inns and their even more questionable food.

"Francine, will you not call for tea?" Emmeline's voice was

brisk with irritation as she swept into the room. "A lack of visitors does not excuse your servant from providing tea at the proper time, especially when you are entertaining a house guest, such as myself. Standards must be maintained. As my dear authoress Fanny Burney would say, *'Insensibility, of all kinds and on all occasions, most moves my imperial displeasure.'*"

Francine blinked and hastily tucked away her distressed thoughts.

"I do fear I am insensible, of time certainly. My apologies, sister. Life here at Barton Cottage passes in a far less formal style than it did at Norland."

Her sister shot her a speaking look. "Life passes in the way we direct it, Fran."

The dart struck deep, with a sting. But Francine knew not how to direct her own life, or even how to determine a course. Her only experience with giving direction was bidding her servants, and even that made her uneasy. With so little money, what life choices were open to her? What direction could even be considered? Life was like being lost at sea, was it not?—although her own feet had never left the shore.

She rose and called for tea.

"Will that be all, ma'am?" Betsy asked after laying a tray of all things necessary for a proper tea, one that would meet Emmeline's exacting standards.

"Yes. Thank you."

Whilst Emmeline took a turn about the room, gazing out of each of the two small windows in turn, Francine poured. Even today's welcome spring sunlight could not dissuade her of a sense that time was marching on. And with that came a troubling vision of herself, dwindling into a lonely old age—a regrettable but not infrequent consequence of having married a much older man.

After Henry's death, her daughter Elinor's cool practical judgement had guided the Dashwood household. To own the truth, even before that sad episode, Francine had allowed her eldest to assume many of the mistress's duties of their fine estate at Norland Park in Sussex. As a child, Francine herself had been allowed to indulge her own girlish inclinations, imaginings, and artistic expressions whilst her parents indulged themselves at engagements of their own. As a married woman living at Norland Park, Francine had preferred to read romances and poetry, produce artful needlework, and tend to her hothouse flowers rather than oversee the household. But here, at Barton Cottage, there was less time for reading—and no library. Needlework now involved more repair than artful expression. And there was no hothouse. Her desolation at losing dear Henry was compounded by the passing of beloved Norland to her step-son. Francine and her daughters were forced to retrench to a small cottage on her cousin Sir John Middleton's estate, Barton Park, deep in Devonshire.

Francine had a kindred soul in her second daughter, who shared her mother's romantic sensibility. Marianne's lilting voice and well-executed notes on the pianoforte were greatly missed now, as was her impassioned recitation of poetry when the family gathered in the evening—all lost to Francine after Marianne's marriage to Colonel Brandon and her move to his estate at Delaford. It hardly seemed a family now with just herself and Margaret, who was no replacement for Marianne.

Her youngest daughter favoured exploration and was enraptured with the idea of world travel and adventure—things Francine had no desire to experience, especially at her present age, which was known to be four and forty. At nearly seventeen, Margaret was expected to begin to move in society, with a proper chaperone of course. Such social opportunities were less than abundant in the Devon countryside but Francine put her daughter forward where she could, although she still found it awkward to socialize without a husband. Fortunately, Sir John loved nothing more than to give parties, and the Dashwoods had made the acquaintance of several amiable families in the neighbourhood, being regularly included in the local array of invitations and outings. Barton wasn't Norland, but it was pleasant enough.

"Fran," said Emmeline as she sat down and reached for a biscuit, "Margaret will soon be off making her life with someone or other, somewhere or other—and you will be alone. Have you found no eligible men hereabouts?"

Francine spluttered over her tea. "Eligible men? Why, I … do you mean … for marriage? For me?" Whilst she enjoyed reading novels about romance, she had not envisioned someone her own age having such notions or experiencing such affairs.

Emmeline frowned. "To be sure. Do not tell me you have given it no thought? Although your girls are not far away, they have their own lives. Elinor has not the space to accommodate you at the vicarage. You are wise enough, I hope, to refuse the role of permanent guest to Marianne at Delaford. However will you manage all alone?"

Francine's heart froze.

Emmeline continued her observations between sips of the fragrant tea. "Perhaps you *are* resigned to staying with Marianne? And visiting Margaret, wherever she ends up?" Emmeline sniffed. "*I* would wish for a home of my own, where I was not just a guest, always to be flitting here and there like a butterfly, forever at the whim of others." She set her cup down with a clink and stared hard at her sister.

Francine was all astonishment. That was *exactly* the future she had envisioned for herself—that of a guest, hopefully a welcome one. She was close to all her daughters, in different ways, yet she did not wish to burden them or interfere in their lives. As the image of being a perpetual guest was held up in front of her, she found the concept wanting indeed. But her other choice—staying at Barton Cottage alone—caused the dismal spectre of those dark rainy months to creep back even now and overshadow the lovely spring day. At present—with her sister visiting and Margaret still about—Francine could brush off such melancholy, but it loomed like an ominous cloud on the not-so-distant-horizon.

Before Henry died, she had never pondered the future. He had taken care of everything ... everything except the future of his wife and daughters. Francine had been told about the legalities that caused Norland—and much of what she had always considered hers—to be left to her less-than-generous stepson and his horrid wife. But such details were tedious and she had not the patience to make sense of them, then or now.

She watched as her sister nibbled at a piece of cake. Emmeline's son was away at school; but when he married, he would inherit Hawthorn Hall and Emmeline would become a dowager and be displaced from the great house, as Francine herself had been displaced from Norland.

Emmeline was now six and forty, and widowed for more than a year. Her womanly curves were draped in lavender, a colour that became her well and flattered her sculpted silver coiffure. She would surely capture the interest of widowers in search of a mistress for their manor or estate—a role for which Emmeline was eminently suited.

Francine was curious. "And what of you, Em? Now that you've cast off your widow's weeds, do *you* think of marrying again?"

"How could I *not*? And I am blessed with a far better situation than you, Fran—no thanks to your Henry, bless his dear departed soul. Yes, I will lose the great house to my son—who has a strong interest in a certain young lady and will likely marry soon—but at least I will have the Hawthorn dowager house as my own, to run as I choose." A smile played about her lips. "Unless ..." her eyes sparkled "... I can contrive something more desirable." She took a sip of tea, then locked eyes with Francine. "There have been some tolerable men in attendance at our recent social activities. What of Mr Cecil Walford? Or that vicar in the neighbouring parish—he is also single, I hear. And people talked much of an admiral coming to visit—who has a splendid estate near the sea. I wonder when he shall arrive? And what of Colonel Brandon's brother-in-law, just recently widowed, that Mr Creighton? He is said to be quite handsome."

The faces of these men spun through Francine's fragmented mind. She was somewhat acquainted with Charles Creighton, a friendly man with a kindly air who lived nearby. His wife—the colonel's sister—had died at their home in the lake country some months ago, and Mr Creighton had not yet returned into Devonshire. Francine was as acquainted as she wished to be with Mr Walford, a lusty man of portly build with a cynical disposition and a small but unencumbered estate. She recalled hearing of other single men at times, but had paid no attention. Any matrimonial thoughts she had at present, or in the near future, were for Margaret. She could not think of herself whilst Margaret was in need of a match ... could she? No. Certainly not.

Francine looked at her sister with consideration. "I admit, Em, that I have at times let my imagination run wild, like in the romantic affairs one reads about in novels." She sighed. "And I *would* welcome someone to make decisions and such, especially now that Elinor is married and in a home of her own." She looked down at her empty teacup, then leveled her green eyes at her sister. "Do you have a plan for ... romance? At our age?"

Emmeline lifted a knowing brow.

CHAPTER TWO

*T*he two sisters and Margaret were preparing to walk over the downs when their manservant, Thomas, announced morning callers. They set their bonnets aside and gathered in the drawing room where they were presently joined by Sir John of Barton Park and Mr Cecil Walford of Southleigh. Sir John's dogs circled outside the cottage, barking raucously.

"Good morning Sir John, Mr Walford." Francine was as rattled by the noise of the dogs as she was by the early hour of the call. "How nice to see you again." The ladies curtsied.

"Thank you," Mr Walford said with a bow. He flushed. "My apologies for the early hour of our call." His eyes moved to Emmeline and lingered there.

"No need for apologies, Walford." Sir John slapped his friend's shoulder and laughed. "We don't stand on ceremony here, do we!" he cried, winking at the ladies. "Indeed, indeed. Ready to go off, are ye ladies? Well, we won't keep ye. Off ourselves we are, for some shooting. The dogs are eager, yes indeed!" He guffawed and then remembered his errand. "Yes, well, I *am* here with a particular purpose: to invite you all to dinner and cards at the Park. Tuesday next. The Whittakers, the Careys, Walford here, Creighton—if he has returned from the North—and young Rees Newbury"—here he eyed Margaret—"plus a few others will attend; oh, and of course my dear mama-in-law; she is staying with us you know. I shall send the carriage at four. Now put on those bonnets and off ye go!" He grabbed his friend by the arm and with a quick bow the gentlemen were gone.

Emmeline turned to her sister and rolled her eyes. "That man! What is he thinking, calling so early? And such an invitation! He did not even allow you to answer. How *can* you tolerate such coarse behaviour, Francine? I would not put up with it if I were you." She huffed as she tied her bonnet ribbons under her left ear.

A soft giggle escaped Margaret.

Francine shook her head. "Now, Emmeline, things are different here in the country. And what can I say to him? I am obliged to my cousin for the very roof over my head. I dare not quarrel on etiquette, although at times things do get awkward ..." She worked diligently at her own ribbons.

Margaret looked at them both. "I like him. He always speaks his mind, and very directly. Sometimes such 'properness' as you speak of, Aunt, results in laughable blunders, or worse—don't you agree?"

The sisters exchanged a meaningful look.

Emmeline shook her head. "Country manners may have more scope, Margaret—especially for gentlemen—but see that your own courtesy meets society's expectations and you will avoid all manner of problems. Mark my words."

"I rather doubt it is that simple," Margaret replied as she stepped out the door.

The sisters traded another look and followed after her.

~

On the appointed day, the carriage arrived promptly at four.

"I haven't seen Rose in almost a fortnight," Margaret said, her eyes alight. "I hope her life has been more exciting than mine of late. With Mr Newbury in London these several days, the only thing I can call fine is the weather." She stared out of the carriage window at the blossoms filling the fragrant spring landscape.

"At least we shall see some faces other than our own tonight," Emmeline said. "Besides, the meals at Barton Park are almost worth the questionable propriety of some of the company, and the total lack of intelligent conversation. Is Lady Middleton always so insipid?"

"Emmeline! Lady Middleton's manner is everything proper."

"And everything boring," added Margaret. "I have never heard an interesting comment or intelligent observation pass her lips. She talks only of her children. I am glad others will be there tonight for relief, else we shall be as dull as a clowder of cats."

Soon enough they entered the drawing room at Barton Park. After paying her respects to Lady Middleton, Margaret hastened to join her friend, Rose Carey, and it looked to be a lively exchange.

Sir John's mother-in-law, Mrs Jennings, bustled up, took an arm of each of the sisters, and joined them in watching the interactions amongst the younger people. "Two such spirited and lovely young ladies," she remarked. "I hope tonight will give them a good deal to talk about. I have reason to believe it will when Miss Dashwood discovers that a certain young man is back from town." Her hooting laughter filled the room, momentarily turning many heads their way.

Francine cringed.

The three watched as young Rees Newbury approached Margaret from behind. When he stepped before her, her face lit up. Francine expected Margaret wished to jump up and down with excitement but she was pleased her daughter managed to limit her delight to her smile and the sparkle in her eyes. Mr Newbury could be in no doubt of her pleasure at seeing him. He had also brought a friend with him from town, which would certainly increase the gaiety for the young people.

Mrs Jennings nodded towards them. "I am sure Mrs Smith wishes she could leave Allenham to young Newbury; he is said to be her favourite grandson. But there are two ahead of him in the succession set out by her late husband. Ah, such a lively, handsome young man, with his dark curls —and those blue eyes. How could any young lady resist him?"

"All the young ladies must resist him now," Francine said. "He is for the Navy. I wonder when he departs?"

"We can be sure Margaret will discover that tonight," Emmeline said. Her countenance held a wistful cast. "Young love. So precious. Can it really have been so long ago?" A sigh escaped her.

"Young or old, love is no longer a card in *my* hand," Mrs Jennings observed, "except for the part I can play in bringing two souls together." She narrowed her eyes at the sisters. "Two souls of *any* age, you may be sure."

Francine's eyes grew large but Emmeline's mouth turned up with pleasure and she said, "Indeed, love has no age limits, in my estimation. Perhaps that card is yet hidden in your hand, Mrs Jennings?" Emmeline's eyes twinkled in a teasing way.

Mrs Jennings roared with laughter, her ample bosom and multiple chins shaking like currant jelly.

Francine lowered her eyes to avoid the stares aimed at them.

Emmeline glanced over the guests in attendance. "Now tell us, who might be eligible hereabouts?"

Mrs Jennings shook her head. "As a match for me, I cannot say. Most of the men my age are dead, or equally not worth having. Now for you two, there *are* some eligible widowers and maybe even single men in the larger neighbourhood. Sad to say, the war has depleted the selection. Ah, here is Mrs Whittaker who can surely add to our knowledge. What do you say, Camelia? We are talking of eligible matches for these two handsome sisters. They are finished with mourning and eager to marry again," she declared as her eyes scanned the room.

Crimson flooded Francine's cheeks at such presumption. "Mrs Jennings jokes, of course," she mumbled.

The tiny woman with a cloud of white hair looked at Mrs Jennings and smiled. "She does joke—better than most—but never about love. She fancies herself a matchmaker. I must say, with my bewitching insight and her talent for making people appear out of hedgerows, we have made a fair number of matches between us, have we not Lucretia?" She tilted her head.

"We have indeed. And I will continue to do until I am planted in the ground." Mrs Jennings' laughter again trilled about the room.

Francine blushed as several eyes turned their way. Mrs Jennings was the loudest voice and the largest presence at any gathering. Fortunately, her kind heart endeared her to most everyone.

Dinner was announced and a lively time it was. Margaret sat next to Mr Newbury, her face wreathed in smiles. He seemed equally pleased, especially when he could make her laugh. Many conversations crossed the large table and people often seemed to speak to no one in particular—especially Sir John, whose jovial voice rang above the others. Cecil Walford was seated next to Emmeline—Francine suspected Mrs Jennings' hand in that.

"Mrs Harrington, pray, how long will be your stay in our county?" He asked as he shoved a bite of roast mutton into a mouth already bulging in the cheeks.

Emmeline's eyes flamed. It was just dinner conversation, but Francine knew her sister found Cecil Walford's company particularly annoying.

"I do not know, sir. And now, do refresh my memory— where is your home?" She was adept at turning a question back unanswered on an unwelcome inquisitor.

After a gulp of wine he replied, "Southleigh, my estate, is located between here and Sidmouth, which is a village by the sea you know. Tell me about your home, Mrs Harrington. Do I remember correctly you are from the Midlands? Are there any millworks in your area?"

"Millworks? Heavens, no. Hawthorn Hall is in the country and a very respectable estate. My son has inherited and shall soon take charge, when he has completed his schooling and married."

"You are a widow then." He looked her up and down. "Plenty of good years left, I wager." He glanced at her clothing. "Are you in light mourning? Or do you wear lavender because it becomes you so well?" His eyes glinted at her over his wine glass as he chugged on it.

Emmeline bristled. "I thank you for the … compliment, sir. My husband passed a twelve-month ago, or a little more. And you—are you a widower?"

"My sympathies, madam," he said, lightly laying his hand on hers. He seemed not to notice her slight shudder. "A widower? Oh, my. Yes. Sadly, my dear Sophie died … mmm … ten years ago now. They say I am a confirmed loner. But *I* say

I am merely particular. And I am in need of a wife ... to run household things, you know? I have other demands on my time and can spare none trying to manage this and that."

Emmeline slid her hand away and into her lap. "Mr Walford, are you in trade? Perhaps with the mills?" Her eyes flashed as the barb was delivered.

He stuffed a piece of buttered bread into his mouth and washed it down with more wine. "I am not in trade myself, but do take a rather personal interest in the mills." If he interpreted the insult as meant, he gave no indication.

Francine stifled a chuckle. Emmeline would be full of fury once the ladies went through.

After the noisy dinner, the more sedate structure of cards was welcome, but Francine never played well. She found studying the trim on a gown or the structure of a headdress more in her line of interest—although that line was far less interesting here, deep in the country. She stared at the cards in her hand and tried to make sense of them. She never knew which to keep and which to discard.

During a break for cake and tea, she let her eyes wander about the room, noticing the few men she knew to be single. Not one piqued her interest.

Years ago, Henry had won her heart with captivating poems and romantic rides in the countryside; and dancing— he had been such a fine dancer. She could still feel the admiring glances as he twirled her about the room. Fortunate enough to marry for love, their years together had passed like a dream. Her daily life now was much less dreamlike. The hollow ache of loss within her had dwindled, but those memories of Henry still precluded any romantic notions for herself.

Henry had loved her so well; how could anyone else compare? Her matchmaking friends had their work cut out for them.

CHAPTER THREE

The sweet scent of spring freshened the cottage through the wide-open windows. Francine sat by the largest casement, her needlework lying idle in her lap whilst she gazed at the colourful show of flowering currants, viburnums, and quinces in the yard. Snippets of poetry floated through her head. Spring was a season of romance. Of hope. Nothing here at Barton was as grand as Norland, but there was a certain poetic charm to the wildness of the countryside and the simplicity of her new life. It put her in mind of her carefree days as a young woman, before the responsibilities of running a house were thrust upon her. Although even those duties had been exciting in the first flushes of marriage, after a short time she was content to hand them off to an able housekeeper and other servants. Now, in some kind of wicked game she had been unaware of playing, those duties had been handed back to her in this new place and situation. Young Margaret shared her mother's disinterest in domestic management, being much more inclined for the outdoors or socializing and so was of little help. Francine now had to do her best to manage the household alone, with only the two servants to assist her.

Earlier, Emmeline and Margaret had departed for a walk down the lane. Francine had declined, desiring some time to reflect on the comments her sister had made about marrying again. The idea rolled around in her head like an unraveling ball of yarn, tangling her thoughts and making it difficult to accomplish any task.

Could she really love another man? Why did her heart hesitate? Mrs Jennings and Mrs Whittaker seemed in support of the notion, and her own daughters were encouraging. She had certainly been in mourning long enough to satisfy the most fastidious expectations. But whom would she find that might be interested in marrying an older woman with no particular gifts or talents or beauty?—and no money. Certainly no sensible man. No, she must be content to—

The clip-clop of hooves interrupted her reverie. She could not see the road from her chair and so ignored the passing horses, instead taking up her needlework to tackle a particularly challenging place where the colours needed to cross and change out.

But the clip-clop ceased. She frowned. Booted feet approached the cottage, followed by a rap at the door. Oh dear, she had hoped for some time to herself.

Thomas announced Mr Cecil Walford and Mr Charles Creighton, who was the brother-in-law of Colonel Brandon. Francine rose, brushed the wrinkles from her skirt and tweaked her cheeks— even at this age she did not wish to appear sickly or … old. She nodded at Thomas to admit the visitors.

"Good morning, Mrs Dashwood," said the gentlemen, bowing in unison.

She curtseyed. "How kind of you to call. I regret my sister

and Margaret are out walking. Did you happen to see them in the lanes?"

"We did not, but we rode mostly cross-country. The ground is dry enough at last," replied Mr Creighton.

"Yes, I believe it is. We have been enjoying very fine weather. May I offer you refreshments?"

"Thank you."

Francine murmured to Thomas, then returned to her chair and motioned the callers to take a seat. Her heart fluttered. She was unused to conversing alone with gentlemen. They usually talked of the weather, roads, hunting, and politics—none of which interested her.

Mr Creighton looked rather cast down. She knew the pain he now endured and her heart went out to him.

"May I welcome you back to the neighbourhood, Mr Creighton, after your absence; and offer my sympathies for your loss. A loss I know only too well myself. If there is any way I may be of assistance …"

He shook his head. "Thank you. You are most thoughtful, but I believe only time may assist in this case. My wife was ill for many months but I had not given up hope for a recovery. I suppose one is never prepared for the finality …"

A moment of uncomfortable silence ensued.

Francine found her voice. "Indeed not."

"Indeed not," repeated Mr Walford, grabbing a handful of biscuits from the tray offered by Betsy. "You are right Creighton—time is the thing, and answered in my case. I have also been told that a new love may speed such a recovery, but I have not been so lucky to experience that noble state again … yet."

Francine eyed Mr Walford. She believed he had developed a *tendre* for her sister.

Mr Creighton gave Francine a wistful smile, twisting his gloves in his hands. She remembered how, in the immediate aftermath of her loss, even mundane conversation had seemed intolerable.

The silence was broken by a commotion at the back door and in moments her sister and daughter entered the room. Margaret curtsied and greeted the visitors with a smile, but Emmeline drew up short at the sight of Mr Walford. Her brows flew high but she collected herself.

The gentlemen rose and bowed.

"You are just in time for tea," Mr Walford announced with a pointed look at Emmeline.

Francine rose. "Emmeline, may I present Mr Charles Creighton. He has been at his home in the North, attending his wife, who was unwell. Sadly, she did not recover. She was Colonel Brandon's dear sister, you know. Mr Creighton's seat is at Whitwell, between here and Delaford. Mr Creighton, my sister, Mrs Harrington of Hawthorn Hall."

Emmeline and Mr Creighton exchanged a bow and a curtsey.

"I am so sorry for your loss, sir," she said. "I am a widow myself these twelve months."

Mr Walford looked at each member of the group. "We all share the same wound, do we not? Comrades in mourning we are," he said, popping another biscuit into his mouth. "Excepting you, of course, Miss Dashwood."

The sisters exchanged a look and Margaret giggled.

Margaret had already taken a seat and Emmeline, with a puckered brow, sank into the only remaining place, next to Mr Walford on the settee.

He gave her a wink and a smile, then continued. "The moon is full on Saturday next and I propose a dinner party at Southleigh. The Careys, my nearest neighbours, have already accepted—well, those Careys old enough to attend such a dinner as there are a great many Careys—so Miss Dashwood shall have Miss Rose and Miss Ruth for company in addition to we dull old people."

He then turned to Margaret. "And what of your beau, Mr Newbury? Can he attend or will he be off to sea by then?"

Margaret looked at her mother then back at Mr Walford and said, with great composure, "My *friend*, Mr Newbury, departs for duty in three days and so will be unable to accept your kind invitation."

"A pity, that. Months at sea can indeed prove an obstacle to love. Well, well, the Miss Careys can commiserate with you and perhaps bring you some comfort."

Francine shifted uncomfortably. It occurred to her that they had no means to …

"Mrs Dashwood, may I offer my carriage to escort you ladies to the event? Barton Cottage is but a few miles out of my way, and the company and conversation would be most welcome."

"How very kind. You are sure it is not an imposition?"

"After my long journey alone from the North, I do not look on it. I would much prefer the companionship of three lovely ladies to my own solitude—especially now, as you surely understand. Will it be agreeable if I call for you around three o'clock that day?"

"Most agreeable, Mr Creighton, thank you. Mr Walford, we shall be delighted to visit you and dine at Southleigh."

The gentlemen soon departed and Margaret went upstairs.

"Now *there* is an eligible gentleman!" Emmeline said, a little flushed. "Fine manners, and as handsome as one could wish. A home here *and* in the Lake Country? I daresay I could imagine marrying such a man."

Francine's eyes twinkled. "What? When you have already made such a conquest of Mr Walford? Will you cast him off to me then?"

"With all my heart!"

CHAPTER FOUR

*M*argaret was distraught and in no mood to socialize. Francine was hard-put to convince her that seeing friends at Southleigh would be of greater comfort than spilling more tears into her pillow. Although Margaret had dressed for the dinner engagement, she now refused to leave her room.

It had been six days since Mr Rees Newbury departed for his ship and Margaret had commenced her own kind of mourning, walking the lanes and hills alone or keeping to her room with tearful eyes and many sighs. The days preceding his leave-taking were marked by long meanders with him—under the watchful, if distant, eyes of her mother or her aunt.

Young Newbury had not spoken to Francine of any intentions, so she assumed he had not made Margaret an offer. And that was just as well. Awaiting a beau's return from the sea was a romantic notion, to be sure, but Francine felt it not useful in Margaret's case. She was young and had not moved much in society, nor met more than a few eligible gentlemen. And, as Marianne had pointed out recently, Margaret had not experienced a season in town or attended any real balls.

Francine subscribed to one of several romantic notions—that, if it were meant to be, it would be—but these words of advice only caused Margaret to stare at her stupidly and storm off.

With a wince, Francine recalled she had felt little consolation herself when her own father had used those same stilted words to comfort her after learning Henry's family refused to sanction their match. It had taken some weeks and much convincing for his family to accept her. She was, after all, a second wife for him, brought little to the marriage financially, and he already had an heir in John.

Francine was at the point of giving up Margaret as a lost cause for Southleigh when the girl's voice rang out from upstairs. "A coach has arrived, and also a curricle!"

Margaret clambered down the stairway. Emmeline followed in a more elegant manner.

Mr Creighton approached the cottage with a younger man; and as they drew near Margaret, peering from the window, cried out, "Mr James!"

The ladies, with much cheek pinching and gown smoothing, assembled in the drawing room to receive the gentlemen.

Charles Creighton spoke to Emmeline. "Mrs Harrington, may I present my son, James Creighton?"

The young man bowed, his dark curls bobbing. He had his father's blue eyes and fine build and appeared more than delighted to see Margaret. The two had been in company several times over the years, particularly at the frequent events Sir John held at Barton Park, where Francine had first made the acquaintance of Charles Creighton. Young James had been at Cambridge until recently when he had joined his father in the North for their sad farewells to the late Mrs Creighton.

Emmeline's mouth fell open in surprise. "You ... have a child ... a young man ... still at home, Mr Creighton?" She then recovered herself. "He will certainly help cheer up Miss Margaret here, who has been in the dismals now Mr Newbury has gone away."

Francine frowned at her sister's candour.

Mr Creighton nodded. "Friends can be of great help during times of affliction, Mrs Harrington."

Then he turned to Margaret. "James has chosen to drive his curricle, being of the opinion that one extra would make the carriage too crowded. If your mother approves—"

"Miss Margaret," James said, stepping forward, "I would be honoured if you would join me in my equipage—to better see the countryside to and from Southleigh. The scenery is quite splendid and the weather very fine. And of course, the coach will be traveling right behind us, everything proper. Mrs Dashwood—?"

The air was heady with the beguiling scents of spring all about them as the two vehicles set off. The fresh green grasses and budding trees were a delight. Francine's heart warmed when she saw, at the turns, Margaret happily conversing with Mr James in the curricle. She vowed to speak to Mrs Jennings concerning how soon to allow Margaret a season in town. It hardly seemed possible her daughter could be that much grown. Was it really so long ago she had cradled the child in her arms? Yet, in many ways, Margaret seemed ready for the next step in life. She had always been curious and independent and rarely needed reassurance—traits she must have inherited from Henry. His confidence had been as attractive as his romantic idealism. Their courtship had been the stuff of novels and even now she blushed at some of those memories.

Mr Creighton required some encouragement to talk about more than the weather. He was persuaded to tell the company about his home in the North and share a little of his sorrow. The mood in the carriage was subdued, as clouds might dim the sunlight. Francine—bereft the longest—felt it her duty to turn the conversation and began a discussion of travel, specifically to the seaside. She and Marianne had been speaking of such a trip but neither knew the southern shore. Time passed in these pleasant exchanges and soon they arrived at Southleigh.

Mr Walford's home was a stately but older building set just below the crest of a hill. It boasted a fine stand of timber to one side, and the other side featured a deep valley surrounded by hills marching into the distance. The park and shrubbery offered winding paths and several benches from which to enjoy the views—one picturesquely situated near a small lake. The sky softened into wisps of cloud, creating an almost magical ambiance.

"Well, this is a charming setting, even if the house is quite old," remarked Emmeline as Mr Creighton assisted the sisters from the carriage.

"It's very romantic," Margaret observed, then lowered her eyes at James' smile.

"That is just what I think," Francine quipped, with a wink at her sister. "That seat by the water would be the perfect setting for a proposal, would it not Emmeline?"

Margaret giggled and Emmeline made a wry face and flounced ahead up the path, tossing gravel in her wake.

Mr Creighton gave Francine a curious look but said nothing and the party proceeded to the drawing room.

A lively group awaited them, including the Careys with Miss Ruth and Miss Rose and two of their brothers, along with the Whittakers and two other neighbourhood families. Introductions were made, then Margaret quickly joined the Misses Carey. Francine knew the Careys well. Margaret had stayed with them when Marianne was taken ill at Cleveland. The girls were all but inseparable. If they were not visiting at each other's homes, they were dispatching notes back and forth.

As the group waited for dinner to be announced, Emmeline sidled up to Francine and whispered, "This place is a little shabby. It has not had a woman's touch in many years."

"It is crying out for your domestic skills, Emmeline," Francine replied with a smirk.

Her sister gave her a withering look and stalked off.

The dinner was tasty if somewhat unimaginative. Francine surmised it the work of an older cook of long standing who had Mr Walford's favourite dishes in short rotation. The wine was excellent and softened the taut ends of her nerves. She and her sister sat on either side of their host, who became more conversational as the wine decanters emptied. He was obviously enjoying himself and the company he had assembled—most especially the female company close at hand. Several times he reached over and touched Emmeline's arm as he made a point—not entirely acceptable behaviour but not *too* scandalous. The table was lively and the company agreeable.

Mr Creighton sat at Francine's other hand. He listened to the conversations and made comments here and there. Although he seemed determined to be in company, it was obvious his heart was not engaged. She recalled how difficult it had been for her to join in or feel any enthusiasm at Sir John's lively events even a full year after Henry had died.

Sympathetic, she attempted to involve Mr Creighton in talking about his interests and sporting pursuits. He was especially keen on equestrian events and took great pride in his hunters.

His interest in horses pulled at a long-lost passion that she had not thought of for many years. As a young girl she had loved riding, but when her mother sustained a broken neck falling from a horse, her father immediately forbade Francine and Emmeline to ride, and the girls' ponies were sold before their mother was buried. Even now Francine could not think of her childhood pony without tears. To forestall being overcome, she hastened to ask Mr Creighton about other pursuits and cast her glance around the table to avoid his observant eye.

Camelia Whittaker caught her glance and raised a brow.

Mr Creighton gave Francine a curious look at the quick change of subject, but followed her lead with all politeness. Her inner turmoil gradually settled as his calm voice waxed on about fishing and his admiration for Mr Izaak Walton, author of *The Compleat Angler*.

With many lips loosened by wine, the noise level at the table rose. Emmeline was scowling at Mr Walford. Francine knew by the set of her sister's jaw that she was about to read a peal over him, host or not.

"Mr Walford, whatever possessed you to invite so many people to dinner at one time? You must be aware that eight to twelve guests are the ideal number for a pleasant dining experience. I declare there are more than twenty seated here and the noise level renders meaningful conversation impossible."

Cecil Walford gave Emmeline a puckish grin. "Since when has dinner conversation been meaningful, my dear Mrs Harrington?" At her silent surprise he continued. "You can see my table is large enough and well-laden for the comfort and satisfaction of my many guests. Is that not the purpose of manners and courtesy—the comfort of others? Although, you must allow me to admit that I am willing to be taught otherwise by a woman as informed and beautiful as yourself. Perhaps we might consider the wisdom of that? They say marriage can improve a man, and I am game to test that truism once again." He reached over and covered her hand with his.

Emmeline's eyebrows flew to the sky. "Mr Walford, how can you be so … so …"

He patted her hand. "Ah, I fear my eagerness for a wife of your calibre has overset my self-control. Forgive me."

Their voices had the attention of others at the table. Mr Walford looked at his guests and continued in a louder voice, addressing the group. "Marriage is often said to fill the minds only of women. But I dare say that men of my age—those of us still above ground—have learned to value an attractive and intelligent partner, and for reasons different than in our youth." The faces at the table gawked, but all were drawn in by the unusual topic of conversation. "Come now, gentlemen, what say you in this matter?"

A wall of silence answered him.

Then Francine turned in wonder at the sound of Charles Creighton's deep warm voice.

"Though I am new to the set of the unmarried and cannot yet speak to the topic of marrying again, I can relate that what I miss about my wife is the pleasure of her company. And by that I mean talking, sharing a smile, having a history and family in common. Friends may replace some of these, but nothing can replace the person lost, and I do not believe even a new partner can fill such a void. It would be a most unfair expectation."

There was a quiet murmur around the table and heads nodded.

"Well said, my friend, well said," Mr Walford agreed. "However, it is my opinion that one should *not* expect replacement; rather I think one might hope—after an adequate period of mourning—for a new adventure of the kind."

Many whisperings and mumblings were heard until Camelia Whittaker's soft voice rose and added, "Love may change with age and circumstance, but I do not believe our delight in it expires until we do. There is the romantic notion bandied about that one loves only once. That I do not believe. We are all of us filled with the light of love. Two flames united burn brighter than one alone, offering added warmth to our later years." She and her present husband shared a smile across the table.

A chill ran up Francine's spine at this testimony. She was startled at such a serious turn in the dinner talk and looked at Cecil Walford with admiration at achieving such. Might there be more to him than the lusty enjoyment of food and drink?

The remainder of the dinner passed amiably until it was time for the ladies to go through. Emmeline was quick to link arms with Francine and hustle her to the parlour. There she proceeded to hiss about the many affronts she had endured from Cecil Walford.

"How could he be so presumptuous? Patting my arm I know not how many times. Touching my hand! Keeping me so engaged in his conversation, to the exclusion of others. All but making me an offer! The man is beyond the pale. Certainly I have given him no encouragement. He needs to be taken to task."

Francine tried to subdue a smile. "Perhaps it is *he* who has taken all of *us* to task. You cannot deny the truth of what was said. I thought it almost poetic."

Emmeline huffed and rolled her eyes.

After being served tea, Francine mused, "I wonder if this is Mr Walford's way of courting you? After all, courting must look different at our age, do you think? Certainly one does not spout verses, bring wildflowers, and take long meandering walks and all such romantic things as were done in our youth? Mr Walford may be a little brash at times, but seems a good sort of gentleman—and Emmeline, he does have this nice estate—"

"No, no, I beg you will not say such things!" Emmeline expounded in a loud whisper. "No one annoys me as much as he. You were fortunate to be sitting next to the only attractive and eligible gentleman at the table, Fran. But surely there are other eligible men about; we must somehow cast our net wider." She knit her brows prettily and picked at some cake, then exclaimed, "I have it! We must travel. Not so very far. Were not you and Marianne talking of a trip to the seaside?" She nodded to herself. "Yes, I believe that is just the thing. But whom can we consult? I know nothing of resorts on the south coast. We want to choose a place of fashion and style, for that is where the most eligible men will be found."

Camelia Whittaker slipped into the chair across from them. "Did I overhear you speak of a journey? That has lately been on my mind also. My husband has some acquaintance living on the south Devonshire coast. When the men join us, let us ask his advice. I daresay he will be enthusiastic. Oh, and I believe he and Sir John—and Mr Creighton too—have a friend who is well situated near there, a Mr Stanton. Surely he might have some eligible friends thereabouts. I believe Mr Stanton is also a friend of Admiral Marcus Tennant, who is said to be making a visit here soon. The admiral is a widower, you know, retired from the Navy. A handsome, elegant man by all accounts. I hear he has a fine estate somewhere on the coast. Perhaps he would do for one of you?"

"This is most encouraging, Mrs Whittaker!" Emmeline cried. "An admiral, and other acquaintance of such a man! And with all the society and diversions to be found at the seaside resorts … please excuse me, I must have one more piece of cake before the gentlemen join us." She rose and moved to the table of confections.

Camelia was some ten years older than Francine and possessed an aura of calm wisdom. Francine felt reassured in her company. And now, by her look, Camelia was word-lessly asking about Francine's change of countenance at dinner.

With a kind smile, Camelia prompted gently, "Perhaps, dear, it will be more comforting to share your thoughts than dwell on private regret. Did Mr Creighton say something at dinner to distress you?"

Francine sighed. "No, of course not. He is the perfect gentleman. So much like his brother-in-law in that way; neither ever give offence. I encouraged him to speak of his interests, as I know the difficulty of making social talk when one is grieving. One of his passions is horses, especially his hunters. That shone a light on a painful memory for me, although I tried to disguise it. You saw through me?"

"I did. You looked in momentary pain, and I feared you were unwell."

Francine cringed at the suspicion that her face may have betrayed her emotions whilst in company. Must I always be so inept?

"You are so kind and so attentive. Such a good friend. Perhaps Mr Creighton did not notice?"

Camelia sipped her tea then looked up. "Mr Creighton is an attentive man. I believe he noticed something, but had the good manners to allow you to guide him into a more comfortable topic. Not much escapes him."

That would not be unusual in a fine horseman, Francine mused. Riders were often particularly aware of things unspoken.

Camelia's calm grey eyes engaged Francine's in a comforting way until both ladies' attention swung to the door as the gentlemen entered.

After procuring refreshments, Mr Whittaker joined his wife and Francine. Emmeline took a seat at her sister's side again, whispering, "Mr Walford's cook could benefit from the instruction of a pastry chef. There were only three pastries from which to choose."

Francine nudged her sister in exasperation.

Mr Whittaker listened to his wife's question about travel and warmed to the topic. "There is no place finer for exploring and leisure than the south coast of Devonshire, especially in June or July. Not August, for it is very wet then by most accounts. Indeed, Mrs Whittaker and I have traveled three times to the coast over our happy years together, have we not? Which place captured your heart, my love?"

"I very much treasure the memories of our little cottage near the sea in Paignton, but"—she smiled up at him "—we were seeking seclusion at the time, were we not? Mrs Dashwood and Mrs Harrington will be seeking society, and fashionable society at that. Places to meet eligible new acquaintance. Did not you and Mr Walford have a friend—"

"Indeed we did, and still do. Hugh Stanton. A fine fellow. He and the admiral are to visit our neighbourhood within a fortnight. I shall write to Stanton immediately and ask his recommendation for the most fashionable resorts. I fancy a journey myself. Perhaps we can all travel together? Would young Miss Dashwood be included? If so, perhaps our granddaughter Rose might come along? Surely her family can spare her. It is time she moves out into the world more. The resorts are the very place to see and be seen."

Carriages were summoned and cloaks donned as the guests made ready to leave. The sky was cloudless and the full moon cast a wholesome glow over the countryside. The coach with Emmeline, Francine, and Mr Creighton followed the curricle carrying Margaret and James. Francine wondered if Margaret's affections had transferred from young Newbury to her current companion. Were Margaret's affections so inconstant? Francine had never talked much with her youngest daughter about romance and beaux; it had always seemed Margaret was too young for such things. Had her older sisters advised her? Francine knit her brow and vowed to keep a closer watch on Margaret—and supposed it would not hurt to consult with Elinor and Marianne on the subject.

After a few minutes in the gentle sway of the carriage, her sister was dozing beside her. Francine tucked a blanket around Emmeline and Mr Creighton gave Francine a kindly smile. The moonlight cast a poetic spell and Francine found her mind wandering. In the silvery light Mr Creighton looked more handsome than she remembered. She had always thought him rather plain, with blue eyes and brown hair that showed more than a few strands of grey. His lean athletic build had not escaped her notice, and she concluded it was that which made him seem younger than his forty-nine years. He had a slight limp when he walked but she felt it inappropriate to ask about it.

"Are you warm enough, Mrs Dashwood? I am always concerned for ladies in their lightweight attire. My wife was often cold. We gentlemen have the protection of tall boots and wool jackets and waistcoats. Evenings can turn chillier than anticipated. You must take my blanket."

"Why, thank you. Another blanket would be welcome. And you are right, about ladies. I often find myself asking Thomas to build a fire, even on a summer's evening, especially if the damp mists move in. That is a chill I feel in my very bones."

Charles Creighton sat forward and opened the blanket, leaning to drape it towards Francine. His eyes were kind, and when he tucked the blanket around her shoulders she felt a warmth she had not known since before her dear Henry had taken ill. She looked at this man now so close to her, his face bathed in pearly light, and shivered.

"You are chilled indeed. I trust this blanket will do the trick."

Francine was at a loss for words. She could only gaze at him, until a rut in the road jostled them all and Emmeline moaned a complaint. Francine then stared out the window until her head felt thick with the softest of wool and she drifted into that realm where the real world and the dream world weave themselves together. Surrendering to the rhythm of the carriage, her last view was Charles Creighton's face staring out of the window with a contemplative expression.

CHAPTER FIVE

rancine did not see that face again for some time.
Mr Creighton had not called in nearly a fortnight, and one evening whilst dining at the Park she learned
why.

"I do hope Creighton returns in time," Sir John remarked.
"It is a great tradition for us to attend the fair together. And
his son too. That would please Miss Margaret, yes?"

"I would enjoy Mr James' company anywhere," Margaret
replied with a bright eye. "But where have they gone?"

"To London," Sir John replied. "Some details to work out
with his man of business. Likely, after the death of his dear
wife, some matters might need to be rearranged. He did not
say how long he would be gone."

"Well, I hope they return in time. James and I enjoyed
ourselves so much at the fair last year."

Emmeline looked at the others around the table. "Please,
what is this fair?"

Mrs Jennings explained. "The May Fair at Honiton is a fine
event that gathers folk from all the surrounding countryside.
The best laces and wools and pottery and all other sort of

goods are on display, and there are some good bargains to be made. We will form a merry party, even if Mr Creighton has not returned. It is certainly worth a day—or even two—spent about the town in the shops and booths, and—what can I say —sampling all the delights of the bakers and confectioners. The apple cider is not to be missed. And anything topped with our Devonshire clotted cream and jam, well, I declare .... yes, a fine day to see and be seen by both new and familiar faces," she said, looking first at Margaret and then at Francine and Emmeline.

"But who attends such a festival?" Emmeline asked. " Surely you do not mix with the common hobbledehoy?"

There was a brief silence around the table.

"Ah, about that, my dear," Sir John said, wagging a finger at her, "everyone—man, woman, and child—of every station attends the Honiton Fair. Titled men and local nobility from their great houses to the common craftswoman or bakerman will be seen—and talked with, yes indeed. So many stories to be heard, and jokes—oh, I do love the jokes. Brandon, what do you say?"

Colonel Brandon and Marianne were amongst the dinner guests on this night at Barton Park. Elinor and Edward were away. Colonel Brandon dabbed his mouth with a napkin and spoke in his quiet, deliberate voice. "Mrs Harrington, it is a long-held tradition in Honiton that during this event all manner of people mix together. It is a most pleasant balance of creator and purchaser. We need or desire their creations and they need and desire us to buy. Many of the crafters are actually working at their booths and it can be fascinating to see the skill and detail that go into making the items we enjoy."

"Such as this lace collar I wear," Marianne offered. "A beautiful gift Christopher procured for me at last year's fair. I was so fortunate as to observe the artist begin work on this very piece." She turned her head this way and that, fingering the lace. "I did not receive it until some months after the fair. It can take hours to create a mere finger-length of lace. I not only treasure my husband's thoughtfulness for this gift; I also treasure the artistry of the lacemaker herself. Talent is certainly not limited to those of higher class or education. Think of DaVinci. I am sure you will find something very fine that you will wish to purchase, Aunt."

Emmeline's brow puckered. "Well, this is a new idea to me. I have never been in company with those outside my station, excepting my servants of course. But it seems to me only proper that I participate in this unusual new opportunity—as long as I am with your party."

"That's the spirit!" Sir John exclaimed, pounding the table with his fist, giving the tableware a bounce. "Oh, what a day we shall have!"

Colonel Brandon and Marianne were at Barton Park for the week and whilst the gentlemen rode out together, Marianne came to help her mother and aunt review their wardrobes for the upcoming Honiton Fair, and for a dinner at the Whittakers' to finalize plans for the journey south.

"Mama, do allow my seamstress to make some adjustments to your gowns from Norland," Marianne implored. "It is high time you set aside your mourning and half-mourning attire. With a few changes to the sleeves and necklines, and new overlays, some of your old gowns from Norland could be quite the thing."

"Even you, Aunt Emmeline, need not limit yourself to half-mourning clothes and so few jewels. Has it not been beyond the year and a day required?"

"It has been one year and a couple of months now. I was

not sure of customs here when I packed for this journey, but I did bring a few gowns in colours other than violet and lavender."

"Then let us celebrate by casting off mourning and take our direction from the beauty of spring all around us. It is time to revel in colours and trims and jewels again!" Marianne cried in true romantic fashion.

Talk ensued about which hues flattered each woman and, for the first time, Margaret joined in this discussion and seemed to take a new interest in her own appearance. Francine witnessed this milestone with a mixture of wistfulness and pride. Her child was becoming a woman, and she herself was becoming ... not wishing to think on that she tucked the reflection away.

Tonight's dinner at the Whittakers' had excited nearly as much anticipation amongst some of the ladies as did the fair itself. There were two new gentlemen to be met. Mr Hugh Stanton had accompanied Admiral Marcus Tennant on a visit to the vicinity, and both would attend the dinner. Mr Stanton was a married man with a large family so the focus for the unmarried ladies would be on the admiral.

Emmeline's eyes lit up when she saw herself in the looking glass. Her deep plum gown with silvery trim and rose insets set her complexion aglow. She adjusted a bow on her cap and tossed at the ribbons streaming down in the same three hues.

"I feel divine! Marianne, you really do have the eye. These ribbons are perfect. Why, I look ten years younger—and lively enough to attract the interest of any admiral *and* all of his eligible friends. Yes, yes, I am most pleased! I wish we could rush off to the dinner this moment."

Francine looked on, admiring not only Emmeline's good looks but also her enthusiasm and confidence. Her older sister had always been the lively one, the one people engaged first in conversation any time the sisters were together in society. Francine, whilst also long of limb and elegant of frame, was sure to be outshone by her sister this entire evening. Would the admiral even remember the name Francine? It was fortunate she had been the only eligible young lady when Henry had come into their childhood neigh-bourhood. She often wondered if Henry would have chosen Emmeline instead, had her sister still been there and unmarried.

Henry had been so dashing and romantic. Francine always marveled at his love for her, never feeling she quite deserved him. She was quiet and plain but he seemed pleased to display her limited charms to all. He had courted her lavishly and she had been swept away by his passion and romantic gestures.

Marianne came over and placed her hands on her mother's shoulders, gently drawing her to the looking glass. "Do look, Mama; you are as splendid as a summer day. See how the greens and blues of the gown bring out those very colours in your fine green eyes? With that delicate lace framing your hair and its enticing tendrils—why, you are the picture of loveliness. You really must consider taking someone with you to act as a lady's maid to help you prepare for all the events you will attend at the resorts. I will arrange for one of my servants to accompany you."

Francine took a deep breath and gazed into the glass. Who is this lady? This was by far the most elegant she had appeared since leaving Norland. Dinners at Barton Park had required some effort but nothing like this.

"Are you sure it is not too much, Marianne? After all, it is only the Whittakers. Will I seem too ..."

"Too eager? Indeed not. You simply look elegant and serene. You have worn your mourning garments for far too long. Papa would not have wished it. He loved you and would want you happy. Do be happy. Enjoy your old friends tonight. And welcome the opportunity to be acquainted with new friends. It is not often we meet with new people here in the country. And it will be good practice for when you travel to the coast where there will be much socializing."

"The coast ... oh, dear ... Marianne, I do wish you could come with us. How it tears me up! I want you to be with me, and yet I want you and the baby to be safe. I cannot have both, can I? So I must choose for the safety of you and the baby. Surely you will help me pack for the journey, and advise me on what purchases to make before we depart."

Marianne squeezed her mother's shoulders. "Yes, Mama, I shall help and advise you, to the best of my ability. I do wish I could accompany you. And I ask one thing—you must tell me of resorts where children are welcome and may play safely on the beaches ... nothing too rocky. So next year we may all travel to the seaside together. I shall think of you every day you are gone, and wish you are having a delightful holiday and meeting people of interest. Even, perhaps, a new lover?" Her eyes twinkled at her mother.

Francine felt the colour rush to her cheeks. "Fie, Marianne, do not roast me."

Later that evening, Francine gazed about the well-laid table. Most of her social life seemed to revolve around dinners. Did people her age do nothing else? The men hunted and fished of course, and some still rode about the countryside. It had been many years since she had ridden horseback. When traveling by coach she had often gazed wistfully at the downs or upon woodland paths. Part of her wanted to explore those paths and feel the wind in her face at a full gallop. Such felicity! But then the vision of her mother's broken body and her father's harsh reprimands darkened this joy, and her own grief prevented her even thinking about riding. Grief, and fear. Tears welled in her eyes and she quickly dabbed them away.

Francine did look forward to the Honiton Fair and also to their later journey to the southern coast with hopes that both would provide some change and diversion to a life that was only occasionally punctuated by something other than daily tasks and familiar faces. She trembled at the thought of such an adventure to the seaside, undertaken without a gentleman explicitly in charge of her. It seemed she had left horses and her sense of adventure buried in the past.

Tonight's gathering was much more intimate than the dinner at Southleigh. Mrs Whittaker's purpose was to gather together those who would journey to the coast with those who might assist their entrance into that society. The two gentlemen glad to assist—Mr Hugh Stanton and Admiral Marcus Tennant—were seated at this very table, along with the Whittakers and Cecil Walford. Charles Creighton was not yet returned from town, and it was not certain he would be of the traveling party. It was likely that Sir John and Mrs Jennings would join the journey as well, though they were also not in attendance; but they had insisted Emmeline and Francine be transported in their coach. Mr Whittaker was the only gentleman present with whom Francine was well acquainted; this fact caused her lips to be pressed closed most of the time, but her eyes and ears were fully open. She had not been in fashionable company since her years at Norland—and then she was always on Henry's arm and could bask quietly in his confidence and charm.

Hugh Stanton appeared a kind and cheerful sort of fellow and engaged in conversation with each of them. He offered information on the resorts with which he was familiar and it seemed, by his reckoning, that new resorts were being developed every day—sleepy fishing villages transformed into watering holes for the elite from Exeter, Bath, Reading,

Oxford, and even as far away as London. With France and much of the continent entrenched in the turmoil of war, those sunny beach resorts were no longer the destination of the wealthy English on holiday. Each Devon resort seemed to have its advantages, and Francine listened closely although convinced her opinion would carry no weight on the final choice.

"Sidmouth is the gayest place on the Devon coast," boasted Mr Stanton, cutting into his roast beef. "A fine protected beach, many footpaths and bridle paths winding through the scenic landscape, and every elegance and luxury one can imagine."

The admiral gave a nod and added, "Every luxury indeed— billiard halls, cardrooms, assembly rooms, plays, circulating libraries, milliner shops, even iced creams. Something for everyone." The admiral's deep voice distinguished him, and was in keeping with his tall frame and elegant-though-weathered face. His tone was not animated but Francine imagined he could boom orders to sailors with great authority. Listening to him appeared to have a mesmerizing effect on some at the table—especially Emmeline, whose eyes had not left the admiral's face.

"And the weather should be mild," added Mrs Whittaker. "I confess I enjoy being out of doors at the seaside and watching the people—those fashionable ones on the promenade as well as the more rustic folk and fishermen. I shall take my paints and easel."

Cecil Walford stared at Emmeline, his brows in a knot. She did not return his gaze. Indeed, she seemed completely unaware of him. Her eyes were riveted on the admiral's chiseled countenance. Mr Walford turned to frown at the admiral, gulped down a glass of wine, and then offered, "I have not been there for some years, but Sidmouth itself is located at the end of the Vale of Sid, with hills rising high on the east and west for protection from the stronger winds; and the Honiton Hills themselves close the valley to the north. One can thus truly enjoy the temperate south winds off the sea. There are fishing boats and nets aplenty to paint," he said with a nod at Mrs Whittaker. Unable to draw Emmeline's eye from the admiral with these remarks, Mr Walford speared a piece of beef and chewed intensely.

The admiral continued to savour Emmeline's obvious attention. Francine wasn't sure whether to be amused or envious.

"The promenade is fine, and there is a tea room open to the prospect of the sea. Plenty of opportunities to enjoy the views," added the admiral with a sly grin.

"I hear authoress Fanny Burney herself stayed at Sidmouth," added Mr Whittaker.

"I believe you are right," Mr Stanton said. "At the London Inn."

"Fanny Burney!" exclaimed Emmeline. "I am her greatest admirer. I should dearly like to walk the places she herself has walked and listen to the 'rustling murmur of the waves' as she did."

Forks clinked against plates as they all contemplated these tempting scenes.

Reaching for more potatoes, the admiral added, "But we must not forget Teignmouth. It, too, offers a large assembly room on the seafront—for one-hundred couple—and weekly balls; plus nightly cards for those not inclined to dance," the admiral said, this time engaging Francine's eyes.

She was powerfully drawn in. But did he think she would not wish to dance? Why?

The admiral continued. "Sailing, riding parties, sea bathing —what more could one ask? I shall personally arrange a sailing party, whichever destination is chosen," he offered, holding up his glass.

Francine's heart fluttered. He was committing to be a part of their group! What excitement his presence would lend to their outings and adventures. Could such a fine gentleman take notice of a woman like herself? She thought him likely to be a fine dancer, and prided herself on her own elegant way of moving. If there was anything she did well, it was dancing.

The others joined him in raising their glasses and all were taken in by the prospect of a holiday in a new place. The very air around them vibrated with excitement.

Whilst the admiral entertained them with anecdotes about his adventures both ashore and at sea, Francine detected an uncomfortable undercurrent, especially between Mr Walford and the admiral. She had little experience with such undercurrents and wondered if it might be wise to be more observant of others whilst in company rather than dwelling on her own social discomfort.

CHAPTER SIX

*T*he coaches stood ready to transport eager travelers to the Honiton Fair: Sir John's family coach plus a wagon for the servants who would help with the children; Colonel Brandon and Marianne's equipage; and Cecil Walford's carriage which would deliver Francine, her sister, and Margaret. Emmeline was not pleased with the scheme and spoke her mind as the ladies secured their bonnets before departing. But with Charles Creighton still in London there was no alternative for them but the Walford carriage.

"Oh Fran, might there be any other arrangement? Perhaps I can exchange places with Mrs Jennings?"

"Em, it is but a short journey and such an action would be an affront to Mr Walford, who is most generous in the offer of his carriage. He has gone a good deal out of his way. Now, do you wish to sit next to him? Or across from him? I can offer you that much choice."

Emmeline frowned. "Neither! I wish to escape both his touch and his eyes! Well, I shall sit across from him. At least from his eyes I may look away."

Francine suppressed a smirk.

Margaret settled on the seat next to her aunt. "I hope the Creightons have returned and that I may see Mr James there. Or that we can at least find the Careys. I would like a companion my own age," she said as she fidgeted with her gloves.

Emmeline shook her head and laughed. "What? Are we too old to be interesting company?"

The idea of being 'too old' did not sit so lightly with Francine and she could not laugh at it.

The ladies were handed into the carriage and Emmeline immediately stared out of the window to avoid any eye contact with one fellow passenger in particular.

Mr Walford was uncharacteristically subdued during the ride to Honiton. He responded politely to the conversations at hand but was not his usual opinionated self. Was he pondering the possibility of 'losing' Emmeline to the handsome admiral? Her sister had made no secret of her enthusiasm for the visitor. But it was not like Mr Walford to draw back or give in. Francine had predicted he might make an increased effort to compete for Emmeline's favour. Was he unwell? Did he have pressing business concerns? What else did men worry about? The admiral and Mr Stanton would surely be at the event—and that thought caused a little flutter within her.

Honiton was a veritable hive of activity. The main streets were thronged with fairgoers sampling the wares, watching the craftspeople, striking bargains, and being amazed by the acrobats and fire-eaters. The sun was bright overhead but it was not yet too hot. Dozens of voices competed to be heard amongst the cries of those hawking their goods. Soon it all became a loud buzz that wove itself into the smells of roasting meats, baked goods, and close-quartered humans.

Francine had not attended the fair last year and was overwhelmed by so many people in one place, and in garb that varied from the roughest homespun to the finest laces, silks, and brocades. She hardly knew where to look. A peasant child brushed between herself and Mrs Jennings, who chortled merrily.

Hot meat pies and pasties were devoured first to provide energy for the rest of the day. Emmeline had to be convinced that this was not an affront of manners in this particular situation. To Margaret's delight the Careys found them. She and Rose giggled as much as they ate. The servants had all they could do to contain the Middleton children with so many sights and sounds to tempt them. Sir John seemed not to notice his family and was busy trading jokes with gentlemen and tradesmen alike. Lady Middleton just smiled blandly at her beloved little ones cavorting about and trying to escape the servants.

Cecil Walford made a great effort to secure Emmeline's attention. "Now, which berries are your favourite, Mrs Harrington? I do insist on providing you with tarts of your choice."

Emmeline glanced at her sister with raised brows.

Francine chuckled. Her sister looked like a cornered chicken.

Mr Walford stood firm. "I will brook no refusals. Kind sir, please wrap up three of each tart for my three lovely companions." He motioned to his servant, who stood at the ready with a small cart to carry anticipated purchases.

After thanking him graciously, Emmeline moved off. She was certainly making things difficult for him. Francine felt an unexpected pang of sympathy.

A nearby lacemaking booth captured their party's attention. Beautiful collars and shawls were on display, along with narrower lengths of lace for use on bonnets or gentlemen's shirts. Francine had never watched such intricate work being crafted, some by girls much younger than Margaret. They were dutiful about their work but their faces were wan. Francine had not spent much time around the children of servants or peasants. Were they always so listless? So pale? She gazed at Margaret and Rose with their glowing cheeks, gushing over a finely-crafted collar. Losing Henry's estate to her stepson had been shocking, but even with that formidable obstacle she and her daughters had managed to maintain a somewhat genteel life, although at a level far beneath that of Norland. She had Sir John to thank for much of their present good fortune.

Leaning closer to Mrs Carey she said, "Olivia, these laces are lovely, but those poor girls. They look so ... well, it is tedious work."

"I suppose it is. Our girls are fortunate, are they not? They need not labour for others, or even in our own kitchens." She gazed at the young lacemakers and sighed.

Mrs Jennings declared, "Although they may not look as happy as we would like to see youngsters, these girls are fortunate indeed. The Leed Lacemaking School takes on only a few girls each year to train up. 'Tis a skill that will serve them well, and for the rest of their lives— they will always have to work, poor dears. I do hear Mrs Leed is a stern taskmistress, and the girls are fed none too generously, I wager."

Francine's heart went out to them—so young, and boarded away from home, working so hard, having no childhood. Were they allowed to play with dolls? Climb trees? Walk through the woods and upon the downs? Ride horses? Pick wildflowers?

Purchases were made and lengths of lace contracted for, and then the gentlemen proposed a walk to the boxing arena.

Emmeline was wide-eyed. "Do ladies attend such events here?"

Olivia Carey nodded. "Certainly. It is all the rage in London, after all. Mind, one only attends in the company of a proper gentleman escort. And ladies do not bet on the matches—or if they do, they are quite secret about such use of their pin money."

Francine cast a curious glance at her friend.

Mr Walford offered an arm each to Francine and Emmeline and the group made their way along.

As they entered the small boxing pavilion, the smell of cigar smoke pinched at Francine's nostrils. The ladies were escorted to seats on raised benches and the gentlemen then left to join the throngs on the floor encircling the boxing ring. Smoke hung in the air. Voices rose in greeting and recognition. Money and papers quickly changed hands. Francine had never witnessed such activity.

Next to her, Emmeline gasped. Following her sister's gaze Francine saw the admiral, cutting a tall, fine figure in the crowd, surrounded by several other well-dressed gentlemen, including Mr Stanton and also Mr Creighton, clearly returned from London in time for the fair. Sir John, Mr Carey, and Mr Walford soon joined them. Francine looked over to see Colonel Brandon, who remained at Marianne's side. Such a fine man. She could not have wished a finer for her daughter.

Margaret and Rose wore happy smiles as Mr James and two other young men left the ringside and joined them with a polite bow. Emmeline and Francine locked eyes and smiled. Margaret's enjoyment of the day was now assured.

When the master of ceremonies spoke, the noise quieted and the men returned to their ladies to watch the match. Emmeline edged her way closer to the admiral. Francine grinned behind her fan. Her sister had not changed much over the years, at least as far as socializing and flirting. Emmeline always went after what she wanted, and was usually successful at engaging her quarry.

Without knowing what to expect of a boxing match, Francine's attention was drawn to the two men in the ring. Both were well-muscled, one with dark skin and one with an Irish-sounding name. The noise level rose to new heights and she wondered on which boxer her gentlemen friends had bet, then discovered as much when they began to cheer for their choice. All but Mr Creighton and Mr Walford that is, whose heads were bent together in some kind of private conference. What were they talking about so intently in such a boisterous crowd? Had they no interest in the match? Their faces—when she could see them—held no hint of mirth. What could be so urgent?

Men's interests puzzled her. How was it entertaining to watch two men beat one another? She supposed she did not understand the sport, and wondered how the fighting men felt about being bet on like racehorses?

The other ladies in her party joined in the excitement except for Mrs Jennings, who spent more time watching the audience than the fighters, her eye moving from Mr Walford and Mr Creighton to the admiral. Mrs Jennings had a great many friends and connections—in both high and low places it seemed—and an uncanny way of delving into the undercurrents of situations yet being above them at the same time.

After watching three matches—one very short in which one fighter almost immediately hit the floor and was carried away by four men with concerned faces—the gentlemen suggested moving on to other activities. Francine was relieved to depart the violence, the confusing racket, and the smoky air.

Mr Creighton stepped next to her after they quit the

building. He walked beside her for several steps in silence so she ventured to welcome him back.

"How was your journey?" she asked.

He hung his head. "It was not pleasant, but it went as well as can be expected. I find it difficult to keep my mind on transactions and numbers when my heart is so full of sorrow. But Merriweather has long been my man of business and I trust him. Things are now settled in such a way that James' future is also secured. So, tell me, Mrs Dashwood, what news might I need to be—" He swung his head sharply around and stared intently.

Francine followed his gaze just in time to see a stocky bearded man in a round hat glance their way and then disappear into the crowd.

"Do you know him?" she asked.

Mr Creighton shook his head. "He seems in some ways familiar, though I know not how. But what is more unusual is that I caught a glimpse of him twice whilst I was in town. Why would he now be here? Can it be he has followed me from London?"

A twinge of fear shot through her. "Might you be in danger?"

He thought for a moment. "I think not. If he wished to harm me, he would have been wiser to do so in town and then melt into the crowds of London. Perhaps it is just a coincidence. Perhaps it is not even the same man. A mind that is grieving can sometimes play tricks." He looked back again with a puzzled expression.

Francine knew not what to say. Mr Creighton appeared to be at sixes and sevens. She took his offered arm with relief; the crowd seemed to move in waves and she did not wish to be carried away from her own party.

"Now, about the news …"

"Mr Creighton, I dare say you would have far more interesting news to tell from London. Was your son there with you or had he gone back to university?"

"News from town? That is just what I should like to hear!" exclaimed Emmeline, boldly taking Mr Creighton's other arm. As she did, she turned a sweet smile on the admiral, who was walking a few paces behind.

Mr Creighton looked at Francine with a knowing smile. Emmeline did not fool him. Francine found this reassuring, though she did not know why.

"Ladies, I fear I did nothing entertaining whilst in London. Meetings for business, dining alone at the hotel, morning rides in the park, and purchasing supplies and gifts that cannot be easily bought here were my activities. I procured three new books. My son came down from Cambridge and we dined out one evening, then attended a concert. That is the extent of my wild adventures in town."

Looking at Emmeline, whose eyes kept flitting back to the admiral, he said, "It seems all the interesting activity might be happening here, what with two new gentlemen amongst us. Have you become acquainted with Admiral Tennant and Mr Stanton then?"

Emmeline blushed at the observation and looked straight ahead.

"Yes, we were introduced to them," Francine replied, with a speaking look at her sister, "at a dinner at the Whittakers, which was given to discuss our upcoming trip to the seaside. Will you be of the party, Mr Creighton?"

He sighed. "I believe it is too soon. Too much merriment for me at present. I would not be good company. I am still in mourning, you know."

"Of course you are," Emmeline replied, patting his arm. "But surely you could walk along the promenades, and perhaps fish or go on a boating excursion? There is much to do there besides balls. We do not travel until later in June. An exact date has not been set."

"Perhaps I may join the group for the last s'ennight. I cannot say yet. But I *would* enjoy fishing." A small smile played about his lips. "James will be on vacation by then so perhaps he and I may join you towards the end of your visit."

"Margaret will like that," Emmeline revealed. "She and Rose Carey will be of our party. Although I dare say such handsome young ladies will find many potential suitors at the resorts."

"Suitors, yes, but also many rakes and n'er'do'wells, I would think," retorted Francine. "I hardly know how to protect her from such and yet allow her to have adventure and enjoy society. Besides, Margaret is not yet officially 'out' and has not had a season in town, or even in Bath, although I am not sure how such a thing might be arranged ..." Francine frowned. She would need to talk with Marianne more about this.

"My sister lives in Surrey," Mr Creighton said, "and plans to take a house in town for the next season, when her daughter will come out. I could ask her ... Carey and I have talked of such a possible arrangement for his Rose next year ..."

Francine looked at him with some alarm. "Margaret ... in London ... oh, dear, it has come upon us so quickly." She had to catch her breath.

Emmeline laughed. "I doubt Margaret would agree with you!"

The group now paused at a woodworking booth and Margaret claimed her mother's attention for the purchase of a jewel box. "See the fine carving along the edges? I adore the leaves and vines; it is just what I would make if I had such skills. Oh, please may I buy it for my hairpins, shoe flowers, and ribbons and such? I am no longer a child. The price is not *too* dear, is it Mama?"

Francine pursed her lips. She had no idea if the price was fair, or if it was affordable within the confines of the budget Elinor had set for them. How tedious. Money was always tedious. Her lips pursed in frustration.

Mr Creighton touched her arm and gave her an almost-imperceptible nod, to her great relief.

She then turned to Margaret. "Of course you may have it. You are becoming a young lady and will one day have jewels as well to keep in such a lovely box."

Margaret's face burst into a smile. Francine was relieved Elinor was not with them today; likely she would not approve such an expenditure. Nor would she understand the importance of such an item for a young lady soon to be 'out'—a young lady only now showing an interest in feminine things. This interest must be encouraged. Margaret must have the carved box.

The next booth drew the women's attention with its fine ewers and vases and bowls. After watching the clay being thrown on a wheel by a young man, and an older woman shaping a different piece by hand, Francine discovered a vase she liked and looked to her sister for an opinion. Emmeline had fine taste in such things. But her sister was now on the admiral's arm, her face aglow. Francine chuckled. Emmeline, too, would now deem the Honiton Fair a great success.

Francine looked around for Margaret, who just moments ago had been proudly showing Rose and Mrs Carey her new carved box, but the girls were not to be seen.

"Olivia, where have the girls got to?" Her friend handed her Margaret's new box.

"They fancied some candy floss and set off to find that booth. They are together and should be safe enough. After all, this is Honiton, not London." Olivia ran her fingers fondly along the curve of a lovely vase.

Their group visited other displays showing lengths of fine cloth, woven hangings, tools, and then sampled roasted nuts and some excellent cider before Francine again scanned the nearby crowd for Margaret and Rose. They had still not returned. Her breath locked within her chest and her colour rose but then, to her great relief, she heard their voices behind her.

"Let us convince our mothers that we must try the ginger-bread," Rose said and both girls laughed.

"And I am very much in need of some cider—I am parched!" cried Margaret.

Francine turned to see both girls—flushed, their hair blowsy, their gowns no longer fresh— looking as if they had been running.

"Now where have you been? You look a fright. I do hope you have not been climbing trees or engaging in footraces!" Francine scowled at them.

Rose looked at the ground, mumbled something, and moved off to join her mother.

"You are exactly right, Mama. We challenged two young men to a footrace, which we won, and then climbed a tree to gloat over our victory." She flashed her mother a sassy smile.

"Well, no matter," Francine spluttered. "You are here now. Please stay with our group—our entire group—the remainder of the day."

"Certainly, Mama. If I may but have some cider and a slice of gingerbread?"

Francine could not deny her child such sustenance.

After sampling and purchasing the delights at other food booths, taking in the acrobat show, and quaffing a good portion of the local cider on offer, the group made to depart, each in their separate coaches. Margaret managed to escape once more until her mother spied her near the servants' wagon and urgently motioned her daughter to the coach.

"Whatever are you doing with them, Margaret? You have no business there."

With a sheepish expression, Margaret mumbled, "Oh, nothing of importance," and climbed into the coach.

Such shenanigans were exhausting and Francine was happy to settle into the coach for the ride home. She had no energy left to confront Margaret and the incident soon slipped from her mind.

On the return journey both Margaret and Emmeline appeared consumed with their own thoughts. Emmeline clutched a small posy to her heart and looked dreamily out of the window. A gift from the admiral? Mr Walford alternately watched Emmeline with angst then glared through the opposite window. The bearded stranger's face poked into the images of the day that were sifting through Francine's mind and an unsettled mood prevailed in the coach.

CHAPTER SEVEN

*E*mmeline Harrington delayed her return to the Midlands for the chance to travel further south, and Barton Cottage was aflutter with the enthusiastic chaos of packing for the journey. Marianne and Elinor had come over specially to help the travelers choose what to pack, and to make a list of items that might be needed for them to appear in finer society once they reached the seaside. Gowns and other accoutrements draped every surface of the room.

"How I wish I were going with you!" Marianne exclaimed. "The seaside! I have not seen it since our honeymoon. It is no wonder artists and poets often live by the sea—so wild and untamed, so very romantic." Her eyes sparkled and Francine wondered what memories Marianne might have of her honeymoon sojourn on the western coast. Francine herself became lost in images of her own honeymoon at the Lake District years ago until—

"Mama, do you have sufficient funds to cover your planned purchases and any unexpected expenses for this journey? Mama!" Elinor's insistent voice plucked Francine from the nest of wistful memories.

"You must keep your wits about you, Mama, for your own sake and for Margaret's. You know her disposition and her love for adventure. Do try to stay alert. Now where will you keep your cash? I would advise that you not keep it all in one place because if you chance to be robbed, at least some of it may be missed by the thieves."

"Robbed? Oh dear! Elinor, do you really think we will be robbed?"

Elinor laughed gently and touched her mother's shoulder. "Of course not. You are in company with several others—at least on the road and at your lodgings—and have several astute gentlemen amongst your party. But just the same, all the adults must be watchful, including you."

Marianne flounced over with three gowns in her arms and faced her sister with a stern eye. "Dear Elinor, do not take all the joy away from Mama's journey before she has even begun! She need not worry about robbers. This is to be a journey of pleasure, and one put off far too long, in my opinion."

Elinor sighed. "Certainly she must enjoy herself. But Marianne, even you must admit that having one's money stolen would have a dreadful effect on the pleasure of one's journey. Mama does not have any particular gentleman watching the purses for her. There can be a pleasant balance of watchfulness and joy."

Francine wrung her hands. "Oh, dear! Perhaps I ought not undertake such an excursion without a gentleman to watch over me. Perhaps it is beyond—"

"Nonsense!" exclaimed Emmeline, entering from across the hall. "It is just the thing for you to do. Especially if you wish to *find* a gentleman to call your own. After all, I traveled here with no companion besides my maid and experienced no complications and met with no robbers."

"You had no distractions," Elinor added with a sly smile. "You were not on the lookout for —"

"Tish tosh. There are always distractions for an attractive woman in the know. Fine beaux may be met with anywhere. Now, which of these bonnets would be best for the seaside?"

"Take them both!" cried Marianne. "And purchase another at Sidmouth!"

～

The next evening at Whitwell, Sir John and Colonel Brandon handed the ladies down from the carriages and shepherded them into the drawing room for a farewell dinner. The colonel was always so attentive to Marianne. It filled Francine's heart to see the light in their eyes when they looked at each other. A well-matched couple indeed. As Francine looked about she observed Elinor's Edward awkwardly situated with Lady Middleton and two of her children, looking as if he would rather be elsewhere. Margaret was barely within the room when James Creighton appeared at her side. Both looked delighted and immediately made their way to Rose and her family.

The dinner party consisted of the travelers: Francine and Margaret Dashwood, Emmeline Harrington, Sir John Middleton and Mrs Jennings, Rose Carey, Camelia Whittaker and her husband, and Cecil Walford; their guides to the seaside—Hugh Stanton and Admiral Marcus Tennant; and some of the friends and family being left behind. Tonight's host Charles Creighton and his son James were expected to join the travelers for the second fortnight. Mr Walford approached Emmeline and, to Francine's surprise, he had no competition from the admiral, who seemed to have disappeared. Mr Creighton was also missing. Perhaps the men were playing billiards, or had stepped outdoors to smoke?

After some small talk, Francine made her way down the hallway to refresh herself before dinner. Her attention was caught by muffled sobs. It tugged at her heart and she followed the sound to find a girl huddled against the fireplace in one of the side rooms, her eyes swollen and her gown askew. Francine peered in and inquired, "Can I help you, my dear?" Two other servants rushed past her into the room and went immediately to the girl. Feeling helpless and trusting the girl was in good hands, Francine withdrew.

Shortly after she returned to the drawing room the admiral himself swaggered in. Emmeline left Mr Walford's side in an instant, hastening to the admiral and basking in the glory of his apparent favour. Charles Creighton had also returned and stood at the fireplace, gazing into the unlit fire, appearing deep in thought. Had seeing other couples prompted a renewal of his grief and despair? It had been so for herself at times.

Dinner was announced and the large group made their way to the table. The admiral and Hugh Stanton would leave the next morning for their homes in the south of the county. Mr Stanton had offered to secure rooms for the travelers at the London Inn until they found a house to let that was large enough and suitable for the party. All eyes were alight at the thought of their impending journey.

Then, to nearly everyone's surprise, Cecil Walford stood to speak. "There has been a slight change of plans, for my part. I have urgent business in the North but I plan to rejoin the party within a fortnight. In my stead, and to add to the safety of the group, Mr Creighton has offered to travel with you immediately. His son also," he said, with a glance at Margaret. "I am indebted to him as I know the grief he now endures. I pray he will find the excellent fishing near Sidmouth to be a comfort."

"But Walford, surely you can delay—"

Mr Walford held up his hand to Sir John. "I am the best

judge of my own business, and shall depart at first light." With that he left the room without so much as a goodbye.

Those at the table exchanged puzzled looks. Charles Creighton lingered at his self-appointed post in front of the fireplace.

Francine became aware again of an undercurrent of disease. Mr Creighton remained distracted and aloof whilst the admiral readily commanded the attention of all, especially Emmeline.

In an effort to comfort herself, Francine imagined that— whilst the admiral showed no interest in her—she would likely meet with many other equally suitable men once the party were ensconced at Sidmouth. Such self-assurances smoothed her countenance but did nothing to alleviate her sense of disappointment about the admiral, or dispel the underlying uncertainty that she could manage to attract any man at all.

Perhaps she should resign herself to purchase paints and canvas and join Mrs Whittaker. A little smile escaped her— Marianne would *not* approve of that plan.

CHAPTER EIGHT

*T*he travelers departed in the late morning on the appointed day. The relative quiet of the carriage ride was a welcome respite after the flurry of packing for the journey of four weeks at the southern coast of Devonshire. Mr Creighton's carriage was comfortably familiar. This time Margaret joined her mother and aunt in its enclosure as the day was overcast and blustery. Charles Creighton gallantly joined his son on horseback; consequently the ladies were free to share their hopes and excitement about the resort without the judgement of male ears. Emmeline and Margaret chatted excitedly, but Francine was content to listen—and neither seemed to notice her silence.

Partway on the journey the Whittaker's coach joined their entourage—that entourage consisting of Mr Creighton's coach, and Sir John's coach carrying himself and Mrs Jennings. Lady Middleton preferred to stay at home with the children and there was no protest to this from any quarter.

As the group reached the far end of the Honiton Hills, the fog lifted somewhat and the sea came into view, sparkling in the distance. The village, below the red cliffs, was snugged into the curve of the bay and partially hidden by remnants of low-lying clouds.

Francine's stomach fluttered up into her throat. This was really happening. She was truly on a journey of pleasure. A momentous journey, undertaken alone, or leastways not in the company of any specific man to care for her. A shudder moved through her, part fear and part delight.

Soon the coaches pulled up in front of the London Inn.

In her excitement, Emmeline cried, *"How will my soul find room for its happiness? It seems already bursting!'* Oh, my dear Fanny Burney was right!" Emmeline looked about her, this way and that, and laughed aloud.

Margaret and her mother exchanged an eyeroll and a smile. The ladies disembarked and were joined by Mrs Jennings, Mrs Whittaker, and her granddaughter Rose. Tendrils of fog curled around the corners of buildings, and Francine's cloak and hair held a touch of the seaside damp. Her body swayed softly to the steady rhythm of the waves breaking endlessly on shore. A tangy smell accosted her nose, reminding her she was now far from the fields and hills of Honiton, and even farther from Norland—truly away from every home she had ever known. Although the reason was not clear, she felt like a young girl again, as if many layers had been peeled away.

The men supervised the unloading of the luggage by the coachmen and gave the grooms instructions about the horses and coaches. Sir John's voice and laughter could be heard above the jostling. Such a cheerful man, and so generous. Francine's heart was suddenly full of appreciation—he had done so much for her and her daughters. And now, this holiday was an opportunity for Margaret to move in a less confined and more varied society, an opportunity Francine could not herself give to her daughter but for which she was most grateful.

As they stood waiting, she peered down the street in each direction to see what shops might be found. A few people strolled on the promenade. One older couple. Three young ladies carrying parasols, whom Margaret watched closely. Some little distance behind them strode two young men in fine dress, their tall hats and walking sticks adding a swagger to their appearance. A fishing boat was slowly pulling into shore. Fishwives stood at the ready to process the day's catch.

Mrs Jennings turned to the ladies. "Well, my dears, it is time for tea. I, for one, am famished. A lovely fruit tart would be just the thing."

Mr Whittaker joined them. "A splendid idea, Mrs Jennings. But first let us change out of our dusty travel attire. I have been recommended a tea house not many steps away—it has a fine view to the sea. I warrant refreshments will be welcomed by all?" He raised an eyebrow to the ladies, and everyone bustled to their rooms to prepare for their first exploration of Sidmouth.

The gentlemen were waiting in the public room as the ladies descended the stairs in fresh gowns and hats. A hum of anticipation filled the air. The Whittakers led the way, followed by Rose and Margaret—each on one of young James' arms, then Sir John and Mrs Jennings, and Mr Creighton with Francine and Emmeline on each arm. The invigorating breeze stung sharp in their nostrils. Summer presented itself quite differently here.

Soon all were seated at a large window with a splendid view of the beach, and a cart of culinary delights was brought about whilst tea was poured. The tea house was abuzz with customers and the travelers' eyes were agog with the variety of people to be seen and wondered about. Margaret and Rose were deep in whispers and muffled giggles, and there was no lack of young gentlemen eyeing them with interest. Francine recalled Marianne's encouragements ("Be out in public as much as possible and ensure Margaret smiles"), and Elinor's cautions ("Some of society's norms may be set at naught at the seaside; Margaret must temper her friendly nature with caution and be always properly chaperoned"). Yes, my mothering duties will continue to be required here.

"I have been told the seafood on offer down the way is excellent, and I recommend that establishment for our dinner tonight," Sir John said. "Beyond that, we shall see what invitations come to us. I have sent word to Stanton and to Admiral Tennant that we are now arrived. We must also seek accommodations that will suit our group for the coming weeks. The innkeeper has given me some names and I will send inquiries immediately."

"Be sure there is a room for Walford when he arrives," added Creighton.

"Aye, that."

"We must also make arrangements for fishing—discover the best spots and what bait and tackle are needed," Mr Creighton said, answered by nods of agreement from Sir John and Mr Whittaker. "And perhaps one day a jaunt on a fishing boat? See, here, this pamphlet gives some details." He passed it over to Sir John. The men were in enthusiastic agreement, even young James.

The admiral had offered to arrange a pleasure cruise on his boat for both gentlemen and ladies, with a few stops for exploring, and had also mentioned hosting a dinner at what he called his castle, but days and times were yet to be settled upon.

Rose ventured, "I would like a walk down the promenade this evening, as far in each direction as possible, to see what might offer and to see and be seen."

"And to determine what we might need to purchase at the shops," added Emmeline. "I wonder if it is always so breezy here? It is difficult to keep one's hat in place. And what does one wear to a dinner at a castle?"

"The ladies in the shops will likely be helpful in that regard," said Mrs Whittaker. "As we promenade, I will scout for places to set up my easel, look for picturesque scenes, and observe the light. I do so enjoy the light at the seaside; it has a much different quality from that at home in the hills."

"May we not also explore on horseback?" asked Margaret, reaching for a piece of cake. "Not only along the beach, but also in the woods and hills? I wager the views from higher up will be worth the ride. And I see many large birds soaring above the hills. I wonder about them."

Francine cringed at the thought of riding horseback. While Henry had taught all his daughters the finer points of riding, it had been many years since Francine sat a saddle. She doubted her skills after so many years and feared her awkwardness would hinder the party, yet she did not wish Margaret to be unsupervised. Mrs Jennings and Mrs Whittaker would not participate in such a ride. That left herself and Emmeline to chaperone.

"A good thought, Miss Dashwood. I am all for exploring, and I myself would much prefer to ride than walk," said Mr Creighton. "The hills and cliffs look like a great adventure. I shall talk to the innkeeper and the ostler to see what can be arranged."

His comment put Francine in mind of his limp and she wondered again how the injury had occurred. Walking on steep terrain would indeed be difficult for him.

Mrs Jennings folded her napkin. "Well, we have a good many things to tempt us, do we not? I say after tea we promenade, and then over dinner we might concoct some plans. Oh, and I also wish to see what the circulating library has on offer.

I am a great reader, you know. I wonder what their hours are?" she mused as she rose from the table.

"Fanny Burney tells us that *'Books are perhaps the mind's first luxury'*," Emmeline offered.

"Must we always hear what Fanny Burney thinks?" exclaimed Margaret.

The listeners traded bemused expressions.

Emmeline gave Margaret a hard stare. "Yes, we must. We are traveling in her footsteps. Although many women may have journeyed so, only she has left us words to share her experience. Her voice enriches every sight and sound for me."

"And my sister enjoys sharing her every thought and idea," Francine added with a wry smile at Emmeline.

"What of the balls?" Rose reminded them. "We must see about the balls."

Mr Whittaker held up a pamphlet. "It says here the balls are held every Wednesday. What a delight for the ladies," he said, and with a sly grin added, "and I assume there will be a cardroom ..."

"A weekly ball! Our unmarried ladies will be overjoyed!" exclaimed Mrs Jennings. "We all of us live in such retirement in the country. This will be an opportunity to meet and make new friends—and perhaps some may become much more." She winked, her laughter trilled and, as it did at home, attracted every eye to their party. They stood and made for the door.

Francine took it all in with wonder. She had never been part of such a congenial group. When she had traveled in the past—and that was rarely—Henry had made all the decisions, handled all the arrangements, talked to all their friends. She had simply followed along, drifting in the wake of his charm. An opportunity such as this journey might not come her way again. I must fortify myself to try everything, and pursue any interest that might reveal itself. Hesitancy would only lead to regrets. This was a time to try new things. If not now, when? A sense of exhilaration pulsed through her. She was determined to make many treasured memories—the kind that might fill the cold dark days and nights of the long winters ahead, especially once Margaret was gone. It occurred to her to follow Fanny Burney's example and make a journal of her adventure. Surely the shops would have some type of journal on offer, along with some stationery on which to write to her daughters.

Later, after a fine dinner, as she prepared for bed Francine's thoughts turned to Emmeline's remedy for those dark lonely times ahead—that of finding a husband. But how to meet gentlemen who were strangers? Would her sister lead the way in this endeavour? Or be completely immersed in the attentions of the admiral? Francine's brows knit in thought as she fell asleep to the ceaseless drum of the waves on the shore.

The morning fog wrapped the village in its wooly blanket. The gentlemen braved it and left early for fishing. Once the ladies wakened and had taken a light breakfast at the inn, they set off to investigate the lending library and some of the shops. Each had a list of items to purchase after observing the many elegant women strolling at the seaside the evening prior.

As their party headed towards the door the innkeeper bustled up.

"Pardon me, Mrs Jennings, but a message has come for you and your party from Admiral Tennant."

"Thank you. There's a good man." She dropped a coin in his hand.

His eyes reflected a curious sense of wonder. Was it Mrs Jennings' generosity? Or the identity of the message sender?

"Let us make for that beachside bench we saw last night, ladies, and I shall read it out," she said.

A few rays of sunlight pierced the pall and the fog began to break up as they reached the handsomely crafted wood and stone bench. After taking some few minutes to settle herself, Mrs Jennings broke the seal and unfolded the note.

"My dear friends, I have word you are arrived at the London Inn. Please join me at Bellevue tomorrow evening for dinner. This may be sooner than etiquette recommends, but all the better to enable me to assist you with plans to fill your holiday with pleasure. My daughter Florentina will join us, so do bring the young ladies in your party. Stanton and his wife will also attend. This very evening I shall join you on the promenade to receive your reply. Watch for me. Admiral Tennant"

"Well! He lets no moss grow under his feet, I dare say. Or perhaps he is quite eager for the company of a certain lady?" Mrs Jennings looked at Emmeline with a mischievous eye. "What say you, friends? Shall we dine at Bellevue tomorrow?"

Emmeline flushed with pleasure. "Of course we shall. But we must get ourselves to the shops as soon as may be. I am in need of a few items to add a touch of luxury to my costume."

They all agreed, and so Mrs Jennings rose and led them down the street.

"I wonder how old the admiral's daughter is?" mused Margaret.

"And how many local young people she knows?" added Rose. "Surely it will be beneficial for us to meet Florentina and her friends?"

∼

The ladies returned to the hotel by mid-afternoon, each pleased with her acquisitions. The shop owners had been most helpful in advising on suitable details for dining at Bellevue, the seat of Admiral Tennant.

Francine untied the bow on the box of stationery papers she had purchased at the library on which to write to Elinor and Marianne. She placed the paper carefully on the writing desk in the room she shared with Margaret and Rose and Emmeline, then unwrapped the holiday journal she had purchased and set it next to the stationery. Perching lightly in the chair she dashed off a brief note.

June —

My Dear Elinor,

This note will advise you we have all arrived safely at Sidmouth. We are lodging at the London Inn, which is nice enough. We enjoyed afternoon tea at a seaside tea house and learned of the many diversions available hereabouts. After a fine seafood dinner, we were all of us ready for our beds. The sea air is refreshing. This morning we visited some shops, and this evening we will dine at Bellevue, the seat of Admiral Tennant—we met him at the dinner at the Whittakers. Surely after tonight I will have more news worthy of my pen. I trust you are all safe and well and that Marianne gets on agreeably. Do keep an eye on her. Share this news with her and I shall write again very soon.

Your loving mother

Francine glanced over at her new journal with a wave of excitement. What tales I shall tell! My activities must be memorable enough to write about. She sanded and sealed her letter but there was no silver dish on which to place it for the post. Mrs Jennings would know how to post it, and she handed the letter to her when they met in the parlour on their way out.

The gentlemen returned shortly before teatime, their faces tanned and their smiles wide as they joined the ladies at the tea house. Their sport had been good, their guide knowledgeable, and the very fish they caught would be served to them at dinner. Francine studied each face with curiosity. She could not fathom such joy being the result of catching fish.

Her puckered brow must have caught Charles Creighton's eye. He gave her the broadest grin she had yet seen on him.

"Have you ever been fishing, Mrs Dashwood?"

She laughed. "No. I have not. The idea of catching and killing something has never attracted my interest. I enjoy eating well-prepared fish but I do not wish to know anything about how it gets on my plate."

He chuckled. "Yes, I can imagine that is so. To me, fishing is about much more than obtaining something to eat. There is skill involved, and patience to be sure. But there is something else. Whilst fishing, a person is out in the air, in all kinds of weather, interacting with not only one's fellow sportsmen, but also with the wind and the clouds or sun, with the water and its murky depths or whipped up waves, and with the canny fish themselves. It is a harmony with the bounty of earth and sea and sky. Yes, I find the experience can be so much more."

There was a light in his eyes she had not noticed before. Francine was surprised to see him so pleased, and rather stunned at his explanation. She had never connected such profound notions with fishing. It had seemed just another boring pastime enjoyed by men.

As she reflected on his words, flashes of memory stirred within her—she could almost feel the wind in her hair; the rhythm of a horse beneath her; see clouds floating across the sky or branches moving overhead; trees lining a woody path, scenting the air with resins or blossoms; hear grasses rustling in open meadows. She was surprised to recognize a sudden sadness at such feelings being absent from her recent life—indeed, such feelings had been shut down for years. How could she have forgotten?

With a slight blush she observed, "It is ... encouraging ... to see you in such a state of pleasure."

He nodded. "It is encouraging to feel such joy again. I had doubted that I could."

"Thank you for explaining so clearly, Mr Creighton. I had never thought of fishing in such a way. But, in remembering my girlhood days of riding, I understand you. When I was a girl, riding a horse was not just about getting from one place to another. It was a joining of life and spirit into one movement—mine, the horse's, the grass beneath and the sky above, and the trees and air all around. Yes, I know of what you speak, and am glad for having those memories reawakened for me."

He gave her a quizzical look and seemed about to say something but Sir John asked him a question and the conversation took another turn.

After hearty agreement that their second night's dinner was the finest they had ever eaten—made finer by the gentlemen sharing stories from their day of sport—the group repaired to the promenade for the anticipated rendezvous with Admiral Tennant.

"Come, Fran, take my arm and let us lead the way." Emmeline pulled her sister to the front of their group. "We shall have a better view here and not be distracted by so much conversation." Francine hastened along until they were ahead of the others. Emmeline's restless eyes searched the promenade and the beach while they walked.

"Sister, do not think me ignorant of your true motive," Francine said, shaking her arm free, irritation creeping into her voice. "You wish to be the first sight to greet the admiral."

"What of it? We must put ourselves forward if we wish to accomplish anything. You, too, should be glad to be more visible. As my dear Fanny advises us, *'You must learn not only to judge but to act for yourself.'* If we do not, who will? We neither of us now have anyone to act for our interests. Who knows what strangers may cast their eyes upon us with pleasure? After all, that is why we are here, is it not?"

Francine had to admit that was true but she could not find comfort in feeling so … on display. She would sooner wait at the sidelines for someone to honour her with his notice. The sidelines were a place of comfort. She tried to be easy, now nodding and smiling at those they passed on the promenade, as a form of practice in socializing with strangers. She had almost succeeded when Emmeline stiffened and gasped. "He is here. Oh, he is here!"

The admiral was striding towards them.

"Ahoy Admiral, and well met," Sir John called out. "What a fine dinner we have had," he declared, and then regaled the admiral with details of their gastronomic delights. The admiral smiled and nodded all whilst casting furtive glances at Emmeline.

After surreptitiously dropping her sister's arm, Emmeline gracefully moved herself so as to be next to the admiral.

Francine watched her closely. My sister basks in the admiral's radiance as I once basked in Henry's—the difference being that Emmeline is acting independently, moving towards what she wants. This observation might have been helpful if one had formed a particular goal, but Francine found herself faltering over what it was that she even wanted. The words of a childhood horse master echoed in her head. *'Who is in charge of this ride, young lady—you or the horse? To get where you wish to go, at the pace you wish to take, you must make a plan and give your horse direction or who knows where you will end up?'* This seemed perfectly rational. Why had she never applied it to anything other than riding?

"Let us move nearer the excitement of the waves," the admiral said, offering Emmeline his arm.

"Nothing is as refreshing as the sea spray," said Mrs Whittaker, with a wink at Mrs Jennings.

Margaret and Rose ran ahead, laughing with delight.

In her new frame of mind, Francine was tempted to join them.

CHAPTER NINE

*A*fter admiring the sunset, the group left the beach and gathered around the largest table in the public room at the inn. Smoke wafted about and Francine found it just as disagreeable as she had at the boxing in Honiton. Men indulged in such irritating habits.

"Hire an ostler from here tomorrow," the admiral was saying. "They all know how to reach Bellevue. It is not far, but the road can be challenging and is certainly not to be attempted after nightfall for those unfamiliar. If you leave here mid-afternoon, we shall have time to enjoy tea and tour the grounds before dinner. My guest rooms are ready to accommodate you overnight."

"Sir, that is very kind, but we are rather a large party," Mrs Jennings said with a dubious expression.

"And Bellevue is rather a large house," the admiral replied with a winsome grin. "Some call it a castle, but you must decide for yourselves. Your party will return to the inn after breakfast the following day, as you must prepare for the Sidmouth ball, yes? People come from miles around. Although each resort has its own ballroom, many travellers wish to meet as many new faces as possible whilst on holiday, so the resort towns hold balls on different nights. My daughter and I shall attend as well. The Stantons will join us for dinner at Bellevue but not for the ball. His wife has taken a dislike to crowds; says they give her the headache." After a swig of brandy and a puff on his cigar, he asked, "Now what other pursuits have you fixed on?"

Mr Creighton spoke up about exploring on horseback. "I have made arrangements for Saturday, if the weather permits. We shall have a guide and ride expanses of beach as well as take to the hills on trusty cobs. Our young ladies have expressed a desire for this activity, as has my son, but I would wish for one of the ladies to chaperone. Mrs Dashwood, can I persuade you?"

The colour drained from her face, and Francine was glad of the low light in the room. Recalling her advice to herself— if not now, when?—she gave a measured reply. "I agree there must be a woman to chaperone, and it appears I am the likeliest candidate, unless I can convince my sister. We rode as children, but it has been many years ... Mr Creighton, would it be possible to schedule a shorter ride a day or two before we try the challenge of the cliff paths?"

"I am sure that can be arranged and I am happy to oblige. Anyone who does not ride regularly would benefit from exercising those particular muscles. Miss Dashwood, do you ride often?"

"No sir, I do not, although Rose does. Perhaps she and I might join on the short ride as well?"

James spoke. "Father, I shall be happy to assist our group on any rides." He flashed a smile at Margaret. "The more secure everyone is in the saddle, the more fun and excitement we shall have."

Rose and Margaret beamed at him.

Emmeline had not responded to Francine's remark. Her

attention was on the admiral, who sat next to her, rather than the conversation at hand.

Francine pressed her lips together. People who pursued the things they wanted had the annoying habit of sometimes doing so at the expense of others.

Sir John spoke. "My leg has been giving me the devil of late. I do not wish to encourage it. I regret I must decline this outing."

"Might we persuade you, Admiral, to join us on Saturday? Surely you know the area as well as any guide," Mr Creighton said.

"Sounds like an engaging time. Yes, I will join you. But I spend more time on the water than on land or beast, so do not give up your guide, sir! Now Mrs Harrington," he said, placing his fingers lightly on Emmeline's arm, "you are a lady who enjoys adventure, do you not? Say you will gift us with your company on this ride."

Mrs Jennings and Mrs Whittaker exchanged a speaking look and Emmeline flushed with pleasure. "As my sister says, it has been many years since I have travelled by any means other than carriage. But, if you insist Admiral, I shall make an exception. I *would* like to take in the view from on high."

"Capital!" he said with a nod and a long look at Emmeline. "Then it is settled. Nothing can stop us, short of disagreeable weather."

"Hear. Hear." Glasses clinked and laughter rose.

Admiral Tennant spoke again. "I have taken the liberty of hiring a crew to man my sailing boat for a pleasure cruise offshore whilst you are here. Which of you will join us? It is comfortable for a dozen or more. We will stop at two nearby beaches to explore, and try our hand at some fishing if the winds cooperate."

"My sea legs have long since left me," declared Mrs Jennings. "I will not board a ship of any size nowadays. I am sure those of us who wish to stay on land will find something amusing to do—shopping, cards, perhaps a lecture or a reading."

"That will be a fine time for me to set up my easel and attempt to portray some of the local sights," Mrs Whittaker said.

"I have never been on a boat!" Margaret exclaimed. "A water adventure will give me something exciting to tell Mr Newbury."

James Creighton's face fell, and the others glanced awkwardly amongst themselves.

With a crimson blush Margaret said, "Oh, he is a neighbour who has recently joined the Navy. I had thought occasional correspondence from home might be ... comforting to him ..." She looked across the room and met no one's eye—especially not James'.

The next day was a flurry of dressing, last minute purchases, and packing for the dinner and overnight stay at Bellevue. Was it really a castle, as the admiral said?

The wheels of the two carriages rattled along the byway, the horses turning this way and that as they made the ascent of the red cliffs. Mr Creighton and his son rode on horseback, with Sir John joining the Whittakers in their carriage.

Bellevue was described as sitting high on a bluff.

"Can anything be more romantic?" Emmeline exclaimed. "A castle looking out to sea, owned by a handsome and powerful admiral. He purchased the place when he resigned his commission in the Navy a few years ago, and claims he could never be happy unless he could gaze out to sea. I look forward to hearing more stories of his wartime heroism."

"He does seem to have no lack of tales to tell," observed

Mrs Jennings, jostling along next to Francine in the coach. "I enjoy an exciting story as much as the next person, but why must the admiral be always the hero?"

"Because that is who he is!" retorted Emmeline. "I look forward to seeing him at the helm of his sailing vessel on the cruise. I like a man who knows how to take command."

Francine muffled a laugh. "Do you really, Em? You are, yourself, a person who likes to be in control—of arrangements, of others, of most everything. He does not seem the type of man to share power, but rather would have all listen to him and follow his orders, as he is used to. Do you not think so?" she asked, turning to the others.

Margaret's eyes were wide but she said nothing.

"It is up to each one's personal taste, I suppose," Mrs Jennings opined. "My choice was a man not against sharing certain powers—some he kept for himself, and some I kept for myself. Fortunately, we agreed on these distributions. Seymour has been gone these long years, yet I do still miss him at times. He was a kind but serious sort of man, and my outgoing, saucy nature was just the thing to balance our temperaments. Ah, me, the years pass so quickly." She stared out of the coach window in uncharacteristic reverie.

Bellevue was indeed a castle, but far less impressive than Francine had pictured in her mind's eye. The sea could only be viewed from one end. The building was a sprawling construction but had no towers. In her opinion, a place required a tower or two to be considered a real castle.

Before any comments could be shared or discussion ensue, the admiral strode towards them accompanied by a tall, dark-haired young lady in a ruby gown. She had strong facial features and a tall lean build.

"Welcome to Bellevue my friends! Here, boy, step up and take these horses. You, these things must be carried to the guest wing. Well, well, let us move to the terrace for refreshments."

As they found seats and the servants brought around beverages and cakes, the admiral rose, lifting his daughter by her elbow. "Friends, may I present my daughter Florentina? I think her a great beauty—which she inherited from her mother, God rest her soul. Florrie, we have here two young ladies with whom I trust you will become the best of friends —Miss …"

Mr Creighton stood and supplied the forgotten names. "Miss Rose Carey and Miss Margaret Dashwood." Rose and Margaret stood and curtsied, and the gentlemen present stood and bowed as the rest of the introductions were made. Florentina dipped a small curtsey to the group. Her mouth formed a smile but her dark eyes held no joy.

The guests admired the view and the cakes whilst the young ladies engaged in conversation of their own, and soon the melody of their laughter drifted through the air. Whatever did they find so amusing? Young James joined them and appeared transfixed by attentions from Florrie. Perhaps that was just as well. Margaret did not appear concerned by it, and Francine wanted her daughter to meet many new friends and potential suitors whilst here before considering settling down with seafaring Newbury or young Creighton.

Dinner was generous and well-prepared. Francine found her appetite heartier since arriving at Sidmouth. She credited the sea air, and concluded the pleasures of the table would need to be limited if she were to continue to fit into her gowns. After the meal, Florrie and Rose took turns at the pianoforte, with Margaret lifting her voice in song. The admiral's daughter appeared about the same age as Rose and Margaret, but there was a worldly air about her which made her seem older. Perhaps she had travelled with her father? How had she lost her mother, and when? It was not a question one could ask, and no explanation was offered by either. And such a discussion would not be proper dinner conversation.

Francine turned her attention to her sister. Tonight, when they retired, she would speak to her, remind her of their plan to meet many people. If Emmeline's attention remained fixed on the admiral, Francine would lack the guidance she was depending upon to navigate the world of resort society.

A loud guffaw pierced her thoughts. The admiral appeared to be in his cups, his conversation growing louder and coarser.

Mr Creighton stood. "Admiral, I fear the sea air is having its effect on me. Your hospitality has been most gracious but our recent travel, the fine fare we have just enjoyed, and your excellent wine leave me ready for slumber. The diversions of tomorrow evening will likely run late so perhaps we could be shown to our rooms? Of course, I do not wish to break up the party ..."

"By all means. Yes, the sea air does have that effect until you get used to its bracing nature. Florrie, ring the bell for Burton."

"Oh, but Father ..." she protested, a scowl wrinkling her tall forehead.

"Do not counter me, girl!"

Some drew back at the tone of his voice but Florrie did not flinch. She stood and, before moving to ring the bell, directed a sharp gaze at her father.

Margaret, ever sensible of tension and ever eager to assuage it said, "Florrie, it is no matter. We have the ball tomorrow night, and what a grand time we shall have. Let us all go to bed and dream about it."

Florrie reached out to grasp the hands of her new friends

and then did as her father had directed. Soon the servant appeared.

"Burton, take care that my guests want for nothing. Any measures needed for their comfort. Anything at all, you hear me?"

On that somewhat uncomfortable note, they were ushered to their rooms.

"I certainly shall not!" snapped Emmeline, her eyes sparking at Francine as they sat on the bed. "It is no fault of mine that I found my man at the beginning of our holiday. I will take every opportunity to be with him, and perhaps, before we depart for home … no, Fran, you shall have to fend for yourself. I am still here to offer advice, but think on this—if you are seen with the admiral and me, your status will be elevated in the eyes of other men. Having lived here for three years, he is sure to know some who might be keen for an introduction. No, I refuse to see how my devotion to the admiral would hamper our plans. Mine are moving along more quickly than yours, that is all. Now leave me be. I have many words and scenes to review in my mind that should lead to very pleasant dreams. Who knows, in the future I may be welcoming you to Bellevue."

Francine knew her cause was futile. She could only hope that a gentleman more dashing than the admiral would catch her sister's eye. Perhaps at the ball tomorrow night … surely her sister could not dance every dance with the admiral. Mrs Jennings would speak up against that, would she not? Francine turned to appeal to her friend but Mrs Jennings was already fast asleep.

In a short time the ladies were awakened by a rumbling at their door. Clumsy hands tugged at the knob. Francine froze, having no idea what action to take. It was fortunate Mrs Jennings had insisted on locking the door. "Servants, you know ... one can't be too careful these days. I should hate for any of my jewels to go missing." At the noisy disruption the lady arose from her bed, wrapping her dressing gown about her. Emmeline scampered to the fire and fetched her a sturdy piece of wood.

"My dear," whispered Mrs Jennings, "I hope I shall not need a weapon."

Mrs Jennings planted her feet and faced the door. "Who are you, and what do you want? Don't you know it is the middle of the night?" she demanded in a tone that left the sisters quailing.

"Oh ... ma'am ... it is I, your host ... Tennant. My ... apologies on the hour ... just came to me ... forgot to ask Mrs ... uh ... Emmeline ... first ... first dance!" He banged on the door with his fist.

Mrs Jennings' jaw dropped and she turned to Emmeline. "Tell him what you wish, but whatever you do, do not open that door. He is three sheets to the wind."

Emmeline's eyes grew wide but she called out, "Thank you, Admiral, I shall be delighted to dance the first with you tomorrow night." She grinned at her sister and Mrs Jennings, who exchanged an eye roll.

"Capital! ... rest easy ... and I shall ... a very good evening to you." His boots clomped down the hallway, away from the guest wing.

An enticing display of baked goods, meats, eggs, coffee, and chocolate greeted the guests in the breakfast room the next morning. Florrie sat down with them but her father had not yet made an appearance. Emmeline was effusive but the others ate quietly with little talk. A silent buzz charged the air, but Francine knew not if it had to do with the admiral or if minds were simply preoccupied with the busy day ahead in preparation for the ball. Had the others overheard the late-night interlude? Her eyes darted to Margaret. To her relief, her daughter was talking quietly with Mrs Whittaker and Rose, her eyes bright and her brow unperturbed. What would Margaret have done had the admiral bellowed at *her* door? Someone must have a talk with Margaret and Rose about such situations. Someone who possessed more knowledge about how to protect oneself from unwanted intrusions and advances. Francine was grateful for Mrs Jennings' brave presence last night. If it had been myself, alone ... well, she did not wish to think on that.

Florrie looked at the gentlemen. "I have requested the coaches be ready at ten this morning. Is that to your liking?"

"Yes, yes, my dear, that will be splendid," Sir John replied. "Gives us plenty of time. Or, the ladies rather. For the ball, of course. Seems to take them an age to get ready, eh Creighton?"

Mr Creighton turned from the window where he had been standing with his coffee. "What? Sorry, my mind was elsewhere."

"Time. Ten. Agreeable to leave then?"

"Ah, yes, most agreeable. Miss Tennant, you have been so thoughtful and an excellent hostess." He nodded at her then took a sip of coffee. "Do you suppose we might see your father before we depart?"

Florrie turned to him with an almost wearied expression, something more apt to be seen on the countenance of one much older. She pursed her lips into a twist. "Who can tell? My father is unpredictable and does what he will. I apologize for his lack of manners."

"No my dear, do not think on it," Mrs Whittaker said in

her soft voice. "You have performed commendably, and we are all so pleased to make your acquaintance and visit you here at your lovely home. I am sure you young ladies will enjoy yourselves tonight. You are welcome to visit us and even stay with us once we have our accommodations arranged. Sir John, have you had any response as to a house to let?"

"Only one on offer, and I have yet to see it," he replied. "After tonight's ball, we will settle things."

The coaches arrived at the door punctually and the guests departed. The admiral did not make an appearance.

Once in the coach Mrs Jennings observed, "Our admiral has a tendency to overindulge. I noticed it when he visited us. A habit from his rowdy days as a sailor, I dare say. He would do better to leave that behind, in my estimation."

"Do you mean he drinks too much? Did something happen last night?" Margaret said, looking at Rose and then back at Mrs Jennings.

"We had a rather rowdy caller at our chamber door last night, girls. Fortunately, I had insisted on using the lock—more to protect my jewels from wayward servants, but it served its purpose nonetheless. I hope you young ladies locked your door?"

Rose nodded. "I insisted. Father taught me to do so whenever I stay from home, or even at home when we have guests."

"I am glad you have someone looking out for you in that way," Mrs Jennings said. "And Miss Margaret, do you know how to deal with unwanted advances and intrusions? A chaperone will not always be to hand, you know."

"No, ma'am, I have never thought on it. I believed most of

the dangerous people to be in London or on the roads. Is that not the case?"

Mrs Jennings shook her head. "No, I am sorry to say there are also petty criminals and worse even in the country. And perhaps more so in the resorts. Young ladies must be especially wary, although young men, too, can be conned out of their guineas by those who might appear respectable. Not all swindlers and debauchers are of the lower orders. That is precisely why we travel as a group, and keep to established shops and tea houses and such, and the larger public balls—with trusted gentlemen such as Mr Creighton and young Creighton, Sir John, and Mr Whittaker to keep a watchful eye."

The young ladies exchanged a glance and folded their hands for a few moments, but before long they were chattering about gowns and ribbons for the evening's event.

CHAPTER TEN

This was to be Margaret's first public ball. Was she ready? Francine knew Margaret to be an excellent dancer, spirited yet graceful. New gowns could not be afforded but the young ladies had chosen ribbons, new shoe roses, and flowers for their hair. Francine studied herself in the mirror whilst her sister did her the service of securing a lovely feather in her faded brown curls.

"There. It is perfect. Fran, you look divine."

Francine's eyes found her sister's. Emmeline's sparkled with anticipation. Francine noted that her own did not. She felt more trepidation than anything. This would also be her first public ball since Henry died. How should she act? She had never paid much attention to the single ladies at a ball. Gliding about on Henry's arm was all she remembered about such events, and floating across the room in his arms—he had been a wonderful dancer. He socialized with everyone. She worked the long gloves up her arms. Would she actually be in another gentleman's arms tonight? Her stomach lurched. She could not picture herself so. Neither did she wish to spend the evening on the sidelines, with the older matrons who were beyond dancing ...

"Come, Fran. Let us look in on the girls."

Motherly duties. Francine was thankful for such; those would slip away soon enough, like the retreating tide.

To Francine's surprise, the girls were ready. Bubbles of excitement burst about the room as they laughed and posed in the long mirror and danced about.

"Mama, how do I look? Is everything as it should be? My flower?" Margaret twirled before her mother, her cheeks flushed and her eyes alight.

Could this be her youngest? This handsome creature? Francine felt the assault of the many years that had passed. A tear welled in her eye. How could this be happening when she herself felt as awkward as she remembered being at Margaret's age? She blinked rapidly so the pressing tear would not fall.

Emmeline stared at her speechless sister. With a nudge she said, "Fran, is she not ravishing? That shade of blue flatters her, do you not agree?"

Francine brushed away the clouds of regret flitting through her own mind and smiled at Margaret. "This will do very well, my dear. You look just as you should. I am a little in shock at what a young lady you have become ... when did this happen? Why, I clearly remember—like it was yesterday— being your age and attending my own first ball. Yes, you look splendid indeed. And Rose, you look fetching as well. You shall be the loveliest young ladies at the ball. I wonder how many will be in attendance?"

"I hope many, Mama. And I hope enough gentlemen will dance. Mr Creighton says this resort is known for its fishing and many fathers and sons holiday here, so perhaps there will be a good number of young men. And we *do* have Mr James to partner us." Margaret looked at Rose and the girls giggled at some private joke.

Emmeline nodded. "Fran, that is good news for you as well. The fathers. Robust sportsmen tend to be fine dancers, in my experience. We shall have partners aplenty, I dare say. And there is the admiral. A man with sea legs is surely adept on the dance floor."

Emmeline's predictions were all correct. Their party entered the ballroom where hundreds of candles blazed, refracting off the sparkling crystal into thousands of fiery stars. The sky's rosy hues painted a watercolour of light in the windows. With the doors flung open to the sea, the soothing rush of the tide under-girded the murmur of conversation and the musical notes of the players tuning up. Francine's heart leapt in spite of her attempts to contain it. She set her shoulders. *Why should I not be excited? After all, this is my second chance, a gift from the heavens that many would wish to experience.* She steadied her breathing and smoothed her face into the pleasant expression she had practiced in the mirror. Many eyes turned their way. There were indeed gentlemen aplenty. She tugged at her necklace and smiled.

Francine and Emmeline, arm in arm, made their way about the room, pausing near the open doors to take in the enchanting view and breathe deeply. No wonder so many extoll the sea air. The salty tang drifted about the ballroom, mingled with the aroma of burning candles, of food being prepared, and of the many bodies present. Emmeline's eyes darted about, kindling a slight misgiving in Francine. Surely the admiral would not disappoint her sister?

Margaret and Rose had also circled the room and were now engaged in conversation with two young men and a young lady. Francine wondered at them conversing without a proper introduction, then saw Mrs Jennings' eyes on the girls. If this was improper, would she not intervene? Mrs Whittaker followed her friend's gaze, and the two matrons nodded and smiled. All must be well. Francine had been advised that manners at the seaside were much eased from the more formal encounters deemed proper in London, or even in Bath and Brighton. But how much were they eased?

As if on a signal, the orchestra fell silent. A dignified gentleman took to the center of the room. After welcoming the guests to the ball, he announced the first dance and the musicians began a prelude. Gentlemen hurried about, seeking their first partner. Margaret and Rose joined Francine and Emmeline and introduced their new friends—a brother and sister, and the brother's friend. Charles Creighton and James Creighton approached as well.

The brother bowed to Rose, reached out his hand for hers, and they followed the sister and the other young man onto the floor, trailed by Margaret and James. He had simply extended his hand and Margaret, as if an understanding existed, happily glanced at her mother and then joined the formation.

"You will excuse me, ladies," Mr Creighton said. "I would happily partner either of you on the dance floor but this old leg injury has sadly put an end to my dancing days. I shall join the Whittakers and Mrs Jennings on the sidelines so as not to discourage other gentlemen from requesting your company." He bowed and departed.

Francine leaned closer to Emmeline and whispered, "I have wondered how he was wounded."

"Wounded? Who cares for that? I wonder the admiral has not yet appeared. I hope he has not met with an accident on his treacherous road." From their position at the edge of the room Emmeline scanned the crowd. "Shall I look into the cardroom, do you think?"

Francine frowned. "I would think not. Such blatant pursuit would not be proper, in my estimation. I may not be informed on all the social graces, but I do believe—even at the seaside—it is still expected the gentleman pursues the lady, not the other way around."

A rather plain gentleman approached. "I am confident you will dance when asked, Em. So if the admiral arrives later, you will be able to dance with him. I believe that expectation also still holds."

Emmeline's smiling countenance did not waver. "I would never commit such a social *faux pas.* I wonder which of us this gentleman will ask?"

He bowed to them both but it was no surprise to Francine when he made his request to Emmeline, who honoured him with a curtsey and moved onto the dance floor.

Standing alone in a ballroom was not something Francine had planned for. What should she do? Skitter over to Mrs Jennings on the sidelines? Just as she was ready to make a hasty retreat, a kindly-looking older gentleman appeared at her side.

"Would you do me the honour, madame?" he said with a bow.

It was time to leave doubts behind. Francine's throat croaked the expected words. "I would be delighted, sir."

And with that, Francine Dashwood took her first steps into the social world—for the second time in her life—her heart pounding every bit as wildly as it had when she first entered that world so many years ago.

Her partner was an excellent dancer. To her own surprise, the steps of the dance came back to her as if there had not been a gap of years. To be sure, she had danced a few times at the local parties, or in practice with her daughters, but then there she had not been on display, as she felt now. She comforted herself with the thought of the many lovely younger ladies upon whom the curious could fix their eyes. Including Margaret.

"And are you from the area here?" her partner asked.

"No, sir, we have traveled from north of Honiton." Is that telling him too much? She had forgotten to ask Emmeline—or Mrs Jennings or Mrs Whittaker—what were the limits of proper conversation amongst such strangers as they would find at the seaside.

"And you, sir—are you a local resident?"

"No ma'am. I am returning to London from visiting my sister near Cornwall."

They happened to move past where Mrs Jennings and Mrs Whittaker sat and Francine caught a wink from dear Mrs Jennings. There. All was well. She could now breathe and smile, and move lightly to the music, surrendering herself to the guidance of her expert partner.

"Do tell me more of Cornwall, sir; I have never been there. Do you find it agreeable?"

That first dance buoyed her confidence. To her surprise, she danced several times throughout the evening. When not on the floor, she joined Mrs Jennings and the Whittakers and Charles Creighton, with whom she now sat.

"What a charming event," Mrs Whittaker commented. "Such an array of interesting people—dancers, nondancers, chaperones … and men escaping to the cardroom." She chuckled. Sir John had long since absconded to that gentleman's enclave.

"And a pleasant atmosphere too," remarked Mrs Jennings. "I was not sure what the seaside would offer, but so far I have witnessed no untoward behaviour."

Mr Creighton offered a wry smile. "The night is young. Likely the rowdiness will come later, and hopefully out of doors, away from the more refined company." He turned to Francine. "Oh, how I miss dancing. I enjoy watching the couples. And you, Mrs Dashwood, are a most graceful creature gliding about." He looked into her eyes and smiled.

Colour raced from her bosom to the top of her head. "Why ... thank you, Mr Creighton. I do love dancing, although it has been many years. My late husband ... he was a wonderful dancer, and quite the social charmer. It feels very ... strange, being at such an event without him."

Mrs Jennings raised an eyebrow at her.

"I am sure it does," Mr Creighton said with a nod.

"But I am enjoying myself, very much. I feel almost a young girl again."

Her eyes searched the floor for Margaret and found her daughter dancing to a lively tune with her new friend's brother, but the newly-formed party remained close to each other in the formation.

"Shall I encourage Margaret to ... well ... to step away from her new group so she might meet other young people?"

"I think not," Mr Creighton replied. "Friendships take time to form, if you wish your daughter to find companions of a deeper sort, rather than many mere acquaintances. Time together, shared experiences—those are the glue of friendship, and more."

Francine's heart jumped within her chest. His comment seemed wise, but why did she feel he was speaking of more than just the young people they were watching? Margaret and her partner sashayed down the line. Francine gave Mr Creighton a sidelong glance. No, how silly of me. Surely he is speaking in generalities.

"Did your late wife enjoy dancing?" Mrs Whittaker asked.

He smiled fondly. "Indeed she did. We met at a ball in Bath. I was there visiting a chum from Cambridge, and she was on holiday with friends of her family. She, too, was a most graceful dancer." He caught Francine's eye, then continued. "I am sure tongues wagged because we danced together more times than was considered proper. I was light on my feet in those days, and whilst partnering her it was as if we were flying through the clouds. I do miss dancing. And such romantic times," he said with a sigh.

"If I may ask, how did you injure your leg? And is there no remedy to restore it so you might dance again? But perhaps it is none of my affair," Mrs Whittaker said.

He smiled kindly at her. "I do not mind speaking of it. I am sure others have wondered."

Francine blinked, wondering if this comment referred to her.

"It happened some twenty years ago now, and I blame myself. I was a hell-for-leather rider back in those days, one of the boldest hunters—*ventre a terra* as they say. Reckless, I must admit." He shook his head and continued. "I had been working with a fine young horse, full of spirit he was. But instead of exercising caution and waiting until he was truly ready, I took him out on the final hunt of the season. The recent rain had left the ground boggy in spots. A more seasoned mount—and a wiser rider—would have paid more heed to those conditions. But once he and I were on the field, it was as if we ignited each other. We were on fire, unstoppable. It was the most thrilling ride of my life until it turned to disaster. We hit a boggy spot, his leg sunk and threw him off balance. I went down with him. We each of us broke a leg in multiple places. I suffered a great deal of pain, but the greatest of all was losing him—and knowing I was at fault. I will never forget his eye, that last look … well, suffice it to say, I did not return to the saddle for some time, and at long last only at the kind insistence of my brother-in-law, Colonel Brandon. He helped restore my confidence, and—each of us harbouring deep regrets from our pasts—we grew very close.

His sister is … was … very like him. So kind. My leg healed enough to return to most activities, but dancing and strenuous hiking in the hills have had to be left behind. Still, I am lucky … it could have gone much the worse for me.

"But now, let us focus on gladder things. We are, after all, on holiday and at a ball. Mrs Dashwood must continue to dance and so—" he turned to the older gentleman—"Whittaker, perhaps we should wander over to the cardroom to see if Sir John has had his usual luck?"

Mr Whittaker smiled. "A fine idea. And my dear," he said, turning to his wife, "do remember to save the last for me."

Her smile was full of affection and she nodded.

"We neither of us dance much anymore, but we keep to our tradition of dancing the last together." He squeezed her shoulder and the gentlemen walked off.

The ladies were silent for some time, watching the dancers and pondering the history Mr Creighton had shared. At the next break, a flushed Emmeline sank into one of the empty chairs. She had danced nearly every dance so far, though her face reflected no joy.

"You seem to be rather the belle of the ball, Mrs Harrington." Mrs Jennings' comment did not solicit even a smile from Emmeline.

"Certainly I have been kept on my feet," she replied, surreptitiously rubbing an ankle underneath her gown, "but that is not what I had hoped for this evening. I am grievously disappointed in the admiral—to beg me for the first dance, in such an unusual manner—and then not have the courtesy to even show up. What am I to think?"

"I wonder if he did not recall making the offer?" Mrs Jennings mused. "He was, after all, in … quite a state, if you remember."

"True. But did his daughter not also look forward to attending tonight? I have not seen her amongst the company either. She will be quite disappointed. And here it is, almost time to go in for supper. I had imagined being on his arm—"

"And so you shall," Francine murmured, seeing the admiral and his daughter enter the room.

"What?"

Francine nodded towards the door.

The admiral strode across the room with commanding style—making directly for them—his daughter on his arm, her face holding the same empty smile that Francine had observed the night before.

"My dear ladies, I fear I am beyond reproach," he said with a lavish bow. "I wish I could blame my tardiness on my daughter taking too much time in her dress, but alas! our late arrival is my own fault, as she will attest." He glanced at Florrie, who refused to engage with him and instead stared out across the room. "I fear the lateness of last night left me far more tired than I had anticipated. With various business tasks to attend to in the morning, I later found myself napping, of all things! When I finally awoke, the sky was already taking on romantic hues"—here he nodded and smiled at Emmeline— "and you know the state of my road—after dark one must exercise great caution to arrive anywhere in safety. I have taken rooms in town for tonight—I presumed on some old acquaintance—so my daughter and I may enjoy the ball to the final end, and perhaps follow it with a stroll on the beach under the moonlight?" He stared again at Emmeline, who blushed at his directness.

Francine bristled but kept her own counsel. How dare he be so cavalier about such rudeness? She and Mrs Whittaker shared a knowing look.

"Indeed, I am surprised to hear of a hale and hearty young man, such as yourself, in need of a nap. But to each his own," Mrs Jennings remarked, her eyes attempting to penetrate his glossy countenance.

As if he did not hear her, he said, "I see we are in time for the refreshments. Mrs Harrington, might I persuade you to allow me the honour of accompanying you to the supper room? Might we all go in together? Where are the other gentlemen?"

"They will meet us there," Mrs Whittaker said. "They are in the cardroom and have promised to save us some seats."

Francine rose. "Ah, here are Margaret and Rose and their party—a group visiting from Somerset. Miss Tennant, they have been dancing all night but would be delighted for you to join them, I am sure."

"Florrie!" Margaret exclaimed, grasping her friend's hands. "You are here at last. What a beautiful gown." Introductions were made. Florrie's striking colouring and jewel-toned dress stood apart amongst the pale gowns worn by most of the young ladies.

"Mrs Harrington?" The admiral extended his arm and another smile.

Francine held her breath. Would Emmeline refuse him? Her haughty countenance was certainly discouraging.

"Admiral, you do try a lady's patience, not even sending word of your tardiness. I did not know what to do about the first dance, having promised it to you. Did you not remember? I worried you might have met with an accident." Her eyes searched his face, which remained impenetrable. "I shall grant you a chance to return to my good graces," she said, her countenance smooth and smiling but her eyes fiery. "One chance." She rose and placed her hand on his arm.

The gentlemen were true to their word, having saved nine seats altogether.

"Good evening, Admiral," Sir John said, his eyes taking in

the newcomers. "Our party is much enlarged. I fear the young people may have to gather about us, on their feet."

Charles Creighton chuckled. "That hardly seems fair, Sir John, as they have been on their feet dancing all evening, whilst we have been sitting on the sidelines or at cards. Might I suggest ... I did see several benches lining the terrace ... that they might welcome the fresh air as much as a seat."

"A capital idea, Father," James said. "What say you?" he asked, looking at the other young people.

"Let us arm ourselves with food and drink and make for the wild outdoors!" the brother said.

Mrs Jennings placed a hand on Margaret's arm. "Take care that you keep to the benches near the doors, in the lighted areas, and stay together with your group." She gave Margaret and Rose a directive look.

"Be assured, Mrs Jennings, I shall keep our ladies in good care," James offered with a slight bow. "All of our ladies," he added, with an admiring look at Florrie.

Mr Creighton gave his son a nod and the younger folk made for the buffet.

A selection of refreshing beverages was offered to those now seated at the table and the usual treats tempted them to remain even after the music resumed. Francine noted that, although he sat next to Emmeline, the admiral did not ask her for the next dance. Instead he talked of his travels in the area whilst hunting for an estate after he resigned from the Navy. Emmeline's expression towards him had softened, and Francine was rather disappointed her sister could be so easily manipulated. But then, who am I to think poorly of her? I have no suitor knocking at my door. She turned to Mrs Jennings and said, "Perhaps we ought to look in on the young people?"

"Yes, yes, we must not let them stray onto a prodigal path. Whilst we know little of their new friends, I believe our young people to have the finest of characters. Let us be sure those are preserved."

Mr Creighton offered Francine his arm. "It is easy to see where your daughters get their own fine characters. You are ever the attentive mother."

"Oh … well … I try my best, and I *am* proud of the young ladies they have become," she said, her face hot at the direct compliment. "We must do for them what we can, while we can."

The dancing had resumed; after the young people returned to the dance floor, the older members of the party found seats together again. At last the admiral rose and stood before Emmeline. With a sweeping bow he said, "Lovely lady, am I sufficiently forgiven to be allowed to delight you on the dance floor?"

His words worked their magic and Emmeline nodded with unabated pleasure. Mrs Jennings rolled her eyes at the dramatic display, and Mr Creighton frowned.

Francine leaned over and whispered to him. "Do you not approve of the admiral, sir?"

He stared at the backs of the couple as they made for the dance floor. "It is not my way to disparage others, especially on short acquaintance. But there are, shall we say, contradictory facets to his behaviour that leave me … uneasy regarding his sense of honour. I believe your sister to be deserving of better. I hope she will be on her guard. That is all I can say at present."

Francine studied his face. Did he envy the admiral? Wish to court Emmeline himself? He did not look angry; rather his expression reflected honest concern. He turned to Mr Whittaker. "Shall we try our luck again?"

"Certainly, Creighton. I have no great interest in watching others dance. Ladies, I am sure you will not miss us." The men rose and returned to the cardroom.

Meanwhile, Francine noticed Margaret partnered with a different young man—so she *had*, on her own, branched out from her new group, which Francine found both commendable and yet a little unsettling. Such familiarity amongst strangers was still very new.

Her eyes searched the floor for Emmeline and quickly found the admiral's tall frame. They made an elegant couple, and both were exceptional dancers. Her sister's eyes shone at the marked attention being paid her by her partner, and Emmeline would also be aware of the many admiring eyes upon them. Francine was contemplating how sincere the admiral's admiration might be when she was asked to dance again and so lost sight of her sister for a time.

At the next break the party gathered together again, adding more new acquaintance. The older ladies on the sidelines had struck up a conversation with some visitors from Ireland. The younger ladies had another female friend in tow, and a pack of young men now followed in their wake. Conversation was lively. When the dancing was about to begin again, one of the gentlemen from the Irish group requested Francine's company on the floor. He was quite handsome, and Francine was stunned that he asked her when Emmeline was present.

Mr Maher proved a fine dancer and an entertaining conversationalist. He had traveled somewhat—at least a great deal more than Francine had done. As he accompanied her back to her party he said, "I know we must follow society's protocol, but I would sooner dance with you the rest of the evening than any of the other ladies present. Am I too presumptuous to ask … might you honour me with the last dance of the evening, Mrs Dashwood?"

Francine caught her breath. "Oh! Well, I have not yet saved it for anyone else." She winced. It was not an encouraging reply but she was not versed in how to acquiesce without appearing too eager.

He bowed and caught her eye. "Thank you. I am most pleased." He gave her a long look and turned away as she sank into her chair to ponder this unexpected request.

Emmeline returned to her seat at the hand of another gentleman. The admiral was not to be seen.

"Where is—"

Her sister gritted her teeth behind a brittle smile. "Admiral Tennant found it necessary to spend some time with the gentlemen. It seems such a thing is expected of the local residents—to make the visitors welcome and to recommend activities and such." She sighed.

The older ladies exchanged a look of disbelief.

"So, how did you find your last partner, Mrs Dashwood?" Mrs Whittaker asked. "He seems an interesting fellow."

"Indeed, he is. He entertained me with stories of his travels. And I was greatly surprised when he asked me to reserve the last dance for him. Am I right in understanding that this shows a particular interest in me?"

Emmeline's eyes widened.

"You most certainly are," Mrs Jennings replied. "It not only shows his interest, but also his respect for the conventions of the dance, and thus for you. Such things are best followed, even here at the resorts," she said with a side eye at Emmeline, who had danced several dances in a row with the admiral. "For myself, I look forward to becoming better acquainted with Mr Maher, and indeed with the Irish party. We have all arranged to promenade tomorrow."

A small smile crept across Francine's lips. That would be perfect. She should very much like to know Mr Maher better herself, but doing so within her own familiar party would be most comfortable. Whilst he excited her interest, she did not trust her own judgement of character. The Willoughby affair had lowered her confidence there.

Charles Creighton appeared with a servant bearing a tray of lemonades and the ladies were grateful. After a few moments of conversation, he returned to the cardroom.

"So thoughtful," Mrs Jennings commented. "Very like his brother-in-law. Kindly. Always looking out for others, even in his time of sorrow."

"And his son follows his example, I believe," Francine said, watching James hand a glass of lemonade to Margaret and wondering about her daughter's opinion of the young man. Were they simply friends? Francine thought she had detected more than friendly interest on James' part.

The music began again and the young people partnered up. Florrie fit well into the group, and her smiles now seemed genuine. It must be difficult for a girl with no mother. Florrie spent no time on the sidelines either.

A gasp escaped Emmeline, and the colour drained from her face. The ladies followed her gaze. Admiral Tennant was on the floor, an attractive younger lady in his arms beaming up at him. The three exchanged puzzled looks.

Fran spoke first. "He cannot dance only with you all evening, Em. You have danced with many other gentlemen yourself."

Emmeline sat up very straight. "I suppose you are right, sister. Still, why would he not say so? Instead he tells me he has 'duties' in the cardroom."

The ladies fell silent again. Emmeline was right. The situation did feel deceptive.

"Perhaps he was even now returning to you, then saw someone he knows and felt obliged to dance with her. You must gather yourself." Francine could see her words were not comforting. Her sister would not be second in any man's eye.

Emmeline maintained her elegant posture and refined expression but her eyes focused only on Admiral Tennant.

When the final dance of the evening was announced, Mr Maher appeared for Francine's hand. As they strolled away, the admiral was bowing before Emmeline. Her sister's usual haughtiness and high standards seemed to have again been melted by the admiral's swagger. Francine had a moment of concern but then her partner engaged her attention and her sister drifted out of her mind.

The wraps and shawls they had brought proved welcome when some of the party chose to lengthen their return by way of a seaside walk. Admiral Tennant had been most insistent and the younger gentlemen eagerly agreed. Margaret's questioning eyes caught her mother's and Francine knew that pleading look.

Charles Creighton appeared at Francine's side. "If you like, I shall join the seaside stroll, Mrs Dashwood. The older members of our party wish to return to their rooms immediately, and there must be at least one wise old gentleman to keep the younger ones—and others," he said with a glance at Emmeline and the admiral—"on the path of propriety. Will you allow me?"

"Yes sir. Your company will be most welcome. I am not adequate to chaperone so many, and surely a gentleman's voice will carry far more … well, I fear our only other gentleman is too distracted to supervise even his own daughter. He has not spoken a word to her all evening," Francine remarked in a whisper. The admiral whisked a flask from his coat pocket and quaffed a long drink. Emmeline was gazing at the sea so Francine could not see her face. He and her sister stood close together, at some distance from the others.

Silvery moonlight cast a soft glow on the scene, and the water slipped further and further from shore as the tide moved out. How romantic this setting is! Why, it is right out of a novel. No wonder Miss Fanny Burney stayed here. It was inspiring indeed.

The young people remained in high spirits and thankfully also remained in a group, none wandering off to the more private alcoves. It was the older couple, the admiral and Emmeline, who lingered behind and needed an eye kept on them.

"Mrs Harrington. Admiral. Do keep up. Your assistance is needed as chaperones." Mr Creighton's tone was neutral but assumed compliance.

Florrie's head turned towards her father and then back at Mr Creighton. After glaring at her father, she returned her attention to her friends, which now consisted of five young ladies and seven gentlemen, along with a few other adults whom Francine assumed belonged to some of those young people. All behaved appropriately. This was just what Francine had hoped for Margaret to experience, and her manners at present would have made any mother proud.

After skipping some stones and chasing the tide up and down, the entire group crossed the road and made for their various hotels with promises to meet on the morrow.

"This seems a good group of young people. Do you not agree, Mr Creighton?"

"For the most part, yes. There is one fellow I am keeping an eye on. He seems quite dependent on the flask in his pocket. But nothing for alarm at present. We shall be back at the hotel soon. James and I shall see that you and the young ladies … and your sister if I may speak plainly … get safely to your rooms."

When they reached the hotel, Mr Creighton and his son

made for the stairs but the elder stopped at the landing when the admiral did not immediately depart.

Fearing her sister might be in some danger, Francine took her arm and said, "Thank you for your escort, Admiral. Miss Tennant, it has been wonderful to see you again. Shall you both join us at the promenade tomorrow?"

"Yes, I look forward to it." Florrie dipped a curtsey and turned to leave.

The admiral glanced up the stairs. Seeing Mr Creighton waiting he said, "Until tomorrow then," and turned on his heel and was off, catching up to his daughter.

The ladies ascended and entered their room and Mr Creighton did the same. Francine took care to lock and bolt the door.

"Fran, why did you not go up ahead of me? I had wished for a moment alone with Marcus."

Francine stiffened at the use of his Christian name. Had things really progressed this far in only a few days?

CHAPTER ELEVEN

*I*t was fortunate the largest holiday house on offer met all the requirements of the Honiton party. Sir John and Mr Creighton had seen and approved it, arrangements were made for supplies and servants, and they might all move in on the following day. Francine spent the morning packing some of her things and writing letters to Elinor and Marianne with the new direction for their replies.

June —
  My dearest Elinor,
  How lovely it is here. Breezy, but the air is fresh and invigorating. We have enjoyed some wonderful meals, and our hotel is quite passable. Tomorrow we move quarters to our holiday house. I have not seen the place but Sir John likes it, and more importantly, Mr Creighton approves. I believe he has a more thorough understanding of the amenities required by the female portion of our party. Please send your letters to Seaview Place, Sidmouth.
  Admiral Tennant hosted a fine dinner at his home, Bellevue, where we made the acquaintance of his daughter, Florentina, whom

we now call Florrie. She is one year older than Margaret but seems more knowledgeable of the world, and less happy. His wife died but he told us no particulars. How difficult for a young lady without a mother. In my observation he is not the most attentive father.

Balls are held weekly and last night we attended our first. To my surprise, I danced several dances. We met a friendly group from Ireland and will promenade with them this afternoon. A Mr Maher of that party has paid me some particular attention and I find his conversation interesting. I shall rely heavily on the wisdom of Mrs Jennings and Mrs Whittaker in ascertaining the character of those we meet so as not to be duped by another Willoughby. Manners here are much relaxed and it is not frowned upon to strike up conversations with strangers, and later dine with them. Margaret and Rose danced every dance. They met new young ladies, and now have a group of young men following them and desiring their company. Of course, James Creighton is of that group. I had thought he had more than friendly interest in Margaret but his eye seems now to have been caught by Florrie. Mr Creighton assists me in the supervision of so many. I am sure your sister will write to you about these things in more detail. I know you will provide her with wise counsel. So far, her behaviour is everything appropriate.

My sister remains much taken with Admiral Tennant and my hope lies in her meeting some other gentleman who captures her fancy. This is a popular place for fishing, and there are many gentlemen about.

After moving quarters tomorrow, a horseback ride on the beach is planned for the following day to prepare for a more strenuous ride into the beautiful hillsides above the resort. My sister and I must serve as chaperones for our young ladies who proposed this activity. It has been many years since I have ridden, although I loved it when I was a girl. Mr Creighton, James, and the admiral shall join us on both rides. I must admit to a curiosity to take in the view from atop the cliffs. The scenery here is beautiful, and I highly recommend this location for a future holiday for you and Edward. This would be a fine place for you to capture scenes with your drawing. The faces of the cliffs are red! A lovely contrast with the green trees, the sky, and the sea.

I trust Marianne remains well. I am confident you will keep a watchful eye over her in my absence.

Much love,

Mama

Here Francine paused to send for another cup of tea and to pack a few more items. Her window framed the dramatic red cliffs, striking in contrast to the green of the trees and dots of colourful wildflowers. Yes, Fanny Burney must have found this place quite inspiring. When the hot water arrived, Francine poured a cup, took another sheaf of paper and readied her pen.

June —

My darling Marianne,

I hope you are well. What news of your condition? The Colonel must be overcome with joy every day. I am certain he will provide you the best of care. Whilst I am enjoying myself, I also wish to be with you to protect you from every harmful thing.

How you would love it here at the seaside. Very picturesque. One can imagine poets and artists being enraptured and inspired. Tomorrow we move quarters to our holiday house, which only Sir John and Mr Creighton have seen, but I trust Mr Creighton's judgement that it will suit the females in our party. Please send your letters to Seaview Place, Sidmouth. I hope the place is as romantic as it sounds. It is said to be only a short walk to the beach, and some rooms have a view of the sea whilst others view the red cliffs rising behind the village.

Admiral Tennant hosted us at a fine dinner at Bellevue, his castle-like home on a cliff overlooking the sea. We made the acquaintance of his daughter, Florentina, whom we now call Florrie. She and Margaret and Rose have struck up a friendship. He told us his wife died but we have heard no particulars.

Balls are held weekly here and last night we attended our first, at a lovely seaside setting with terrace doors open to the breeze. I danced several times and felt very like a young girl first moving into society. A group we met from Ireland will promenade with us this afternoon. A Mr Maher of that party has paid me some particular attention. He is handsome, a fine dancer, and shares fascinating tales of his travels.

At the ball Margaret and Rose danced every dance. They, along with Florrie, met two other young ladies and now have a group of handsome young men desiring their company. James Creighton is of that group. I had thought him to have a romantic interest in Margaret—had you noticed this before? Whilst he remains attentive to her, his eye now seems drawn to Florrie, who is more sophisticated, and her appearance is striking. Her brown skin and dark eyes and hair are set off by the rich colours she wears, unlike most other young ladies here who wear white and pastels.

Mr Creighton assists me in supervising the young people as I find it quite overwhelming. I am sure Margaret will write to you in more detail. Do offer her your wisdom.

A ride on the beach is planned to prepare for a more strenuous foray into the beautiful hillsides above the resort. Our young ladies proposed this activity, and my sister and I must serve as chaperones. I have not ridden for years, but loved it as a young girl. Mr Creighton, James, and the admiral will join us on both rides. The view is said to be breathtaking from atop the cliffs.

A sail about the coast will take place on the admiral's boat, and I am also determined to try sea bathing. There are wide expanses of beach as well as rocky coves. All in all, I think it would be delightful to explore with a young child. I am thrilled for you to be a mother,

although I cannot quite conceive of myself as a grandmother. Where
has the time gone?

    Do take care of yourself, Marianne.
    Much love,
    Mama

When the group reached the promenade, Florrie was greeted
with enthusiasm by Margaret and Rose, but her father was
nowhere in sight. Only Emmeline seemed surprised at this.
The Irish party soon joined them, making for a substantial
gathering along the waterfront. Mr Maher's eyes caught
Francine's and a smile lit his face. He nodded at her but did
not immediately join her. Instead, it was Emmeline who took
her arm.

"I think Marcus must not be an early riser," she said, a
forlorn look etched on her face.

"I wonder why that would be? One would think a Navy
officer might have a lifelong habit of rising early to effectively
lead his men. It is after midday. You slept late enough yourself. I wrote and posted letters to Elinor and Marianne this
morning, telling them about Bellevue and the ball and
supplying our new direction." She glanced ahead at Margaret,
who was arm in arm with Rose and the admiral's daughter.
"Florrie seems pleased to be here." The young ladies were
deep in laughing counsel.

"They must have enjoyed the ball a great deal. There were
so many young men to dance with, and they seemed to attract
their share."

"As did you, Em. You danced most of the evening. Did not
any of those gentlemen pique your interest?"

"There were some who were interesting and some who

were attractive, but few who were both. None compare with the admiral." Emmeline sighed.

"I am sorry to hear it. I did meet with one man who is of particular interest. Or, at least, he has shown particular interest in me."

Emmeline looked surprised. "The one with whom you danced the last?"

"The very one. And he is with us now. He greeted me with a smile and a nod but has not yet approached me. What do you think of that, Em?"

"Who can say? Gentlemen are unpredictable and puzzling, and at times I am happier to be alone and not be drawn into their intrigues."

"Not all are that way. Take Mr Creighton, a most reliable sort. I was grateful for his help in supervising at the beach last night. If there had been any unacceptable behaviour, I hardly know what I would have done."

"True. He does seem a constant type. But there is something missing there, an excitement that one wishes for in a romance. Perhaps it is due to his mourning state?"

Francine pondered on his attentions to herself. Mere politeness? Or something more? She felt a flush of excitement at that possibility but was not yet ready to share that thought with anyone.

"With Rose here, Margaret has not confided in me as of yet. I shall make a point of speaking with her privately, but I am pleased for her—meeting so many new people—and her manners and behaviour are everything they ought to be."

Emmeline gave the girls a wistful glance. The group had stopped, the older members resting on a stone bench. James and other young men crowded around the girls in lively conversation.

"It was all so effortless when we were young, was it not?

Everything just bowled along—the excitement, the intrigue, the competing for attention ..."

Francine looked at her sister. Was she really so unaware?

"Perhaps for you, Em. It was not effortless for me. In spite of following in your social wake, the first man who paid me any real attention was Henry, and of course by then you were gone off and married. I was just pleased to be chosen."

"Chosen? I do not understand."

"Of course not. Because—back then—you were the one doing the choosing, were you not?"

Before Emmeline could reply, three gentlemen joined them.

"Good day ladies," Mr Maher greeted them. "The weather is with us today. May I introduce my two friends, Lord Marlborough and Mr Findley?" The proper bows and curtsies took place and he then turned his eye on Francine. "I see last night's late hour has not affected your loveliness, Mrs Dashwood. I am pleased to see you again."

I must not blush at every compliment, Francine silently chided herself. She steadied her voice and replied, "Thank you, sir. I slept well. I believe the sea air agrees with me. And how long will your party be staying?"

Conversation carried on, then the group was moving again. This time, Mr Maher offered Francine his arm, and the other two gentlemen accompanied Emmeline. This time, *both* sisters had been chosen. Francine stepped lightly along the path.

"I know not the plans of our entire group, or yours, but I would be honoured if you would dine with me, Mrs Dashwood. Would tonight be agreeable?"

Her heart pounded. Visions of a romantic repast swirled in her head. But then she remembered their plans. "I should very much enjoy dining with you, but later today we move into our holiday house and I fear everything might be in uproar. Perhaps we can choose another evening? I can consult others in my party for certainly some of them may wish for … well, for some activities outside our larger group. Will that be agreeable?"

He did not seem put off. "That would be a fine arrangement, and I will be pleased whenever you can accommodate me. The Mariner offers a fine selection; would that establishment please you?"

She hoped her sister might be making a similar arrangement with one of the gentlemen accompanying her. Either of them might provide a diversion from the admiral. Someone must.

Francine's first glimpse of Seaview Place was mostly pleasing. Located just two streets uphill from the promenade, the stone house was situated in a small but delightful garden and faced the sea. It did not look large enough to accommodate their party, but sometimes houses could be deceiving that way. Mr Creighton had reassured her that the sharing of rooms would be nearly the same as at the hotel, with an extra bed for Walford, when he joined them.

"Oh, I do hope our room has a view of the sea," Emmeline remarked as they entered the front door. *"Nothing is more enchanting than the placid Sea whose waves, in gentle ripplings, play on the shore."*

"That is lovely. Is that from Fanny Burney?"

"No. A man wrote it. I forget his name. But if our room has a view of the sea, I shall be enchanted."

It was so. Francine and Emmeline would share a corner room, with views of both the sea and the red cliffs. I must thank Mr Creighton for this, as surely he is behind it. Servants flurried about with last-minute fetching. The sisters met the housekeeper, who was in charge of the upstairs maids and valets as well as the footmen. There was also a cook and her staff of young maids, available for the times the group did not take their meals out. It was homey enough, and rather more luxurious than her own accommodations at Barton Cottage. Francine sighed with satisfaction that these arrangements were taken care of by someone other than herself.

A hearty tea was served and the entire party gathered in the drawing room. All seemed satisfied with the accommodations.

"What a fine place you have found for us," Mrs Dashwood said as Mr Creighton settled in the chair across from her. "And I believe I have you to thank for the lovely room my sister and I share? I very much value someone looking out for such things."

His face shone with pleasure. "I thought you might be more appreciative than the others of the variety of views. Although I hope you don't spend much time in your room with so much else on offer here. Will you still wish to ride tomorrow on the beach, weather permitting?"

"I am willing, yes. As a child it came so naturally to me, but I wonder if it shall come back at this age?"

"It will. A little exercising of the muscles and you shall feel like you never left the saddle. At least it was so for me when I had not ridden for some years. I am ever thankful to Brandon for urging me to ride again. And here there is always a hot bath or sea bathing to sooth any soreness."

"Sea bathing? When shall we try it?" Margaret settled on a nearby stool. "Oh, there is so much to do here; how shall we ever be content at Barton Cottage again?"

Francine chuckled. "Tomorrow is our ride on the beach. Let us focus on just one day at a time."

Mr Creighton looked at Margaret. "I predict you shall have several more seaside holidays in your future, Miss Dashwood. You appear to be making a friend of Miss Tennant, and others besides. Your friendliness and kindness will render you a desired companion of many."

Margaret looked at him with a bright smile. "Thank you! I have sent a message on to Florrie, telling her of our new accommodations. Perhaps we can invite her and some of the others to the house in poor weather, or to the garden in fairer? I do enjoy the weather here. The breeze is fresh, and even the fog—it feels so cozy one would like to sit by a fire and play games or chat with a friend."

"You are certainly appreciating the seaside atmosphere," her mother remarked.

Dinner was taken in that night and the cook provided a fine selection of meats, seafood, and accompaniments, along with fruits and puddings and cakes.

"Surely we must walk off some of this fine dinner," Mrs Jennings said. Some of the group accompanied her. Daylight lingered long this time of year, and since the girls were of the party, both Creightons accompanied the group on a walk.

Emmeline's attention was claimed by one of her Fanny Burney books. Francine was content to sit by the fire and reflect on activities enjoyed, relationships being formed, and adventures to come.

CHAPTER TWELVE

og wrapped the coastline in a downy blanket, drawn aside here and there to permit beams of golden sunlight to pierce its shroud. When the riders entered the hushed warmth of the stable, Francine reveled in the familiar but long-forgotten smell—a mixture of horse, hay, human, and leather. It hurtled her back to cherished childhood hours spent in the barn grooming her pony, braiding its mane, and tying ribbons in the mane and tail. Her mother, a devoted horsewoman, had usually been nearby doing much the same. Precious memories of a safe and blissful time—a time cut short by the tragic fall of a woman from her saddle, by the loss of a mother from a little girl's life.

When this present holiday's horseback activity had first been talked of, Francine had commissioned riding habits for herself and Margaret, as they had none. An extravagance, perhaps, but in light of the plans here and Margaret's upcoming season Francine felt it justified. She made the decision and refused to be gainsaid on the matter.

As they rode, Francine smoothed the fine blue wool of her skirt and admired Margaret's elegance in a deep green habit.

Rose wore, fittingly, a rose-coloured habit that flattered her lighter coloring. Emmeline's deep violet ensemble had been refitted and a new feather worked into her hat.

Neither the admiral nor Florrie made an appearance. Perhaps they had gone back to Bellevue instead? The Creighton men helped the ladies into their saddles and performed a final check on the tack, then mounted up, and they all made for the beach.

The breathing and snorting of the horses and the fall of each hoof on the road echoed as they rode along into what felt like a secret adventure, hidden in the fog. James was in the lead, followed by Margaret and Rose, then Emmeline and Francine, with Charles Creighton bringing up the rear, keeping a watch eye for any problems. The leather, now warmed with the heat of the horse's body and her own, released its rich fragrance and mingled with that of the horse, a sturdy piebald cob. Francine adjusted her right knee around the top of the sidesaddle. It was a bit of a stretch, not a position used in her daily life. The easy motion of the creature walking beneath her was soothing, and her back and shoulders loosened to move in harmony with the horse. It was a good idea, this, of starting with an easy ride after so many years. Francine reached down to pat her mount's neck.

Their destination was not far. The upper part of the beach near the promenade had a good deal of shingle and rock which the horses expertly picked their way through. The tide was still out. They followed James down to the water's edge, where there was more sand than rock. The fog was lifting, revealing the sun riding rather high in the sky. Fishing boats bobbed in the distance, dancing on a jeweled sea.

James' face reflected his enthusiasm, but whether for the ride itself or for the young ladies following him was impossible to speculate. He had no competition this morning.

"Shall we pick up the pace a bit?" he asked.

The girls nodded with enthusiasm.

"Ladies?" Mr Creighton asked. "If you are not ready—"

"I believe we are, Mr Creighton," Francine answered, her face relaxed in a pleasant smile that was impossible to vanquish whilst on a horse. She turned to her sister, who had been unusually quiet. "Emmeline?"

"Oh, yes. Let us trot out a bit, by all means."

"Keep your horses in hand," Mr Creighton reminded them all, "and no racing ahead," he said, with a stern look at his son.

James simply smiled and turned his horse on its hind quarters to lead the group off. There was some head-tossing by a few of the horses, those ones eager to flatten their bodies for speed and careen down the beach, *ventre a terre*. Francine laughed aloud as they all trotted away.

"What are these odd contraptions?" Margaret asked as they passed what looked like tiny cabins on wheels.

"Those are the bathing machines," Mr Creighton replied. "A place for ladies to don their bathing gowns in privacy. Horses then haul the machines out into the water."

Rose wrinkled her nose. "It seems a lot of bother. Can we not just walk out into the water?"

Emmeline sniffed. "That is just the way it is done. We ladies must follow protocol or be cast out of good society forever." Her countenance was serious but there was a mischievous twinkle in her eyes and they all laughed wholeheartedly.

Eventually James circled his horse and brought them all together again. Once all were halted, he said, "There is still a good stretch of beach ahead. Do you all have your horses well in hand? Shall we let them run?"

Mr Creighton said, "Ladies, let us allow the young people to head off first." He steadied his mount and held up his hand as the young riders departed. "Now, circle your horses with me, and then we shall pick up a canter. When you are ready, cue your horse."

Francine's horse tossed its head. She gathered her reins and sat deep in the saddle. That was all the cue her mount needed to be off. Blood rushed in Francine's veins. She felt tingly and alive in a way she had not in many years. The wind rushed past her face in a familiar way and the salty spray tinged the air. It all came back to her! Her body remembered exactly what to do. Heady. Glorious. Why did I abandon this for so long? I shall never let it go now I have found it again.

By the time they caught up to the younger people, Francine was breathless. She hoped they could ride often whilst at Sidmouth. And—at home—might Sir John have a horse suitable for her amongst his herd at Barton Park? She was determined to pursue this.

After cantering again partway back, then slowing to a trot, they settled into an easy walk to take in the views of the red cliffs behind the village and to the east, and to allow the horses to cool down.

"There, on the near side of Salcombe Hill, you can see part of the admiral's home." Mr Creighton pointed to it. "A rock promontory partially hides Bellevue."

"Yes, I do believe you are right, although it is a little blurry to me," Emmeline replied. With a sigh she added, "I wonder where he is? And what he is doing now? What if he were watching us, here on the beach, from up there?"

Francine was able to see it well. It did look familiar, although quite different from this angle. She was fortunate to need her spectacles only for needlework or reading.

Mr Creighton added, "There are said to be several elegant homes along the crown of the Salcombe. We may see some of them on our cliff ride."

Francine was intrigued. "I should like that very much. Fine homes are always interesting. I wish I knew more about the architecture, as some do, and be able to tell the style, when it was built and so on."

"I did not know you had such an interest. It is one I share."

Emmeline joined in the conversation. "For myself, I just know when I like a place. When I am taken by it. I find Bellevue very elegant, unlike … say … Mr Walford's Southleigh. That place is far too old-fashioned for my taste."

"Furnishings and landscaping can go a long way towards imparting an impression, I find," Mr Creighton continued. "Perhaps Southleigh might benefit from a renewal. However, I think a place says much about the owner, and even about the previous owners going back generations. One can also learn much about the economy and trade in the area."

James interrupted the discussion. "Father, I am famished. Let us return for tea before I fall from my horse in a faint." He laughed, the girls giggled, and his father smiled and nodded in agreement.

They joined the others back at Seaview Place for refreshment and a lively discussion of their day's adventure and upcoming outings. Later that evening the group played cards and relished a fine dinner at home. Francine was particularly ravenous. That sea air.

CHAPTER THIRTEEN

*F*rancine woke with a start and rushed to the window. Today was the day they would first try sea bathing. She pulled the drapery aside and peered out at the foggy gloom. "Oh, no. I had no idea the seaside would so often be this foggy." Her enthusiasm was instantly quelled. At present she found her cozy bed far more appealing.

"Come, sister," Emmeline coaxed. "We must not disappoint the young ladies. They cannot go sea bathing without us, you know. Besides, I hear many of the visiting men take to the bracing water in the morning. Who knows? You may meet your future husband there on the sand! And perhaps the fog will lift by the time we reach the water."

Once again, Emmeline's prediction was correct. By the time they stood on the sand, the sun was climbing brightly over Salcombe Hill and the brisk breezes of dawn had subsided. Rose and Margaret began laughing in anticipation of what had been described as "a shocking plunge that takes one's breath away." Francine was not convinced she wanted to experience such a thing. But then she remembered her own rallying cry—"If not now, when?"

The gentlemen walked the ladies to the bathing machines.

"Mr Creighton, we none of us knows how to swim."

"Not to worry, Mrs Dashwood." He then turned to the attendants. "This is the first sea bathing event for these ladies, who do not swim. Not too deep for them, if you please."

The attendants dropped a quick curtsey. "Yes sir."

"Good luck then, ladies. Make what you can of the experience. We shall return to accompany you back to Seaview Place." With that, the Creightons made their way down the beach to where the men took the plunge, free of any hindering clothing.

Rose and Margaret entered one machine whilst Emmeline and Francine entered the other. None of them knew what to expect but the attendants gave instructions.

Once the bathing gowns and caps were donned and the horses had hauled the machines into the water, the sisters opened their door. The water sparkled before them, as if they were to dip themselves into a field of stars. Margaret and Rose were already down the steps, shrieking and laughing and paddling about. Both had fully dipped their heads below the surface.

Francine and Emmeline looked at each other, wide-eyed.

"Well, we've done many daring things together, Fran. Why not one more?"

Emmeline descended the steps into water slightly above her waist, reached out a hand for the attendant and, taking a large breath, immersed herself. A moment later she burst through the surface with a scream. "Oh! My! Indeed, it does take my breath away. But in a good way, an exciting way. Your turn now, Fran. It will shock new life into your body."

Francine descended the steps, gasping as the shocking chill rose in her body. She paddled her arms and looked at her sister.

"Do it, Fran!"

She did. Her entire body felt ablaze with cold—on fire and frozen at the same time. How could that be? She emerged in a moment and shook her head, sending drops of shining crystals flying in every direction. "Oh!" She gasped, then threw her head back in laughter.

Both sisters paddled about, chortling at the sting of salt against their hands and faces. Who knew sea bathing could be the source of such gaiety and joy? The girls joined them and they all walked out a little deeper until the attendant called out, "Stop, ladies! No further, if you please. Sometimes the bottom drops away, and if one cannot swim …"

Francine instantly turned to go back.

"Don't be such a wet blanket, sister," Emmeline said. "We are safe right here, all together. Now I have been in the water for a time, it does not seem cold at all."

The younger ladies agreed, laughing whilst they splashed their faces and arms.

"Please, Mama. Here, we shall walk back just a few steps to calm your mind. Is it not fine in the water?"

Rose pointed some distance out. "There. The two Creighton gentlemen, am I correct?"

They all turned and saw two men, bare backed, swimming several yards further out.

"I believe you are right, Rose." Swimming was not something Francine had ever desired to learn. As a young child she had seen other children swimming about in ponds or rivers, but even then it had not tempted her. Now, possessing that skill seemed of greater import.

In a short while they made their way back to the bathing machines.

"Oh dear. Look at my fingers. They are wrinkled like an old crone's!" Emmeline held her hands up, turning them this way and that.

Francine's own looked the same. "I wager the shops will

have some lotion or ointment to help with this. After all, it must be a common affliction in a spa town."

"Yes. We must get something to remedy it. I will ask the attendant for a recommendation."

They returned to the machine, climbed the steps, dried off and dressed; then the horses pulled the machines back to shore. The men strode towards them from down the beach.

"I need not ask if you enjoyed the experience," Charles Creighton said with a knowing grin. "Your glowing faces tell all. Many folks come to the seaside during the season precisely to do this every morning. It is said to greatly improve one's health."

"How could it not? I feel such energy," Emmeline said. "We should sea bathe every morning, unless we have had a very late night, in which case sleep might be more restorative."

"It was very cold at first," Margaret opined, "but once past the initial shock, I found it most invigorating. I would agree to sea bathing most mornings." Then she turned to the Creightons. "Did I see you gentlemen swimming? You were much further out than we were allowed."

James nodded. "Yes, indeed, we both swim well. Perhaps you might wish to learn?"

"It does not look that difficult," Rose said.

"This is the ideal place to learn. The body is particularly buoyant in the salt water," Mr Creighton said. "James and I should be pleased to teach you the basics, although it may be more difficult for you—having to deal with the encumbrance of a gown billowing about your limbs in the water." He frowned. "But I do not know any other way that would preserve a lady's modesty. And perhaps it may not be proper for gentlemen and ladies to be so adjacent while in swimming attire."

"With so many lakes and rivers about, and actually living

on an island, it would seem prudent for all to at least know how to stay afloat," Francine mused.

"Let me ponder on it," Mr Creighton said, "and perhaps consult with Mrs Jennings."

During the whole of the walk back to Seaview Place, Francine's limbs tingled with renewed life. This was an experience she had not anticipated, and the feeling of youthful energy was one she wished to enjoy again and again. It gave her pause to consider the reality of living on an island yet being landlocked all her life.

The entire party met for tea later that afternoon. Some had been shopping—Francine and Emmeline had obtained a concoction said to soothe the skin after sea bathing. Others of their party had attended a lecture, and some had procured books from the circulating library. Mrs Jennings passed around a leaflet about an upcoming concert series, and they all agreed on a night to attend. Sir John would make the arrangements.

Francine began to share Margaret's concern—however would they be content at Barton Cottage after enjoying such an array of entertainments and places to visit? This made Francine more determined to write in her holiday journal daily about everything they were experiencing. It might keep these memories alive during the cold wet months ahead.

She found herself seated next to Mr Creighton at the tea house. She always felt comfortable in his presence, though she did not know exactly why. Perhaps it was because he was such a reliable gentleman, and someone with whom she was beginning to feel familiar in a community of strangers.

He cleared his throat. "On sea bathing. Mrs Jennings believes there is no appropriate way for me—for James and me—to teach ladies to swim. However, she says Mrs Whittaker does swim; so I spoke to her and she agreed to teach the young ladies, who are likely to learn quickly, both being an active sort of person. Then they could teach you and your sister. Does that sound agreeable?"

"You have followed up so quickly, Mr Creighton. I am grateful. Learning from my daughter—that will be something of a turnaround, will it not?"

"Have you not learned things from your other daughters?"

"Well, certainly. But they are much older and ..."

His kind smile was encouraging.

"Mrs Dashwood, your Margaret has become quite a young lady, although it is sometimes difficult for us, as their parent, to see it—and especially to accept it—particularly when it is our only or last child. James has had to remind me on many occasions that he is now a man, not a boy. The time is not far off when he will complete his schooling and be ready to take possession of Whitwell, at least in part."

His words gave Francine pause. "Well, sir, if our children are grown—or practically so—that means ..." She stared at him with some alarm.

He chuckled. "... that we are old."

At her shocked look he laughed aloud. "Yes, that is precisely it. Not only must we see them differently, we must also see ourselves in a new light. I liken it to a new chapter in an unread book. Now that I am alone—widowed—this idea of a grown child is far more ... poignant ... and to not share it with my wife, as I had always pictured, makes it all the more difficult to imagine or accept. For a woman, even more so, I think. Our society sometimes looks on women as—vulgar as this sounds—breeding stock; and once beyond that use, tends to cast them off, giving no heed to the wisdom and insight gained over the years. Nor to the value of their capacity to love and nurture others. Look at Mrs Jennings and Mrs Whittaker, and what they do for friends and neighbours. You are most fortunate to have three lovely daughters, and two who remain nearby. But—near or far—our children are a mirror for us, are they not?"

Francine gazed into the fire for some minutes. Old. She had never imagined ahead to the idea of one day being old. She had seldom thought further into the future than getting Margaret well married. This new idea would require some reflection. And Margaret—she was a much more adventurous soul than either of her sisters. Would she remain close by?

"I do cherish having Elinor and Marianne relatively near. But Margaret—I suppose it depends on whom she marries— she seems set on a life of adventure, and possibly joining her young Mr Newbury at sea once he attains a ship of his own, as she is certain he must. He will be gone many months at a time, and it may be some years before he earns a ship. We shall see what comes to pass there. I believe he is her first love. As we know, those do not always work out. What about your James? And yourself? What do you predict there?"

Mr Creighton set down his tea cup. "When the time comes, I shall relinquish Whitwell to James. I have been working on adjusting my vision of the path things might take now, after so big and shocking a change in my life. I see a few different directions, and other doors are opening. At present, one might say I am exploring. Not yet set on one vision or one particular path. Not yet ready to conjure a new reality."

He reached into his pocket and handed her a book.

Filled with amazement, she asked, "What is this? Architecture?"

"You had expressed an interest. I have many books on architecture at Whitwell but thought having this one here in Sidmouth might be useful as we explore the houses and buildings of the village as well as those grander estates in the hills. I have this very book at home; it is one of my favourites. This one is yours."

"Why, I don't know what to say. No one has ever gifted me a book." She looked at him closely. "When did you find time—"

"I saw this book in the shop a few days ago. I remembered it when you spoke of your interest. That is all. I consider it an investment in a shared interest with a friend."

"Thank you. I shall definitely—"

"What serious conversation do you two pursue?" Emmeline slid into the chair opposite them. "I am quite entranced."

"Mr Creighton has gifted me this book on architecture, after I spoke of my interest yesterday on our ride. Is that not kind, and most thoughtful?" She smiled at him again, and then paged through the book. Emmeline's shrewd appraisal of Charles Creighton's neutral countenance went unseen by Francine.

He drank his tea and Emmeline replied, "Very thoughtful indeed."

The group dined that evening at the other hotel, the one Admiral Tennant and his daughter had stayed at. Emmeline seemed disappointed the admiral made no plans to see her before the cliff ride but hid her feelings well—only her sister could penetrate the pleasant countenance that Emmeline maintained.

Once in their room, as they prepared for bed, Francine set down her pen. She had been writing in her holiday journal whilst Emmeline paced the room.

"Whatever is the matter, Em?"

"In two days, we shall make the adventurous ride up the cliffs and into the hills."

"Yes." Francine stared at Emmeline. "Do you not wish to go? The riding did not seem difficult for you."

"It is not the riding. It is the admiral. Do you not find it strange that he has made no plans to see me until that time? Even you—you have a dinner tomorrow evening with that Irish gentleman, Mr—"

"Mr Maher, yes. But Em, we are here on holiday, as is Mr Maher. The admiral likely has business affairs to continue to manage. He is *not* on holiday." Francine wondered if she should express her own concerns as she, too, had been puzzled by the admiral's waxing and waning attention to her sister—paying her lavish and dramatic courtesies and then seeming to not acknowledge her existence. If she were Emmeline, she would be most confused. Not wishing to set off a drama, yet feeling she could not ignore her sister's apprehensions, Francine ventured an opening comment.

"But I must admit, the admiral's behaviour seems a riddle. He pays you marked attention, but makes no effort to see you again. You have more experience than I, and more understanding of the male sex. What do you make of it?"

Emmeline sighed and flounced onto the bed. "I do not know, sister. I like him very much. I find myself dreaming of such a wonderful life with him. I do see that he is moody and of a strong temperament, which gives some of our party pause—I am referring to Mrs Jennings and Mrs Whittaker and their eye rolling—but he is exciting. Dashing. Quite different from my husband, God rest his soul. Bernard was steadfast. Reliable. Clever. A fine dancer and very handsome in his youth. But our life was so ... predictable. I want something different this time. Someone more like your Henry was."

Francine's eyebrows shot up. This was a new wrinkle. Could it be that Emmeline envied her?

"I have had much time to think on this myself. Henry *was* dashing and romantic, and I felt like a jewel on his arm. But a jewel that knew little, and had even less to say. He dominated everything—not only our private conversations, which were all about him and his interests and desires—but our social interactions as well. I had no friends of my own. And whilst he was attentive to me in public, in private he did not take actions that would provide for me and our daughters after he was gone, as you know. I always assumed he had made some plan. How could he not? Yes, the estate was entailed to the male line. But I believe some arrangement might have been made for our benefit, to protect us. I loved him greatly, and I miss him; but lately I have resented how much he left me—and the girls—to flounder in our grief."

Emmeline played with the end of her long braid. "Yes, I suppose that is true. Isn't it odd? It seems we are each seeking what the other had. How ironic!"

Both were lost in thought for some minutes. Then Emmeline announced, "I am still determined on securing the admiral. It is the life I want. The future I see for myself. There must be some way to engage his attention on a more regular basis. Naturally, that is easier when we inhabit the same setting, and the more we are in company together. I must redouble my efforts whilst we are here. Honour him. Flatter him. Let him know what a wonderful addition I would be to his world."

Francine pursed her lips. "Just do not be too eager to give up your own world. I suspect his world may not be all that it seems."

"Really! Fran, what do you mean by that?"

"I cannot say. It is just an inkling inspired by his unpredictability, how he charms you but then disregards you. But I do not wish to put a crimp in your happiness."

Emmeline scowled. "Then don't. I will see my way through, somehow."

Francine closed her journal and crawled into bed where tangled thoughts wove their way into restless dreams.

CHAPTER FOURTEEN

*T*he next morning brought letters from both Elinor and Marianne. No one else had come down yet so Francine procured a cup of tea and settled in the drawing room near the fireplace to ward off the chill of the usual morning fog. She carefully unfolded the first missive, from Elinor. Her eldest daughter's hand was legible and feminine, with a regularity about it.

June —

Dear Mama,

I am so pleased you are enjoying yourself. Perhaps once you return to watch over Marianne, Edward and I might slip away for a short time, and the seaside would be just the thing.

Be assured all is well here. Marianne no longer suffers the morning sickness. She has energy now and we have made an effort to take a daily turn about the grounds. Fortunately, the weather has been fair. She has a good appetite but an odd affinity for figs—it seems she cannot get enough of them! Luckily the colonel's glass house gives her an endless supply. She is enlarging and has a pleasing bloom about her. I believe you have no worries on that score. We and Lady Middleton employ our time in sewing for the baby. He or she will be well supplied.

I did not know you enjoyed riding. You have never spoken of it and did not ride at Norland. Why ever did you give it up? I suspect there is a story behind this and I shall play the role of Mrs Jennings and attempt to winkle it out of you.

Edward enjoys sermon-making and seems to have a gift for it, as long as it is written down for him to read aloud. He is no orator. But he is very effective in the parish. People find him easy to talk to. I also enjoy my parish duties of visiting Colonel Brandon's tenants, bringing extra food from the colonel and giving what counsel I can. Whether I go out alone (with the maid) or with Edward, I take my sketch book as the quaint cottages and countryside are so picturesque. Marianne has even accompanied me twice on shorter outings. The tenants are always pleased by a visit from the Lady. So you see, we are all happy and content.

I look forward to hearing from you again soon, about the beach ride and the cliff ride, another ball, and of the mysterious Mr M. And the stories of riding as a child, if you are willing.

Much love, Elinor

Francine leaned back in her chair and gazed into the fire. She had not spoken to her daughters much about her childhood, thinking it best to not burden them with such sadness. All they knew was that their grandmother had died when Francine was young. The memories had been so painful that she could not speak of them, and so had tucked them away in the darker parts of her heart. Being around Emmeline so much recently had brought these memories more to mind; and when exposed to the light of day, they were not quite so dark and did not loom quite so large. Even she and Emmeline had not spoken much of that time, ever. Their father had forbidden speaking their dead mother's name. For Francine it was as if that part of her life had been swept away and, like a child's bad dream, faded in the light of dawn. She sighed as the flames flickered low, then noticed the sun had brightened at the window. The blanket of fog had been pulled away.

She finished her tea, which had grown tepid, then opened a multi-page letter from Marianne. She smiled seeing Marianne's large script, full of flourishes and hearts. Her middle daughter did not believe in crossing over the writing, and it was fortunate indeed that she could afford to use so much paper.

June —

My dearest and sweetest and much-missed Mama,

I rejoice about (and I must say, envy) your retreat to the sea. You must tell me all about what your eyes take in at every moment! Every flower that blooms. Every blade of grass that waves in the breeze. June is a lovely month here at Delaford with the gardens full of flowers. I pick and arrange many blooms each day. Elinor and I have been taking walks in the garden, and even down the lane to the first orchard, which I enjoy immensely now that I am feeling better. That wretched morning sickness nearly took away my will to live! I could not bear to eat or drink anything, and grew ever so weak. Tepid tea and toast are not enough to nourish this new life within me. But fear not, that seems behind me now. And I must praise Christopher's figs, for they seem to have brought me out of it. I cannot get enough of them. I eat several each day. Oh, be assured, he sees that I eat a variety of other things too, now that my appetite has returned. And the results are visible! I am certainly enlarging. What if I were to have twins? Oh dear, I hope not, not for the first confinement. Elinor and I have been sewing the most delightful things for the baby. Lady Middleton has joined us on occasion, and I am able to tolerate her insipid company as long as Elinor is here. Lady M is an excellent seamstress and the items she is making will be most welcome. I do wonder if the baby will be a boy or a girl? I cannot decide which I shall prefer, but my arms eagerly await holding my infant, and cooing over and kissing him or her. Oh, Mama, it is all so exciting!

Your ball, how I enjoyed hearing about it. And you dancing, how I should love to see that, especially at a large and public event. Dancing by the seaside, how romantic! Which gown did you wear? And what type of headdress? What are the fashions like? Perhaps we may all go there next year, together.

I must say you disappointed me by giving no description of Mr Maher. What are his looks? What are his interests? I do hope you will not marry him and move to Ireland! I could not bear to have you so far away! Do send me your reassurance that you will do no such thing. If you truly love him, perhaps he could buy an estate here. Christopher would certainly know of one nearby.

I continue my practice on the Broadwood Grande. What a fine instrument it is! Christopher continually supplies me with new music to learn—and with books to read, at his recommendation—and I must say I sometimes feel like a concert musician or a bluestocking! I am full of admiration for him, for his kindness and his effective management of Delaford. All the tenants love him! I have visited a few of them in recent days, in the company of Elinor as she performs her parish duties. But I do not visit where anyone in the house is ill. I am most careful in that regard. Their cottages are so quaint and picturesque. I have convinced Elinor to bring her sketch pad when she visits them, and to allow for some time to sit and capture the divine views of such a peaceful countryside. I am encouraging her to also bring her watercolours, and have purchased for her a new easel that folds handily so she may take it along. I picnic and enjoy the glorious sky and clouds and breeze fluttering the new leaves in the trees whilst she draws the same. We have a blissful life! I am so very grateful you brought us here, to Devonshire, although being torn from the beauty of Norland was one of my greatest tragedies. I have learnt one must come to accept change, and one also must open their heart to new and pleasurable possibilities, even though one might be heartbroken. How else would I have found such a great love as that between myself and Christopher? Oh thank you, Mama, for your wisdom in everything.

I have been making lists of names for the baby and I have several for each sex. Christopher has his favourites but he will not share them until the baby is here. He likes to surprise me. What a delight my life is with him!

Whilst I wish for you to hurry back home, I also wish for you to have a wonderful, magical time at the seaside. Tell me about your holiday house, all the rooms, and does it have a garden? Describe for me the beach and the water, the rocks and the trees. Have you been to any more balls? A ball every week! What could be more delightful! How was your ride at the beach? I was not aware that you cared for riding. And then to take on the adventure of a ride up the cliffs! How daring you are! But do, please, be careful. Then tell me of the view far out to sea from the top of those cliffs. I hope it was a clear day. Did you see many ships? And what of the fine manor houses?

Give our greetings to everyone from myself and Christopher. And especially to dear Mrs Jennings. I am sure having her nearby is a great comfort.

And tell my wayward sister Margaret to write to me! I have not yet received a letter from her. How can I advise her when I do not know her adventures and activities? I can only hope she is enjoying herself too much to find the time.

All my love, as always, with affection, your dear daughter, Marianne

She pressed the letter to her heart. Dear Marianne, always the enthusiast, and as romantic as ever. By reading letters from each daughter one after the other, Francine was struck by how different they were in temperament. She wondered she did not notice this when they wrote from Chelsea whilst there with Mrs Jennings, during the Willoughby debacle. Her own mind must have been fixed rather on their events instead, and on them marrying well. That desire had now been fulfilled, much to Francine's relief and joy. And now one daughter left to guide to the same. A daughter that presented challenges of her own.

Hearing voices in the dining room, Francine folded her letters and stood. Sir John's voice rose, as usual, above the rest. As she entered the room, Mrs Whittaker's eyes caught hers.

"I hear you went sea bathing yesterday. Was it what you expected? Shall you indulge yourselves again today?"

Francine gazed at those around the table, and heard the swish and clatter of Margaret and Rose on the stairs. Emmeline had not yet joined them.

"Do the others wish to do so? I am willing. I have nothing planned for today until an evening dinner with Mr Maher." She could not help blushing at the disclosure.

"Aha!" exclaimed Sir John. "You are making quick work of that business, Mrs Dashwood." He laughed heartily, though his was the only laughter.

Francine felt her face colour furiously. If only Sir John realized how mortifying some of his comments were!

Mrs Jennings broke into the one-man ruckus. "It looks to be a fine morning, friends. What say you, Camelia? Shall we join them at the beach?"

All eyes turned to her, and her jolly laugh filled the room. "Not to sea bathe, goodness no. Camelia might wish to paint, and I have an engrossing novel to finish from a sunny bench. So we could accompany you there and back."

Mrs Whittaker nodded her assent as she buttered her toast.

Francine chose a muffin and poured more tea, then sat down.

"James and I plan on swimming again. We would be delighted to walk with you ladies," said Charles Creighton.

Sir John spoke again. "What say you, Whittaker? Let us join the group this morning. Sounds like a good deal of activity at the water's edge. We must have our share!"

"Indeed. That's what we are here for, to enjoy the seaside—including its variable weather. Keeps us young, eh?" He put a forkful of eggs into his mouth. "And it certainly gives us a healthy appetite, does it not?"

The girls entered the room and helped themselves to toast and cups of chocolate. "Sea bathing again? How wonderful! We can be ready in a trice." Margaret smiled happily at her mother. "And when might we learn to swim?"

Francine looked to Mrs Whittaker for the answer. "I am honoured to have been chosen—as apparently the only female here who knows how to swim—to teach you girls. Whilst I am not prepared to go sea bathing this morning, there are things I can instruct about from the shore. You can practice those, and then tomorrow—if the weather is kind—I shall join you in the water. How does that sound?"

The girls looked at each other and then at Mrs Whittaker. "Wonderful!" they cried in unison.

Mrs Jennings mused, "I remember swimming as a child. I don't even know how I learnt. From other children, I suppose. However, I recall nothing of the techniques and wonder if I could still float? Good on you, Camelia, for teaching these girls. A lady's accomplishments must span many areas, I think." She winked at her friend.

When breakfast had ended, beverages been lingered over, and the party disbursed to prepare for departure, Mr Creighton stopped by Francine's chair. "Where is your sister? I hope she is not unwell?"

"I was just wondering that myself. I shall check on her now. Thank you for your concern."

He gave a small bow and Francine went upstairs and entered their room.

Emmeline looked up at her, startled. "I thought you would be gone somewhere by now." She was still in her nightdress.

"Whatever is the matter, sister? Are you ill? Did you not sleep well? Can I get you something?"

"No, no, I am well. But I am distraught." She put her head in her hands.

Francine moved to the bed to sit beside her.

Emmeline looked at her and said, "I hope I did not wake you last night?"

"Last night? Certainly not. So you did not sleep well?"

"Indeed no. My mind and heart were in restless tumult."

"About …?"

Emmeline looked away to avoid her sister's eye.

"The admiral and me. What else? I feel like a schoolgirl. This was not the sort of romantic adventure I had wished for at the seaside. But I simply could not rest until I put some of my thoughts on paper, and I did so last night by the light of the candle. I was distressed, and hardly knew what I wrote. Oh, I am such a fool! I then sealed the note and roused a footman to deliver it immediately!"

"In the middle of the night?!"

"Yes … yes, to my eternal shame."

"Whatever did you say to the admiral? Did you scold him?"

"From what I remember, it was part scolding and part pleading. Oh, Fran, I will be mortified to see him. I cannot leave this room ever again."

Francine gave her sister a stern look. "You know that is not rational, or even possible. Of course you must leave this room, and this house, every single day." She paused for a few moments to ponder the situation. "What is done, is done. It is now out of your control. He will respond however he sees fit —or however he desires. If he cuts you, then … well, he cuts you. There are many other men to turn your eyes to. Nothing can be known until he responds. Now get yourself dressed. Breakfast is done, and we are all of us making for the water. Will you sea bathe with us? The shock may do you good."

Emmeline shook her head. "No, I think not. But I promise to sea bathe tomorrow. All of you? Surely Mrs Jennings will not be bathing?" They exchanged a look and a smirk.

"No, she declines. And Mrs Whittaker will paint today, but also give the girls some direction from the water's edge. Tomorrow she will join them in the water for further swimming instruction."

"That settles it. Tomorrow I will do the same. Today I will pay my penance by spending time on shore with our esteemed matrons. Perhaps I will soak in some wisdom so I never do such a foolish thing again."

"Then you must make haste. The party is nearly ready to leave."

Their time at the beach was jolly and the sun bright and steady. On the return walk, a plan was made for the rest of the day. They would promenade before stopping at the tea house, then retreat to Seaview to play cards by the fire, inviting a few of the Irish party to join them. The fog began to gather offshore.

"I declare, I do feel the cold in my bones, the early and late dampness of the mists and fog," Mrs Jennings said. "The fire is most welcome at those times, although in this bright sunshine I feel at least twenty years younger." She laughed merrily.

"And so it is with me!" cried Sir John. "I feel the ache in my shoulder, and the damp aggravates that dashed old leg wound.

But better than some, I must say, for I am still walking about on two legs, and grateful I am for that!"

Emmeline and Francine trailed the group, arm in arm.

"I would value your advice on choosing what to wear to my dinner engagement this evening."

Emmeline looked puzzled.

"My dinner. With Mr Maher. Can you have forgotten?"

Emmeline's eyes grew wide and then sparkled with delight. "Of course. Yes, I shall be honoured to serve as your lady's maid," she quipped. "Thankfully, manners are somewhat relaxed here. Still, a dinner alone is suggestive of much more than, say, a luncheon or teatime *tete a tete*," she said with a teasing look.

"Emmeline, if you do nothing but mock me, I shall prepare without you."

"No, please, I am sorry. But sometimes I cannot resist teasing you for your serious outlook on, well, everything."

"At least I don't send muddled missives in the middle of the night!" Francine exclaimed.

After a moment of silence Emmeline admitted that was true. "Sometimes being serious—or cautious—is the prudent choice. Just not all the time, agreed?"

"Agreed."

After the promenade and a lively time at tea, the party retreated to Seaview Place to read and await dinner whilst Francine went to her room to prepare for dining with Mr Maher.

"Are you not nervous?" Emmeline asked her sister as she fastened the clasp of her necklace. "The Francine I know would be nervous." Her eyes questioned her sister's in the mirror.

"No, frankly I am not. It is only a dinner, and only in Sidmouth. It is not like we are dining at some fine establishment in London. In fact, here at the seaside, I have discovered a slightly different Francine. One who dares to try new things, who speaks to new people. I believe I have left the old, unsure Francine behind at Barton Cottage. And, perhaps when we return there, the new Francine will shoo the old Francine out for good." She laughed at this vision of herself.

"There is a new confidence in you, and pride. It gladdens my heart to see it," her sister concurred. "*It is in changing that we find purpose,*' as my dear Fanny Burney says.

Francine smiled. This was a quote she found meaningful.

A light rap at their door heralded the arrival of Mrs Jennings and Mrs Whittaker.

"What is this all about?" Francine asked. "Is something amiss?"

Mrs Whittaker walked over and placed her hands on Francine's shoulders. "You look lovely, my dear. It is a fine night and the moon is nearly full."

"Romance!" cried Mrs Jennings. "The night is ripe for romance. If you remember, that is something we wish for both of you. You look quite divine, Mrs Dashwood. Mr Maher is a lucky man. Well, of course, he *is* Irish," she said with a jolly laugh. "We shall be waiting on tenterhooks to hear your account when you return. In the meantime, I think a game of backgammon will divert our minds, do you not agree, Camelia?"

"It certainly shall," Mrs Whittaker said, taking Francine's hand and giving it a light kiss. "Enjoy yourself, my dear."

CHAPTER FIFTEEN

*M*r Maher called properly and promptly at Seaview Place and after a few minutes of friendly discourse with the others the couple departed on foot. The dining establishment was only two streets away. What a unique experience, having so many diverting possibilities immediately outside one's door. What might it be like to live in a town all of the time?

On arriving at The Mariner, Francine noted several other couples and groups at the surrounding tables, even though she and Mr Maher were dining rather unfashionably early. They were shown to a table by the window with a view of the sea. This style of living was vastly different from any she had known. Thinking that a good topic of conversation she said, "This being my first time on holiday here, I notice everything is oriented towards the sea; life revolves around the sea. Having been to several spa towns, what is your own opinion, Mr Maher?" She took a sip of the wine he had poured for them.

"You are correct, Mrs Dashwood. I have visited several resorts in my time, and have observed they all share that involvement with the sea. After all, it is what people come for —sea bathing, walks in the brisk air, fine dining on freshly caught seafood—all a diversion from their daily lives. You live in the countryside. What does your daily life revolve around there?"

Francine was speechless for a moment. "I have never considered it. As a mother, I suppose it is true I have focused on helping my daughters move in society as best I can, so they might find appropriate suitors and gain a secure and happy future." She reached for the wineglass again to steady her nerves.

"And that sounds very appropriate, as a motherly duty. But what of yourself? What does your own mind focus on in the country? Are you one for long walks? Do you draw? Do you ride out on horseback, or drive a pony and phaeton? Do people frequently give parties or balls in the country? What are your interests and pursuits?"

Oh my. Francine's mind began to spin. She did none of the things of which he spoke. And her motherly duties would soon be coming to a close, or at least changing in a major way. She was aware of this, but had avoided thinking beyond, caring not to contemplate the unknown, especially when that unknown did not appear merry. "Certainly the country is … well, the diversions are far fewer … we have been settled there only a short time … my second daughter was recently married … I do enjoy needlework …" As she faltered for an answer, images of her pony galloped through her mind. "My time recently has not been my own, with so many duties required of me. However, here, the other day, a ride on the beach recalled to me my passion for horses. A childhood passion I have not pursued for many years. I may consider taking it up again. There are many lovely lanes and grassy downs to be explored on horseback in the countryside."

"Indeed. What a fine pursuit for a lady. If you wish for help in setting up your stables and finding the perfect lady's mount, may I offer my services?"

She tried to disguise her surprise. *Does he assume I am a widow of some wealth and importance? I was merely hoping to borrow one of Sir John's horses from time to time.* She nearly confided her dilemma to him, but of a sudden thought the better of it. Elinor had always cautioned her from talking about money with anyone outside of one's family.

"Thank you for your kind offer. I shall keep that in mind. Now, do tell me about the concerns and pursuits of *your* daily life. You have spoken of your estate in the Irish countryside. I wonder if your time spent is at all similar to mine? Are you a horseman?" She watched his expressions as he spoke. He was very gentlemanly and courteous, his manners everything fine. He added more wine to her glass again.

"I do not spend much time at my estate because of business affairs in Dublin, therefore my horses are somewhat neglected. My duties are fully to my business as my son and daughter are both grown and married, on their own for some time, and my wife departed many years ago."

"My sympathies. And what is your business, if I may ask?"

He took another drink of wine. "My family has long been in trade. Imports and exports of various sorts."

"I see." She wondered he was not more specific, but just then their dinner was served and the concern went out of her head.

The meal was exceptional, especially the salmon. Mr Maher spoke more about his travels around England and Ireland and she listened with interest, wondering if she might ever see some of those places. Each time she reached for her wine glass she found it full again. He certainly was an attentive dining partner. His conversation then circled around to her situation again.

"Besides your estate in the countryside, do you also have a

home in town, perhaps in London?" he asked. "Will you spend the season there for your daughter's benefit? She is a fine young lady, as is her friend—both quite beautiful, in fact. One could not help but notice them on the dance floor."

Her body tensed. His questions had become rather pointed, yet his answers to her own questions remained vague. She reined in her inclination to confide in him, instead turning the conversation another direction. "I have never cared for London, sir. Too noisy and too smoky. Country living is my ideal, although I must say I am enjoying the seaside very much. Your Irish friends from the ball, are some of them in business with you? Did you all travel here together?"

He carefully studied the selection of cakes on the tray. "No, they are not business associates. We did all take the same ship from Dublin to Exeter but I do not know them otherwise. They seem a jolly bunch. As does your group, Mrs Dashwood. You are fortunate in your friends."

She noticed her wineglass was full again. So he was not of the Irish party. Was Mrs Jennings aware of this? Had they all made this assumption in error? Or had he deliberately chosen to project such an image?

Francine was suddenly overcome with a desire to be back at Seaview Place, cozy by the fire, amongst her trusted friends. She was indeed fortunate in these friends, and felt her affection for them grow. Now, how to end dinner graciously? Did she dare walk back alone? Did she dare walk back with him?

She glanced about the dining establishment, seeking she knew not what. But ... how could this be? Here were the very rescuers she might have wished for! Charles Creighton and Emmeline approached the table.

"We have discovered you," she said with a lift of her brow.

Francine mouthed a silent "thank you."

"If you are finished dining, might we join you for dessert and tea?" Mr Creighton asked. Mr Maher's face was stony, but with his nod of assent, Charles Creighton motioned for the attendant to bring two chairs.

"Thank you. Our companions at Seaview Place are very dull this evening," Emmeline said, "and the fire so fierce in the drawing room that Mr Creighton and I felt we might expire from the heat. Our party has not yet dined here. Tell us, how were your meals, and what did you have?"

Emmeline was unusually chatty. Francine wondered whose idea it had been to seek out herself and Mr Maher—and why. Whilst relieved at the rescue, she also chafed at being watched over as one might a child. The gentlemen spoke some of the fishing, and when the cakes had been consumed and the tea drunk, the foursome departed for Seaview Place.

Mr Maher offered Francine his arm but did not meet her eye. His step was brisk and it took effort on her part to keep up, especially being full from the meal and a little hazy from the wine. The fog had moved in so there was no night sky to exclaim over and the party reached Seaview Place with little conversation.

"Would you wish to come in and warm up, Maher?"

"Thank you, Creighton but no, I shall return to my lodgings before this fog obscures the way," he said with an awkward laugh.

"I enjoyed learning more about you and about your travels this evening, Mr Maher, and taking such a fine dinner in your company," Francine said, wondering if she was obliged to say or do anything else.

Mr Maher steadied his hat, said "Good evening to you all," and with a quick bow turned abruptly and disappeared into the thickening miasma.

Francine let out a deep breath when the servant closed the

door. She gave her sister and Mr Creighton a quizzical look. The house was quiet.

"Let us adjourn to the drawing room," Mr Creighton suggested. "I believe we can be private there." He went to the fireplace and stirred the logs, then dismissed the servant.

"Are you angry with us?" Emmeline said, taking her sister's hand as they sank onto the settee.

Mr Creighton turned his head from the fireplace and caught Francine's eye.

"No, I am not angry. In truth, I was relieved to see you. But I am more than a little puzzled." She looked from one face to the other.

"When Mr Creighton learned you were dining alone with Mr Maher, he expressed concern. I became alarmed and insisted we follow you to ensure your safety."

"My safety?"

Mr Creighton nodded. "It is not propriety that is the concern, not here at the seaside. It is the company—the often-unknown character of that company one finds in the ever-changing cast of travelers. It can be difficult to determine if persons are who they present themselves to be." He took a seat in a chair opposite the sisters. "In further conversation with members of the party from Ireland, I asked about Maher, knowing he had made you an invitation. Perhaps none of my business, and my apologies for my interference, but my intentions were honourable. When I learned he was *not* of their party, yet had presented himself to be so … well, I would not wish for any of my friends to come to harm … so I discretely asked around about him."

Francine thought back to the dinner. "I had asked about his party as well, and learned the same. He was vague about his business … he would only say 'importing and exporting' … yet he asked me about my situation in detail as far as my holdings in the country and even in town, and commented on the beauty of the girls—"

Emmeline gasped. "Commenting on the girls? A man of his age?"

Mr Creighton raised a hand to quell her reaction. "Now, we might conjecture some kind of Banbury tale when it may have been merely a fatherly sort of comment. We will never know the truth of it. So let us just be aware that we have concerns, and agree to share any knowledge we may collect. He could be a perfectly fine gentleman."

Charles Creighton stood and paced about the room, hands in his tweed coat. "Maher is known hereabouts by name and appearance. He has visited at least twice before, and seems acquainted with a few local businessmen. He speaks of traveling a great deal, and has appeared with parties from London and from as far as Blackpool. Now this time from Ireland."

"Dublin, he told me."

He nodded. "Mrs Dashwood, what did you tell him of your holdings, or your holiday plans … or anything else?" He looked at her keenly.

She returned his gaze with confidence. "He did seem a fine gentleman at first. Then, after a time, his particular questions of me but the vagueness of his answers to my own questions, did put me on my guard. He seems to assume I am in possession of an estate in the country, and a home in London as well. I let him believe such for the time being, and gave him no particulars."

Emmeline grasped both her sister's hands. "Then you told him nothing? Brilliant, sister. Quite brilliant."

Creighton smiled with relief. "Fine work, Mrs Dashwood. You have an instinct for discerning character. Something we all need as we explore a wider world."

"But what do you suspect him of, Mr Creighton?" Francine

was curious as to what else he might have unearthed about her handsome dinner companion.

"Nothing for certain. But perhaps we would be wise—all of us—to have at least one or two others of our own party with us on our outings. We don't want any untoward events to spoil our holiday."

"I think that wise," Emmeline said. "Now, if there is nothing further, we shall retire for the night." They rose, curt-sied to Creighton and made for the door, leaving their friend staring into the fireplace, alone with his thoughts.

After penning the day's events and her own thoughts into her holiday journal, Francine took a sheaf of paper and wrote a letter to each of her daughters.

June —

    My Dear Elinor,

    Seaview Place is comfortable and spacious, two streets uphill from the beach. Emmeline and I share a corner room with a view to the sea and of the red cliffs.

    I did not anticipate how much I would enjoy the horse ride on the beach. The mechanics of riding all came back to me, and I marvel at that, at my "advanced" age. I now look forward to our cliff ride. At one point I had previously expressed an interest in the architecture of the many fine homes hereabouts. The next day Mr Creighton gifted me a book on the very thing. Such a kind man.

    It sets my heart at ease you are nearby Marianne. I rely on your practical knowledge and wisdom. However, this journey has taught me I have relied overly-much on others, especially you—something I wish to change. Being in a new place seems to make change easier to attempt.

Marianne says you have added painting to your artistic skills. I am most eager to see the works you have produced. Mrs Whittaker has done several sketches and is commencing now on a painting. You would enjoy painting and sketching here.

Several of us have taken up sea bathing. It is most invigorating —I might even say shocking! It leaves the body tingling and refreshed. I do not know if I look younger, but I certainly feel younger. No wonder so many come here to partake of it. We plan to sea bathe most mornings.

My dinner with Mr M took an unusual turn. I have never felt much confidence in discerning character, especially after the whole Willoughby affair; but it appears I am more astute than I imagined. During dinner, Mr M asked me many detailed questions about my situation, but when I had asked him similar questions I received only vague answers. This put me on my guard. Mr Creighton says I did very well in not divulging any compromising information to Mr M. I think you, too, would have been proud of me.

My childhood riding is a longer story, probably best told to all three of you girls in front of the fire one evening. Some of it is very sad, thus my reluctance to share it. But you and Marianne are grown now, and Margaret nearly so, and I believe the time is right.

Much love, Mama

She prepared the letter for mailing then promptly began a missive to Marianne so as to have both letters ready for the morning post.

June —

My dear Marianne,

How I enjoyed your long letter. Elinor reports you are well, and this news pleases me. I was amused at your taste for figs! When I carried you, I could not get enough cheese.

I can attempt descriptions of the beauty here, but it will likely not satisfy your romantic and artistic sensibilities. When we rode from the stable to the beach, the fog was thick at first and it felt like we were riding in a fairy story. I was pleased how well my body remembered the mechanics of riding. My childhood passion has been reawakened and I plan to pursue it—perhaps Sir John has a lady's saddle horse or two I might borrow at times?

How kind of you to support your sister's artistic pursuits. You are fortunate to have a sister with whom you are so amiable, even though you are vastly different in temperament. My sister is frustrating me here at times with her indulgence of Admiral Tennant's somewhat unreliable behaviours. But I am grateful for her company in other ways.

The fashions here are of a wide variety, probably more noticeable because ladies from all stations mingle more. Even the fishermen's wives are seen at the beach areas, and people from all parts of the country and even the continent travel here. I did purchase a riding habit for myself, and one for Margaret. I shall try to pay more attention to the fashion details at the next ball so I may give you a better report.

Mr Maher is no longer of any interest to me. I will certainly not be moving to Ireland! Mr Creighton uncovered some questionable connections so I shall set my sights elsewhere.

For now, I look forward to our cliff ride with a mix of eagerness and trepidation. Mr Creighton, an excellent horseman, will be with us, as will the admiral and his daughter Florrie, along with myself and my sister, Margaret, Rose, and James. And with a ball that evening, I dare say I shall have news enough for my next letter.

Do take care of yourself and your little one.

Much love, Mama

She prepared the letter and tip-toed down the stairs to place her missives on the silver tray in the entryway.

CHAPTER SIXTEEN

*T*he nightly fog had kept hold of its rain so their cliff ride was not spoilt and they set out that morning in happy anticipation.

Emmeline had been delighted the previous evening that a note from the admiral confirming the riding rendezvous was addressed to none other than herself.

"He must have forgiven me for my midnight missive," she told her sister. "Or been flattered? I suppose I shall not know for certain until we meet."

The six riders from Seaview Place—and their guide—met the two riders from Bellevue at the appointed crossroads. Florrie gushed happy sentiments at being in the company of Margaret and Rose once again. Her high-spirited mare was fine-boned with a beautiful head and expressive eye, and Florrie appeared to have her well in hand.

Admiral Tennant again showered Emmeline with flattering attention, and made no mention of the middle-of-the-night note whilst in company.

The red clay paths were damp in the shaded areas, yet dusty in the parts baked by the sun. Francine was pleased to ride the same horse again—whose name she learned was Lightning—and laughed at such a name for the sturdy cob.

The riders threaded their way through the rusty red and green tapestry of soil and trees, sunlight and shade. Saddles creaked, birds called, and the pungent smell of the woods filled Francine's nostrils.

"Not long now, sire, 'til the open area," the young guide said.

Florrie's horse had been dancing about—one of those horses averse to staying within the group. It took a calm sense of discipline from an experienced rider to manage such a mount. Francine admired Florrie's horsemanship as she watched the young lady calmly maneuver.

"This pace is far too slow," Florrie exclaimed. "I know another way to the top." She flashed a mischievous smile at the other girls. "Follow me!"

Without as much as a by-your-leave, the girls galloped off after Florrie. Shocked at her daughter showing so little courtesy, Francine's cheeks flushed at such impertinence. She looked to Charles Creighton.

As did James. "Father?" At his nod, James was off in pursuit of the young ladies.

Francine turned to Mr Creighton. "I am so sorry. That was unexpected, and so unlike Margaret. I wonder about the influence of—"

"Admiral," Mr Creighton began, "may we assume your daughter does indeed ..." but when he turned in his saddle, the admiral and Emmeline were nowhere to be seen.

Mr Creighton fumed. "Well, this is a fine situation!" Francine had never seen him look so fierce. "How can I assure the welfare of those who ride off?"

"You may be sure I will speak to Margaret to put an immediate stop to this kind of behaviour," she said, chagrined by Margaret's impetuous choice. "And to Rose as well."

"James will catch up and see to their safety," he said. "However, I fear there is naught I can do for your sister." He shook his head. "We shall follow our guide, if that pleases you?"

Francine's eyes widened at being consulted. She murmured her agreement and the horses resumed a steady walk behind the young guide on his trusty mule.

After some minutes of silent plodding, Francine ventured a comment. "Emmeline loses her good sense when it comes to the admiral. I have spoken to her many times."

Charles Creighton turned with a gentle smile. "We may be able to guide the young, but the others will do as they will."

Misgiving filled her heart. "I fear my sister fancies herself in love."

His eyes caught hers as the horses trod along the hillside path. "Love," he said and turned away. "A word used carelessly by many." His tone was almost bitter.

Had she offended him? Or reopened his recent wound?

"I am attempting to teach James the difference between *falling* in love with someone and *growing* to love someone. The outcomes, I have found, can be quite different."

Francine had never thought of love as having such distinctions. She was certain Elinor had grown to love Edward; and Marianne—once she had got over her infatuation with Willoughby—had grown to love the colonel. Such love took time to grow. How much time? Emmeline's acquaintance with the admiral had been of too short a duration for even a steady affection to begin to grow, had it not?

The party rode on and the trees grew dense, seeming to swallow them as if they rode through a tunnel into another realm. For Francine, riding *was* another realm, in itself. Her love of the sport was rekindled and glowed within her. Energy sparked in her limbs. Even Lightning seemed to perk up, though the path had grown narrow and dark. Then they emerged into the open. She had to shade her eyes to allow them time to adjust to the sudden brightness—a process that took longer these days. But great was the reward. Open ground spread far to the north where it continued to rise, with clumps of trees here and there—which she surmised sheltered manor houses. Red cliffs marched off to the east in varying heights whilst waves dashed against their crumbling bases. One cliff, far off, shone white. To the west tumbled many hills and downs and a long expanse of beach. And stretching before them to the south, the magnificent sea! The great and wonderful sea, disappearing over the edge of the earth in a mist that blended water and sky. Her mind reeled at the vastness of it all, a distance greater than the eye could perceive. What must it be like far out to sea, beyond the sight of all land? Adventurous Margaret would enjoy this view.

Fie! Margaret! Had there been an accident? Francine's heart fell with a thud and dread seized her senses. Lightning's ears twitched and his tail swished from side to side.

But wait … Francine bent her ear. There was a commotion in the trees and soon a party approached them from below a wooded hill. Praise God! It was James, with Margaret and the others following. Francine was overcome with the desire to rush to her daughter and embrace her, hold her, keep her safe, never let her out of her sight again. As she contemplated doing this very thing, she noticed two young men following on fine steeds, one with a hooded bird perched on his arm. The two waited politely at a short distance.

Mr Creighton rode forward and addressed the young ladies.

"Halt where you are please," he said, in a voice that conveyed such authority that the young ladies exchanged nervous glances. "Miss Tennant, these words also apply to you. Although your father has ultimate responsibility for you, that is presently relinquished to me by his … unexpected disappearance with Mrs Harrington, and so—"

"I apologise for his choice, sir, but his disappearance does not surprise me," Florrie said with a hiss.

Charles Creighton's eyebrows rose but he continued. "So, to the three of you I say this: you are each of you aware that chaperones are required in proper society, and I have stepped up to assist Mrs Dashwood in that endeavor. However, neither of us can be successful at our duty if you run away. I do not make these rules, but it is my duty to see they are followed. I therefore offer you a choice."

Florrie's eyes grew large. Margaret and Rose hung their heads.

"We can return to the village immediately and limit the number of adventures with certain friends for the remainder of our holiday …"

Florrie looked away, her cheeks flaming crimson.

"Or you may each offer Mrs Dashwood and myself an apology, and your pledge of honour to stay with the group and follow all directions given by us from here forward. Which shall it be?"

Margaret looked at her friends and then spoke. "We regret letting our enthusiasm take us out of bounds. It was thoughtless and we are sorry. We do wish to have adventures on this holiday—hopefully many—and will follow your lead and guidance, sir, and that of my mother. You have my pledge."

"And mine," echoed Rose.

"Mr Creighton, I am sorry for leading the others off. Such … guidelines … are not often given to me, and I was remiss. I also give you my pledge. I shall be more mindful in the future. And," she turned to James, "I thank your son for following after us to ensure our safety." She aimed a dazzling smile at the young man.

Mr Creighton looked at Francine. "Are you satisfied, Mrs Dashwood?"

Francine, in her great relief to see her daughter again,

would have let the whole matter drop. But now Mr Creighton required her opinion and agreement. She was unused to having her opinion sought. She sat deep in the saddle and summoned her resolve.

"Yes, I am, and I accept their apologies and promises."

"It is settled then. Let us put this incident behind us and look forward to more adventures. Now, who are your new companions?" He motioned the young men to join them, and they rode forward with James.

"Father, may I present Mr Geoffrey Manning of Somerset, and his friend Mr Michael Wheeler. Gentlemen, this is my father, Mr Charles Creighton."

Both young men doffed their hats and nodded in acknowledgement, then said in unison, "We are honoured, sir."

Geoffrey Manning held out his arm, adding, "And here is Seamus, a young hawk I have in training. We were out on exercises when your son and the three young ladies happened upon us, sir." His eyes were a steady grey and his countenance open. He was perhaps thirty years of age. The livery of the pair was of fine make although well worn.

Mr Creighton looked from one to another, and a smile broke over his face. "I am pleased to make your acquaintance. May I presume you live nearby?"

"Indeed sir. Yonder over the downs is my summer residence, Atlas Hall. May I be bold enough to invite you and your party to tea? It is an interesting ride along these clifftop lanes, with some splendid buildings to appreciate as well as commanding sea views. That is, if you have no particular agenda?"

Mr Creighton looked at the young guide on his mule. At the boy's nod, he replied, "We shall gladly oblige you, but we must linger here until two others of our party rejoin us. We had thought to take refreshment as we await them. Will you join us?"

The young men exchanged a look. "We shall be very happy to, sir."

"Good. It is settled then. But before anyone dismounts, do all come round and take in one of the finest vistas I have ever beheld." The riders joined in appreciating the view. Gasps and sighs were heard, hands pointed this way and that.

"Now Miss Tennant, please tell us more about what we see."

She turned to Mr Creighton in surprise. "With pleasure, sir. Down below us, to the left, you can see where the River Sid flows into the sea, near the Ham." She snickered. "So called because … well … that little island looks like a ham!"

Laughter broke the remaining sense of tension.

"What, pray, is that white cliff to the east?" Mrs Dashwood asked. "All the other cliffs are red."

"It stands out, does it not? It is called the Beer, near the town of the same name. Of course, there are many white cliffs further east, nearer to Dover. I have seen them from the water."

"Whoever named these places must have had eating and drinking on their mind!" exclaimed James. "Very like-minded to me, I say. Perhaps we can dismount now for refreshments?"

Mr Creighton stared hard towards the woods. "I am concerned for Mrs Harrington. Miss Tennant, might you have any idea where your father has taken her? She is not in my charge, exactly, but courtesy dictates—"

"I have never ridden with my father," Florrie answered, her chin thrust forward. "I ride often, but my groom accompanies me. I regret I cannot be more helpful, but I do not know my father's habits." The scowl on her face belied the calm propriety of her words.

Questioning looks darted amongst the others.

Mr Creighton frowned. "Well, let us eat and perhaps they

will show their faces yet." He dismounted, and the others did likewise.

Their guide stepped up and bowed. "Sire, if I may … I know these paths well. Might I offer to search while ye fine folk eat?"

Francine nodded at Mr Creighton. "Thank you, young man. That might ease our minds in case they have met with an accident. Half an hour?"

"Aye, half an hour, an' wish me luck!" He tugged at his hat and was off.

Worry and annoyance battled for dominance in Francine's troubled heart—worry for her sister's safety and reputation, and annoyance at her sister putting them all out. How could she?

Although Francine's feelings were upsetting, they did not dampen her appetite. The guide had left behind the pack of food and the explorers and their guests indulged in breads, cheeses, and dried fruits with enough cider to quench their thirsts.

In due time, their young guide returned on his mule with Mrs Harrington following on her horse.

Fran rushed towards her sister. "Emmeline, thank God! I was sure you had met with some terrible accident. Are you hurt?"

Emmeline would not meet her eyes. "Of course not. You fret too much, Fran." A brittle smile appeared on her face as she looked out to the others. "I do hope you have saved a few bites for me? All this exercise has fueled my appetite."

Francine stared hard at her sister. Will she not even apologise?

"Where is the admiral?" Mr Creighton asked. Neither his voice nor his face revealed his state of mind.

"Oh, Marcus did not feel well and made for Bellevue. He invited me to accompany him, but I felt that would disrupt our cliff ride so I attempted to make my way back to you. I was on the correct path when our young guide found me—"

Francine gasped. "The admiral left you alone in the woods? I cannot believe—"

"Pish posh, he gave me directions before he departed. I am certainly not helpless. Is there no place in our world for the autonomous self-determined female? As my dear Fanny Burney says, *You are made a slave in a moment by the world, if you don't begin life by defying it.* Now, can someone bring me a bite of bread and cheese? And some of that cider? I am parched!" She dismounted and looked around expectantly.

Mr Creighton frowned and turned away.

Francine froze in astonishment, and made no move.

Florrie hastened to Emmeline with a napkin of food and a flask, her cheeks bearing a flush that was not born of sunlight. "Here, Mrs Harrington, it is the least I can do to make up for my father's poor manners."

"How kind. Thank you my dear," Emmeline said, then raised the flask to her lips.

An awkward silence hovered over the clearing like a rogue cloud. The new gentlemen busied themselves adjusting their tack, and uneasy glances were exchanged amongst the others.

Charles Creighton cleared his throat and all eyes turned to him. "Mrs Harrington, may I present two young men who have joined our party in your absence?" He introduced them and their hawk, and repeated the invitation to tea. "If there is no objection, let us continue. We are assured of seeing splendid parklands and commanding views on our way to Atlas Hall."

Emmeline curtseyed. "Certainly, let us enjoy this unexpected fellowship. Fine houses and fine views will be just the thing. How far might this journey take us?"

Mr Manning stepped forward. "Not more than a few miles to the west, Mrs Harrington. Atlas Hall is nestled in those high downs and looks out to sea. And from there, a different path leads back into town. Do you know it?" he asked, turning to the young guide.

The boy touched his hat. "Aye."

The party mounted and resumed their journey. James and the guide joined the new acquaintances, followed by Margaret, Rose, and Florrie. Francine and Emmeline rode side by side in silence, followed by Charles Creighton. The path was wide and wound in and out of small copses of wizened trees with stunning views out to sea to the south, and glimpses of fine prospects to the north. Mr Manning related details about the properties they passed, their owners, and their histories. Only one home could be seen clearly, the others being partially obscured by gates and woods and gardens.

The road bent sharply to the north to avoid a series of higher downs and here Mr Manning halted the group.

"We are arrived at Atlas Hall. The day being fine, shall we enjoy tea in the courtyard?"

"I am agreeable to tea whilst sitting on a rock in the rain, as long as there is plenty of it and some cakes to boot!" exclaimed James.

Mr Creighton chuckled. "My son is ever hungry."

The party approached the gates, which were opened promptly, and passed through a small wood to sunlit grounds. The garden was tended but had a more natural look about it that surprised Francine in so ancient a setting. She found the idea of a contained wildness an intriguing contrast. The stone building was not large but boasted a tower on the west end, and Francine deemed Atlas Hall far more a castle than Belle-vue. Stable boys appeared to manage the horses and a man came and carried the hawk away. The group moved towards a partially-walled garden.

An older gentleman appeared and bowed. "My lord."

CHAPTER SEVENTEEN

*G*eoffrey Manning's shoulders shook with laughter at the old retainer's formal address but he maintained his countenance.

"Nichols, we have made some new friends today. Would you kindly see to tea and refreshments? Here, in the outdoors —although the ladies may wish to go indoors first?"

"Certainly, my lord. Ladies, follow me and a maid will assist you."

Francine's and Emmeline's faces mirrored each other's surprise as the females of the group followed along. Once freshened and tidied the ladies returned to the garden where tea, lemonade, and a selection of delicacies awaited them. Young James' plate was heaped high and he nodded at them with a pleasurable grin. Soon everyone procured a drink and a plate and found a seat.

Francine lifted her eyes to the wide expanse of sky above. A few clouds were tossed about on the same breeze that caressed her cheek. It had been so long since her cheek was caressed by a loving hand. Seagulls swooped near and far, crying overhead, and a sense of longing swept through her … for something unnamed yet almost tangible. As she lifted the fine china cup to her lips, she felt someone watching her and looked around. Charles Creighton smiled at her and popped a piece of cake into his mouth. She nodded. So kind.

Geoffrey Manning held up a glass of lemonade. "Welcome to Atlas Hall. I am pleased to enjoy your company, but feel I must explain …" he began with a rueful smile. "We rarely have guests"—he eyed Mr Wheeler for confirmation—"but you seemed such a likeable group, and we sometimes grow bored with our own company." He looked around at the guests, each pair of eyes watching him expectantly. "No doubt most of you heard Nichols, my butler, address me." The sense of expectancy was palpable. "It is true, I am the son of a duke—acting the role because my father is presently incapacitated. Sadly, there is not much hope for his improvement. He has left our seat in Somerset for … further medical help. I was reluctant to introduce myself by my title until I knew you better." He glanced again at Mr Wheeler. "I have spent many summers here; it is a splendid place to pursue my passion of hawking."

Charles Creighton spoke for the group. "We are honoured at your invitation, my lord. We are on holiday from the Honiton area. Do you know it?"

"The town known for its lacemaking?"

"The very one. We each reside on various estates near there and all value our privacy as much as you, I dare say. But Miss Tennant lives here, just northeast of Sidmouth."

Lord Manning looked at her. "Are you the young lady I see riding through the woods and over the downs at times on that sweet mare?"

Florrie's eyes lit up. "Why, yes, my lord. My father and I have lived here for three years. He is retired from the Navy—Admiral Marcus Tennant. Do you know him?"

Lord Manning's brow furrowed. "No, we have never met. But I have heard the name."

Mr Creighton spoke about the others of their party who remained in the village at Seaview Place.

"Another will join us in a few days—Mr Cecil Walford, a fine gentleman I have known for many years."

"Indeed! A gentleman I know myself. I will be happy to renew our acquaintance."

Mr Creighton looked surprised.

"I came into contact with him whilst making arrangements for my father's treatments," Lord Manning said with a shrug of his shoulders. "He was most helpful."

"I am sure he was. He has dedicated his life and wealth to helping those in unfortunate circumstances. I am involved with some of his ventures in that regard. His interests in the North prevented him traveling down with us initially."

"Yes, I am aware of those difficulties."

Francine and Emmeline exchanged a look at Mr Creighton's compliment of Mr Walford, and at Lord Manning being acquainted with him.

"I should like to meet your other friends whilst you are here. I am sure we can make some arrangements. Perhaps a garden party? I can demonstrate some of our hawks, if you are interested?"

Margaret spoke up. "My lord, I would love to know more about hawking. Birds seem so free, soaring high above us. I am curious how you get them to work with you instead of just flying away."

Lord Manning's face broke into a smile. "Then you shall. Perhaps after a demonstration you may, during your visit at Sidmouth, wish to accompany us hawking on horses. But I get ahead of myself."

Margaret beamed. "I would be honoured to be amongst your hawking party."

Francine's own heart leapt at the idea of such, and she silently vowed to also be of the group. After all, Margaret would need a chaperone.

Then Francine's curiosity momentarily shattered her reserve. "Might you tell us more about your residence here, Lord Manning? I am newly interested in architecture, and the name Atlas Hall seems rather unusual. Who is or was Atlas, other than the Greek Titan god?" She drew in a little breath at her own boldness. "If I am not too impertinent …"

"Not at all. I enjoy talking about Atlas Hall. The place was so named when we purchased it. During my research I learned the Atlantic Ocean was, in ancient times, called the Atlas Sea, and I find that fascinating. So we kept the name. For the architectural details, I must defer to Wheeler, who is far more knowledgeable than I on that topic."

Mr Wheeler spoke about the stone used in the building—some local and some imported from surrounding counties and beyond. "Atlas Hall contains many types of stone—basalt, Ashburton marble, limestone, quartzite, travertine, Dartmoor granite—but is mostly made of Salcombe sandstone, quarried just east of here, and slates of various kinds. Those other stones mentioned are used for ornamental effect." He shared what he had learned about the age of the house and who had originally built it, and some of the previous residents. "It has been a project dear to our hearts. Certainly parts of the place have needed repair or been updated over the years. In our own improvements we have been most conscious of keeping details as authentic as possible."

Lord Manning spoke again. "Perhaps you would enjoy a very brief tour before you depart? The days are long this time of year but you will want your dinner and a good fire before it is full dark, I wager. A longer examination of the house and grounds—perhaps guided by Wheeler—can happen at another time."

Mr Creighton replied, "I am sure we should all enjoy a full tour on a future visit. But there is a ball in town this evening that our young ladies are most eager to attend. They will need time to prepare." Three enthusiastic smiles confirmed this.

Lord Manning chuckled. "So it shall be then."

Before departing, they did ascend the tower. The view was spectacular, aided by a fine telescope to view ships passing on the horizon—a view that would soon be blocked by the ominous clouds gathering in the west and darkening the horizon.

Promises to meet again concluded the visit.

It had been Francine's desire for Margaret to meet a variety of people on this holiday, but making the acquaintance of a peer of the realm had not even entered her thoughts. Lord Manning seemed eager to teach Margaret about hawking, and about using the telescope to look at the stars and planets, but beyond that Francine could detect no particular attraction between the two.

As the riders made their way to the village, the wind changed. The sky darkened overhead as the clouds moved in. Just before they reached the stable, Mr Creighton rode up alongside Francine. "I believe it would be wise for Miss Tennant to stay at Seaview for the night. What is your own opinion?"

Francine's eyebrows rose at again being consulted, but in spite of her surprise she found her voice. "Yes. I agree it would be the safer choice for her. We don't really know what state her father was in when he abandoned Emmeline. And the storm approaches."

Mr Creighton tipped his hat in accord.

As they neared the stable, he called out, "Miss Tennant,

may I solicit a word?" She pulled her horse back to ride beside him. "The hour grows late and that treacherous road to Bellevue is even more difficult in the dark. To say nothing of the storm. I invite you to join us for dinner and stay the night with the girls at Seaview Place, if it pleases you."

A smile burst over her face. "I thank you, sir. I would be most obliged."

"I will send a messenger to your father so he knows you are safe."

"You are very good."

"What of the ball this evening?" Emmeline asked as the group dismounted. "Do we have time to prepare? We do not wish to smell like horse whilst on the dance floor."

Florrie looked at her two friends. "I have no gown with me. I do not see how I can attend."

"Surely you can find a gown amongst ours to borrow? I am sure any of us would oblige," Francine offered. "You are taller, closer to my sister's height—"

The talk of gowns was interrupted by James. "These clouds do not bode well for traveling anywhere this evening. I have heard that seaside storms can be quite violent. The chance to watch one might prove more exciting than a ball," he said with an apologetic grin.

They arrived at Seaview Place before the rain began. Whilst they dined, James got his wish—the howling wind smashed the storm clouds against the shoreline, and rain from the south and west battered every building. In less than an hour the streets were flooded whilst lightning and thunder bore down upon the village. James happily stationed himself at the largest window to take in the weather spectacle, although Francine noted he kept one eye on Florrie, especially when her melodious laughter burst from the girls' game table.

CHAPTER EIGHTEEN

Over the next few days dense fog clung like a limpet to the coastline, thwarting all outdoor activities. The gentlemen had planned another fishing outing, and so were disappointed. The girls were not so as Florrie stayed on with them during the inclement weather. When the wind and rain had lessened, the group from Seaview Place did manage to attend an evening concert and were surprised to be approached there by Lord Manning and Mr Wheeler. Introductions were made to Sir John, Mrs Jennings, and the Whittakers.

"We are marooned on an island of cloud," Mr Wheeler said, describing how the heavy fog affected them at the top of the cliffs. "But it does make for a cosy time to pursue reading at the fireside, or to perfect our billiards skills."

Lord Manning extended his garden party invitation to them all and asked, "Do you have any fixed engagements?"

"The admiral had spoken of a boating excursion," Sir John said. "But that is also dependent upon the weather."

Lord Manning's eyes darkened and he exchanged a furtive glance with Mr Wheeler.

"Beyond that, we plan to go fishing again, but that can be done at any time. You would be welcome to join us, if fishing is to your liking." Then Sir John turned to Mrs Jennings for further information.

"We have nothing else," she said, "except more concerts or readings, and the weekly balls—things we cannot get at home. But those are mostly evening events, and dates are not yet set."

"Capital. Then watch the weather and expect an invitation. And yes," he said, turning to Margaret, "I shall fly some of our hawks for you. Perhaps you might wish to try the activity yourself? One of my birds is quite amenable to new handlers, as long as they feed her well."

Margaret's face lit up at this offer. Her eyes sought her mother's and received smiling approval.

"I shall be delighted to learn how to work with the birds."

It *was* out of the ordinary, but then Margaret was not your usual young lady. Francine secretly shared Margaret's desire to work with such a powerful bird—rather like working with a horse, but a bird was not ten times one's size. Might I even consider …?

The day after the concert Admiral Tennant sent a message, via Emmeline, that he would like to call on them. The missive— shared only with Francine—contained the following few words:

My dear Mrs Harrington,

My behaviour on the ride was unforgiveable, yet I am bold enough to beg your forgiveness. May we start anew? May I call on you at Seaview Place?

Your admirer, Admiral Marcus Tennant

. . .

"What do you think, Fran? Shall I relent?" Emmeline had been quite silent about the admiral since the cliff ride.

"It is difficult to say. We have not known him long enough to determine his usual behaviour, or what might be out of character for him. We have seen an equal amount of charmer and scoundrel. Particularly when he's in his cups."

Emmeline nodded slowly. "That is true. Perhaps I was unwise to rush in, but he seemed everything I was looking for."

After a pause, Francine said, "Everything your husband was not?"

A rueful smile appeared on her sister's face. "Yes, I suppose you are right. But why should I not have an exciting companion this time?"

"I hardly think being abandoned in the woods is a desirable kind of excitement, Em." She frowned. "Was he drinking that day?"

Emmeline owned she did recall a flask appearing from his pocket several times during the ride.

"Perhaps you might voice that concern? Even request that he abstain from drinking in your presence? Although, should your dreams come true and you end up betrothed, would he be willing to abstain from drinking altogether? It does seem to contribute to his … misconduct."

"That seems a lot to ask. But I shall consider it."

At dinner Emmeline told of their potential caller.

"About time!" Sir John quipped. "Where has he been keeping himself anyway?"

Mrs Jennings smiled knowingly.

Mr Creighton scowled and said nothing.

Emmeline sent a reply, but did not share those contents.

The storm had lost its ferocity, and despite the continued fog and light rain, the admiral called on the residents of Seaview Place. The visit lasted a few hours and included tea at the fireside and games of backgammon, with the admiral's behaviour everything charming and correct. Florrie then returned home with her father.

Once their guests departed, Charles Creighton took up his station at the hearth, gazing into the fire. The logs popped and hissed. Rain pattered against the windows. After the others had quitted the room, curiosity got the best of Francine and she approached him.

"I do hope I am not interrupting, Mr Creighton?"

He turned at the sound of her voice and a slow smile melted his scowl. "No indeed, your company always brings me pleasure, Mrs Dashwood." He scrutinized her face. "Does something trouble you?"

Her eyes searched his, then she looked into the fire. "We have had a pleasant enough afternoon …" She looked up and he raised his brows. "It is my sister. She still wishes to give the admiral the benefit of the doubt. He was most charming and appropriate today, but … after our other experiences with him, well … I just cannot trust him. I have not moved much in society in recent years and have no experience with the manners of Navy men … perhaps I am overly cautious? Pray, what is your own opinion of this seeming change in him?"

Mr Creighton's gaze was steady and he nodded thoughtfully. "No, I do not think you overly cautious, Mrs Dashwood. I share your concerns about past events and unexplained behaviours—although some of those behaviours might relate to his imbibing in excess. Nevertheless, if your sister might listen to your advice, perhaps you can caution her to proceed slowly?" He wrinkled his brow. "He does not appear to have a reputation as a muslin chaser—no more so than many eligible men about town—but he seems to be known by the free-traders and the like, which are mostly smugglers, although that too is not unheard of for a seafaring man. But I get a feeling there is more going on than we can see. Walford says the same."

"Mr Walford? But might his opinion not be coloured by jealousy?"

Mr Creighton gave her a crooked grin. "Walford does have a *tendre* for your sister, which is obvious to most of us. But no, in a recent letter he cautioned me about the admiral related to something he has learned through his own business in the North, but he would rather not put details on paper. Walford will join us within the week. Perhaps then we can learn more."

"I do hope he can be present for the garden party, and the sailing cruise. As I have come to know Mr Walford better, my opinion of him has improved. He seems more than a fusty old gentleman with a fancy for my sister."

Mr Creighton chuckled. "That might well be one description of him. But you are right, there is much more to Walford, and his integrity is beyond reproach. I have known him for years. He and I have business dealings and I have always found him to be a straight arrow."

"Would that my sister could return his feelings. Ah well, the heart wants what it wants. I thank you for your frank opinions. How quickly our holiday time has passed. With only a few weeks left, I think my sister feels an urgency to secure the admiral. I will do my best to distract her. Now, I must go write in my holiday journal."

They exchanged warm smiles, and when she turned at the door to look back, he was still smiling at her.

CHAPTER NINETEEN

*a*t last the sea calmed and the sun shone. Sea bathing resumed and the gentlemen enjoyed a fishing expedition. A messenger brought an invitation for the garden party at Atlas Hall, which immediately livened the dinner conversation.

"What does one do at a garden party?" asked Rose.

"A garden party," Mrs Jennings explained as she gathered all eyes to her, "is the best of all entertainments, in my estimation. One is outdoors in fine weather, mingling with charming people, and enjoying the best food and drink without the need to stay awake until an unreasonable hour. We will have a wonderful time at Atlas Hall, particularly with the unusual hawking demonstration promised. I have attended many a garden party in my day but this will be my first time to witness hawking. What do you say, Sir John?"

He was equally ready to command the attention of the group. "I have seen hawking occasionally. It is a splendid sight to behold. As we might also say about Lord Manning himself, and his friend Mr Wheeler too, am I right? One of them, or both, are bound to suit some of you young ladies, eh?"

Mrs Whittaker's soft voice interceded, with a remedial glance at Sir John. "Howsoever that may be, girls, a garden party is very pleasant indeed. Besides refreshments and interesting conversation, there are often demonstrations, such as hawking or archery or target shooting. At one party I attended, the host showed off the skills of his herding dogs. Quite amazing. And there are games, such as lawn bowls or pall mall. If there is a lake, boat rides might be possible. I believe you will find it enjoyable, and I hope it will be the first of many garden parties that you attend. Which reminds me, a wide-brimmed bonnet is imperative as the sun will be high and complexions must be protected. Tonight, choose the gown you wish to wear, then perhaps we ladies shall visit the millinery shops tomorrow?"

Smiles spread around the table and the chatter about gowns began.

"Let us go through," suggested Emmeline, "to pursue our topic of interest, and leave the gentlemen to their own conversation. I wonder who else will attend the lord's party?"

The ladies rose and bustled to the parlour.

The day of the garden party saw the early arrival of Cecil Walford in his carriage. He joined those gathered around the breakfast table, his appearance hale and hearty, but Francine detected a cloud of concern in his countenance. Perhaps his business in the North had not gone well?

Determined to be more of an active participant than a silent observer during these final few weeks of their holiday, Francine set her tea cup down and asked, "Is your business situation resolved, Mr Walford? It must have been of grave import."

"Thank you for your kind inquiry, Mrs Dashwood. I have

established an asylum, a hospital, and an orphanage in a certain town in the North—a mill town—and a fire caused great damage and some injuries at the asylum. So I have begun a new building project. Whilst there, I learned things about some of the asylum residents. Surprising truths, one might say. I cannot share more until I confer with those who will be involved in the … actions … needed to set certain things right." He glanced at Charles Creighton as he spoke.

Mr Creighton folded his napkin and said, "Then you will be pleased to learn that the residents of Seaview Place have been invited to a garden party at Atlas Hall, the summer residence of Lord Manning, who professes to know you. We leave here mid-afternoon. Will you be sufficiently refreshed so that you might attend?"

"Aye, it will be most pleasant to meet with him again. Quite the gentleman. The ease of a garden party is just what my soul desires at present." He cast an almost wistful look at Emmeline, who was now engaged in conversation with Mrs Whittaker and did not notice. "Indeed, such a diversion is exactly what I need."

The travelers had engaged two coaches for the short journey to ascend the heights of the cliffs. The four older members of the party rode in one coach, with Francine, Emmeline, Margaret and Rose in the other. James and his father traveled by horse, as did Cecil Walford.

Francine almost wished she were in the saddle as well, the better to take in the stunning view of the sea. Remnants of heavy fog hung over the offshore waves, and beams of sunlight pierced the dense blanket at certain points, setting the water alight with the brilliance of sparkling jewels. The cry of the wheeling gulls brought tears to her eyes—how she would miss the seaside. Who would have thought she could come to love a place so utterly and completely? That a place, rather than a person, could so capture her heart?

Soon enough they were greeted at the gates of Atlas Hall and ushered down the lane. Decorative flags were tastefully strung around the terraces and gardens, in the colours of the livery she had noted before. The servants, busy about the setting, wore the same colours. Windchimes hung from the low branches of trees. How many guests would attend?

As the coach came to a stop, she pinched her cheeks, having come to appreciate the healthy glow of those at the seaside over the wan paleness of the so-called fine ladies who called London their home. She had only been to town a few times and, whilst the parks were lovely, at times the quality of the air was distastefully smoky. It might be difficult to spend a great deal of time outdoors in London.

The gentlemen of their own party stepped up to hand the ladies out of the carriage, with Mr Walford offering his arm to Emmeline. Fran noted her sister seemed not quite so opposed to his presence and wondered if she, too, had sensed the character below the surface? Today might illuminate more as he talked with Lord Manning. This could prove a most interesting event.

Lord Manning stepped forward to welcome them, with Mr Wheeler at his side. She felt like royalty herself being in such elevated company, and was surprised at her own confidence. Certainly the host's kindness contributed to this, but she wondered at her other changes of late—speaking up to Charles Creighton and to Lord Manning, dancing with several men at the ball, even handling the errant Mr Maher. Surprising changes, yet all now seemed molded imperceptibly into her own character. Who knew a holiday could bring about such personal alteration?

Charles Creighton offered his arm and she gladly took it.

"We could not wish for a finer day, could we?" she said, looking up at him.

"No, we could not. Nor for a finer host. I look forward to the hawking demonstration."

"As do I. Despite my age, and my status as a woman, I feel as much excitement about it and desire to learn the skill of it as does Margaret. Is that too improper?"

"Certainly not," said Lord Manning, joining them. "There are many fine ladies throughout history known for their falconry or hawking skills in cultures around the world. Mary, Queen of Scots, enjoyed falconry and flew a merlin. It is claimed she was Grand Master of Falconry for Queen Elisabeth I, who also enjoyed the sport. As did Queens Eleanor of Aquitaine, Mary of Burgundy, Christine of Sweden, and Eleanor of Arborea. You, Mrs Dashwood, would be in fine company."

"I am amazed. And more eager than ever to learn, my lord."

"Good. And now, I must prepare for the presentation." He turned and walked down the hill.

Two families introduced themselves as neighbours of Lord Manning. Mr Walford and Emmeline joined in conversation, although Emmeline's eyes darted about the scene. As if in answer to her query, Admiral Tennant strode towards them with Florrie on his arm, but once introductions were complete, the young lady made for the table occupied by James, Rose, Margaret and the other younger people.

Francine wondered the admiral had not previously met these neighbours, after living in Sidmouth more than three years. With whom did he associate? Or did he keep to himself? The new acquaintances did not appear keen to learn more about him and soon moved off.

"Now that the sea is at peace again, shall I finalize plans for our boating excursion?" he asked. "I think you will find it interesting to experience the coast from the water. It is a wholly different perspective." He smiled and lit a cheroot.

After a moment of uncomfortable silence, Mr Creighton said, "Yes, Sir John is eager for the promised outing. What is the capacity of your vessel?"

"The *Windermere* carries a dozen passengers in comfort, plus the crew. I believe that will encompass most of your party?"

A bell rang. Guests moved towards the edge of an open hill to look down a slope that was wooded below. Francine stayed beside Charles Creighton, nervous excitement coursing through her. Emmeline stood beside her with the admiral slightly behind. Mr Walford had moved some paces away, dividing his focus between Emmeline and those preparing the hawking display.

Lord Manning stood several yards below the guests with three assistants, two holding hooded hawks and one arranging the gear and handing it to him.

"My neighbours have seen our hawks in flight before. One of my guests today, Miss Dashwood, has expressed an especial interest in learning about these birds, and I invite her to join me now as my assistant. Miss Dashwood, would you do me the honour?"

Margaret hurried forward, her smile as large and bright as her eyes. Lord Manning fitted her with a leather gauntlet and gave her some directions in a low voice. He took the larger of the hawks from the boy, placed it on Margaret's arm with a tether, then took the smaller hawk on his own gloved arm.

After removing the hood from Margaret's bird, he said, "Ladies and gentlemen, please meet a hawk I have worked with for many years, Lady Eleanor."

Margaret stared at the hawk, disbelief on her face but no sign of fear. Francine folded her hands together, delighted in her daughter's obvious thrill. She and Mr Creighton exchanged a smile, sharing that happiness from knowing one's child is experiencing something memorable.

"And here, on my arm, is my young hawk-in-training, Seamus." He removed the hood from his bird, who looked about with sharp eyes.

"There is no need to fear these birds. We, as humans, are not their prey. Falconry is an ancient sport, existing for thousands of years. These birds are not pets, like our dogs or cats. They remain wild. Their hunting instinct is strong. We simply teach them that we are a supply of food." Here he reached into a pouch secured about his waist and placed a morsel of meat on Margaret's gauntlet, which Lady Eleanor promptly ate. Seamus flapped his wings whilst Lord Manning reached in the pouch and then deposited a piece of meat on his own glove, which the bird immediately devoured.

"Today's demonstration will simply show the birds in flight, not on an actual hunt. One can hunt with them on foot, or more commonly from horseback. Of course, the horse must be trained to be comfortable in the presence of a large bird; horses fear anything on the back of their neck, where they cannot see and are most vulnerable to attack. It takes a special horse and a special hawk to work together, and an experienced human to guide them."

He untethered Seamus, spoke some words to Margaret, and then lifted his arm into the air, from which the great bird took flight, soaring upward to catch the wind currents. There were sighs and exclamations from the onlookers. After the bird had taken several spirals upward and then swooped down over the woods, Lord Manning held out his arm, placed a morsel of meat on the glove with a tapping motion, and the bird came soaring back, landed gently, and devoured the treat.

The lord handed Seamus to one of the lads, tethered him, then turned to Margaret. He spoke some words to her, she nodded, and then he untethered her bird and helped her lower her arm whilst keeping it level. At the proper moment she lifted her arm swiftly and Lady Eleanor flew off, finding wind currents to ride, going further afield than Seamus had done, then swiftly diving towards the woods below. Lord Manning helped Margaret position herself and place the meat on her gauntlet with a single tap. The bird came speeding towards them yet set down gracefully on Margaret's arm and daintily enjoyed the morsel.

Each bird took two more turns in the sky, riding the wind currents rolling in off the sea, dipping down then rising high, soaring in great circles and making long swoops over the lower land. After giving each bird a final bit of food, Lord Manning hooded them and the lads made off with them, the third boy carrying the equipment.

The onlookers applauded and he took Margaret's hand and bowed as she curtsied. Francine felt ready to burst—her happiness could not be more complete. She was now determined to experience hawking for herself before they returned into the countryside. Surely hawks would also enjoy the rolling hills of the Honiton area?

"How exciting!" Mr Wolford cried, approaching them. "A wonderful experience for the young lady. And, if I do not miss my guess, something her mother hopes to try before we leave Sidmouth?"

"Your guess is shrewd. I do hope I shall have such an opportunity myself, preferably while riding."

"Oh? I did not know you rode, Mrs Dashwood."

She shook her head. "For many years I have not. That interest has been reawakened on this trip, riding at the beach and then, on another day, a ride up the cliffs. That was when we met Lord Manning. What a fascinating person he is."

The admiral walked up and added, "I hope you find our sailing excursion equally memorable, Mrs Dashwood. Florrie tells me Miss Margaret has a beau recently in the Navy. Perhaps she fancies the life of a naval officer's wife?"

After a moment of speechless surprise, Francine found her voice before Mr Creighton could speak for her. "You put the cart before the horse, sir. My daughter is not yet out. She simply has a friend recently signed up and finds the idea of travel exciting, should she ever have the chance."

"'Pon my honour, I did not intend to be presumptuous."

"Of course not," Emmeline chimed in. "Admiral, you simply forgot that although the girls have become fast friends, Margaret is somewhat younger than your Florrie."

"Indeed."

Mr Creighton shifted, appearing uncomfortable. Reaching for Mr Walford's shoulder he said, "Do excuse us. We have some catching up to do." Mr Walford nodded and the two gentlemen walked off.

Her sister took the admiral's offered arm. "Emmeline, you have been here before. Perhaps you can show me about the grounds?" Exchanging smiles, the two set out in the opposite direction, leaving Francine alone and wondering what to do next.

CHAPTER TWENTY

"Yoo-hoo, Mrs Dashwood, do join us for some cake." Relieved to hear Mrs Jennings' friendly invitation, Francine hastened across the courtyard to join them. The group was in disagreement as to the day of the sailing excursion.

"I am sure the admiral said Wednesday next. I heard it from his own lips," Mrs Jennings said, reaching for another slice of cake.

"No, Lucretia, I am certain Wednesday was the day the ship would be ready, but because of business to attend, the cruise would not be until Friday."

The men talked of fishing from the boat or from the beaches of the coves they would explore.

"Are either of you ladies of a mind to join us on the water?" Mr Whittaker asked. "I had thought not?"

The older ladies looked at each other, amused.

"No indeed. I have a wonderful novel awaiting me," Mrs Jennings said.

"And you may read it aloud, sitting at my side as I paint," Mrs Whittaker said.

Francine envied the close relationship of the two, almost like sisters themselves.

"Neither Margaret nor I have been aboard a boat before," she said.

"The open sea never did me a harm," Sir John boasted.

Mr Whittaker spoke up with enthusiasm. "Well, with a Navy man at the helm, I'd prepare for an exciting time on the water. I enjoy it immensely, being at the mercy of the wind and the waves. Such freedom."

"For some, perhaps," his wife said. "Others cannot bear to be out on a boat or ship."

Francine was puzzled.

"Seasickness." Mrs Whittaker shook her head. "Some are made quite ill by the motion of the waves and the swells. Personally, I find them relaxing, although I have never been out on a stormy sea, and pray I never shall. But I have witnessed some who are quite miserable and cannot wait to get back to land, poor souls."

"Take some ginger root with you, or a tincture of ginger," Mrs Jennings advised.

"I have heard peppermint recommended," Mrs Whittaker counseled.

Francine considered this new concern. It had been enough to think about contending with the admiral for several hours on a contained vessel. Now this. "Surely the shops here would have both, would they not? I must remember to purchase some."

"My maid swears by ginger root; she has a brother in the Navy, so you can be sure she would know—"

"My mother always used peppermint for any upset of the digestive sort," Mrs Whittaker countered.

Francine smiled. "And I must find Margaret." With that, Francine rose and wandered off, not sure where to search for her daughter. The courtyard was filled with a somewhat wild assortment of shrubs and small trees, anchored by a few large wizened evergreens. Surely trees at the coastline must be especially hardy. There were various clusters of wooden and stone seating areas, with some partial stone walls and shrubbery offering peace and privacy. Francine caught a glimpse of Margaret and her friends with some of the younger members of the neighbour families setting up wickets for pall mall. The group appeared amiable, chatting and laughing. With Margaret doing well enough, Francine allowed the lure of peace and privacy to convince her to settle on a particularly handsome wooden bench with a carved back and arms, surrounded by what appeared to be a mixture of whitebeams and yellow gorse.

She leaned back, taking in the faint rush of the sea below, the cry of the gulls, and the salty scent of the air. Just in the middle of a deep sigh of satisfaction she heard two familiar voices on the other side of the shrubbery.

"Are you saying it is all a ruse? That he is still married? And has locked her away for no good reason?"

"Oh, I'm sure he thinks having control of her fortune is a very good reason. As she tells it, her father arranged that she would maintain control of the majority of her money until she was dead—or incapacitated. Not the typical nuptial agreement we have here, but they are Spanish and of noble blood. Tennant received only the bride price on wedding her, and taking the daughter to boot. The girl was very young when the mother's disappearance was staged. I'm surprised he didn't pawn the child off to a nunnery—or a brothel. But having a daughter would make him appear a more respectable widower."

"Unconscionable!"

"That poor woman has endured the asylum these many years. And been separated from her beloved daughter. I only wish I had discovered this earlier. I could have spared them both so much heartache. It was in the aftermath of the fire that, hearing reports of her heroism in saving so many others, I took a closer look and examined the intake records at the hospital."

"How does Lord Manning signify? He said he knew you from your help to his father."

"Ah, yes. His father suffers from severe mental illness. We know so little to help them. The elder duke has no hold on reality and often becomes violent—to others and to his own self. The condition is progressing rapidly. Nothing can be done. His son visits often, and is trying to prepare himself to take on the full responsibilities and the title. He is not grasping for power. He has certainly not anticipated this role coming to him so early in life. Living here on the coast, Lord Manning became aware years ago of the many free-traders. Some he became friendly with, and some—the more sinister and the slavers—he did not. But amongst all of them the name Admiral Tennant is well-known. He is believed to be padding his fortune by smuggling liquor, tobacco, and silks mostly, although there is talk that at times he has engaged in the white slave trade."

"But why? Did he not make enough as an admiral? I would think his finances to be well-set."

"One would think. I did. So I made enquiries of a friend of high rank in the Navy, asking him to investigate our admiral."

"And ...?"

"He never was an admiral. He did make captain, and was successful for a time. Took his wife and daughter with him on the high sea. But he was caught red-handed taking bribes from pirates and slavers—and protecting the free-traders too. A dirty business it was. Stripped of his rank and forced to resign. Had to forfeit a good deal of his prize money, it is said."

"So he settled here, where he was unknown. With his Spanish wife and her daughter."

"Yes, and promptly got rid of the wife. Being a seafaring man, and with his connections, he knows the waters and all the coves and such for smuggling. He appears respectable so it is the perfect foil. Some of his connections, like Maher, also appear to be gentlemen. But they are all connected in the underworld of crime and smuggling."

"I am astonished! What are we to do? How is such a man to be worked on?"

There was a moment of silence and Francine held her breath.

"Well, the way I see it, we must set a careful trap and approach this from a few different directions. His wife is now free of the asylum. Doctors have examined her and certified her as mentally competent. But because of our laws, only Tennant can sign for her release. Believe me, Parliament is going to hear about this; she is far from the only woman suffering this fate. I have employed Isabel—his wife—in the orphanage, helping to care for the children. So she is safe, for now. Until he learns that we know of his scheme. And we must prevent him from harming Florentina, or sending her away. She comes into a share of her mother's fortune on her twentieth birthday, if there is any fortune left."

"Perhaps, if we can prove some of the charges, he can be persuaded to sign over Isabel's assets, and mother and daughter will be free of him," Mr Creighton mused.

"Yes, but only Parliament can grant a divorce. He will not want his business dealings scrutinized in the light of day; that gives us some leverage. The Bow Street Runners are already looking for him, mistakenly in the Brighton area. There are only two resolutions to this situation."

The men were silent again, reflecting on the possibilities.

"And Creighton … there's one more thing. Sometimes

those unfortunates who are captured are sold for slave labour, but others—if they come from families of wealth who will pay for their return—are held for ransom. It seems farfetched, but I worry for Mrs Harrington …"

This was too much. Francine burst around the shrubbery and in a hoarse whisper said, "We must act now! We must leave Sidmouth this instant!"

The two men sat back, their eyes round with surprise.

CHAPTER TWENTY-ONE

*C*harles Creighton's face expressed his alarm. "How much did you hear, Mrs Dashwood?" He looked at Cecil Walford and took Francine's hand, pulling her down to a seat.

She began to shake. "Enough. Enough to know all my ill feelings about Admiral Tennant were correct. Admiral indeed." Her eyes blazed.

"Your instincts are good—as they were about Mr Maher, who is really a Mr Bartlett, of a family notorious for smuggling, and worse, in this area."

The whites of Francine's eyes showed as much as that of a frightened horse.

Mr Walford leaned forward and took her hands. "I know this is all a shock. It was for me too. I never did like him, but this is beyond the pale. However, we must plan our actions with great care. We must remain calm. Secretive. Can you do that?"

"Why can we not leave now, and never think of him again? Surely he would not follow us into Honiton, or my sister into—"

Mr Creighton put a hand on her shoulder. "We cannot assume he would not. Some men will take great risks for money. He appears to be one of them. And even if he did leave your sister alone, without being able to spring our trap Isabel and Florentina are left in danger of his retribution."

"Mrs Dashwood," Mr Walford said, "I am sure you know I care very much for your sister. I do truly want to marry her, if she will ever have me. Please believe I would not risk her safety for the world. But neither would I wish this man to continue to prey on others. He must be stopped."

Then Mr Creighton asked, "How do you think Emmeline will react when she learns the truth about the admiral?"

Francine had a ready answer. "She will not believe it. She will think it something Mr Walford has fabricated because he wants her for himself. She is aware of your interest in her, you know. Sadly, she has not returned it. I am sorry. No, Emmeline will assuredly not let go of her fancy unless she catches the admiral in some situation that proves he is not in love with her."

"That is what I feared."

Mr Creighton had something to add. "I personally know him to be a scoundrel. And a violent one at that. He assaulted one of my maids at the dinner I hosted in the spring at Whitwell."

Francine's eyebrows flew up. "I remember. I happened upon her crying, and then the other staff came to tend her so I left. I deduced something had happened. That was *him*?"

"Yes. I confronted him. He denied it, of course. I tried to get her to publicly identify the lout but she would not. Too frightened. I heard he offered her money for her silence. There was nothing more I could do without proof."

Mr Walford folded his arms and frowned. "Perhaps Lord Manning can help us with an accomplice—an experienced woman who may have motivation of her own to get back at Tennant?"

"That should not be too difficult to find hereabouts."

"Meanwhile," Mr Walford cautioned, "we must not tip our hand. I will confer with Lord Manning about our knowledge and our plans. Tennant thinks my dislike of him is based on my desire for Emmeline. Although partially true, that can work to our advantage."

"Then our first task is to detach my sister from the admiral?"

"If we can, yes," Creighton said.

"Then we have an accord," said Walford. "Let us separate now before others become suspicious. I shall meet with the lord at a later time. He has long known of Tennant's exploits and will be an eager ally."

Creighton stood and offered Francine his hand to help her stand. "We two can walk about and converse with others. Let my arm steady you. Do fill your mind with other thoughts now, pleasant thoughts—hawking, perhaps, or architecture. We must not raise suspicion that anything is amiss."

Francine smoothed her dress and her brow and the couple made for a group that was near the apple tree.

"Our new acquaintance will be less familiar with my expressions. Let us begin with them."

None of the subterfuge was shared with others, yet Mrs Jennings seemed aware that something was afoot. Francine noted her watching stealthily whenever Charles Creighton and Cecil Walford talked closely.

A few days later at tea Mrs Jennings commented, "Those men, what are they about? Can they huddle and talk of nothing but business during our holiday? I would swear they are planning some kind of overthrow from the seriousness of their expressions."

Francine thought to distract her. "Who knows what compels gentlemen? I suppose business matters can be quite concerning at times, with much money at stake. Fortunately, we need not worry about such things. With the ball this evening, we have more pleasant topics to discuss, do we not?"

"Indeed we do," said Mrs Whittaker. "We have only one more ball after this before we return to our quiet country lives. What can we do to help the young ladies prepare? Do they need new ribbons or toe roses? For myself, my costume is complete; variation is not needed as attracting a beau is not my goal. But what of you, Mrs Dashwood? And your sister? There may yet be new men to be met. Speaking of variations, it was so kind of Lord Manning to gift us with peacock feathers. I have fashioned the tiny ones behind one of my brooches and am most pleased with the result."

"My maid has worked the small downy feathers into one of my necklaces," said Mrs Jennings.

Francine's interest wandered ... only two more balls. On this holiday, neither she nor her sister had met a man worthy of serious consideration as a husband; and sadly, Emmeline remained smitten with the admiral. When she shared this concern with Charles Creighton, he had reassured her that the gentlemen had set a snare that would surely send her sister's affections off of the rogue. Francine was to watch for signals from himself or Mr Walford at the ball. Being involved in an intrigue was as exciting as it was crucial to extricate Emmeline from a potentially sordid situation, or worse.

"What have you done with your feathers, Mrs Dashwood?" Mrs Whittaker asked. "The colours are especially divine when viewed up close, as you must hope gentlemen will do. Many of your gowns are greens and blues—a good match to set off the feathers, are they not?"

Without waiting for Francine's reply, Mrs Jennings launched into an observation. "Your sister appears to have two suitors to hand. The admiral and Cecil Walford are both quite attentive, and a rivalry of sorts is apparent. I wonder if she will make her choice tonight? One is dashing and one is rich—what a conundrum!"

"My dear Lucretia, do you not think sweet Emmeline should instead look to meet new men? Here at the seaside there are always new men to meet, which is not the case when these two sisters return home."

"If these were younger sisters, I would heartily agree, Camelia. But at their ages, the pickings are slim, with the war and all. My advice is to secure one of the two as soon as may be. These new men may not be all they appear, you know."

"The same might be said of the admiral," Mrs Whittaker mused. "Our acquaintance with Mr Walford is long and steady and we know his character and situation well. The admiral is dashing—I'll grant you that—but of his character and fortune, we know only what he has told us."

Mrs Jennings clutched her throat. "Oh, my! What you say is sensible, Camelia. Perhaps we should ask around about him?"

"There is something in his eyes I do not trust," Mrs Whittaker said, wrinkling her brow. "He meets one's eyes with boldness, but will not hold a steady gaze. He does not wish to be known well by any of us, I think."

"Yes, you may be right. And I found it peculiar that he had never before met with Lord Manning and Mr Wheeler, or their neighbours, despite living here for more than three years." Mrs Jennings' countenance was troubled. "Do you not find that peculiar, Mrs Dashwood?"

Francine looked from one face to another. "It does seem unusual, when weighed against how well I have come to know the two of you and some of our other neighbours within a similar time period. But perhaps men are different? I have seen that, whilst they may take part in the same pursuits, they know very little of each other on a personal level. Does that not seem true?"

"You may be right. Although my husband is very close to Hugh Stanton—we dined with them the night before last you know—I believe I am my husband's closest confidante. Which, in my view, makes for a closer bond than either of us knew in our first marriage." Mrs Whittaker's eyes grew dreamy.

"Well, with all that to consider Mrs Dashwood, it would behoove you to make your best effort tonight and next week to at least make some connections worth pursuing. Perhaps our Mr Creighton or Mr Walford can be encouraged to invite some of your interested gentlemen to visit us in the country— even Sir John can easily be convinced to find a reason to invite guests to Barton Park. Shooting sports always seem to attract the gentlemen," she said in a matter-of-fact way.

Mr Creighton. Why did it feel awkward to think of him inviting gentlemen to get to know herself better? It would seem to go against his own best interest—but that would only be the case if his interest was in her. Could that be? He was such a thoughtful man to all his acquaintance; how would she know if his kindness had gone beyond general civility where she was concerned?

"A penny for your thoughts, Mrs Dashwood. But now, it is time for us to make all speed for the shops, before the best ribbons are sold out. Did the girls wish to accompany us?"

Francine forced her thoughts back to preparing for the ball and facilitating proper connections for Margaret, but her own mind was in rather a state of dreaminess at the thought of Mr Creighton. Mr Charles Creighton.

CHAPTER TWENTY-TWO

The ballroom appeared the same as before, everything elegant and romantic, but this time Francine felt as if she belonged. Gone was the giddy nervousness. Arm in arm with her sister, the two glided about the room, noticing the variety of people to be seen. Mr 'Maher' was not amongst them, to her relief. Emmeline had heard nothing from the admiral since his last visit, so it was not known if he or his daughter would attend tonight. How difficult he made life for Florrie. Perhaps they could invite her to visit them in the country, once the crisis of the current situation had passed. Surely it would pass. She had to believe it would pass. The local country dances at home were neither as large nor as elegant, but true character could be more readily known. Usually. If one was determined to not let wishful thinking colour one's view. She bit her lip, thinking of how Mr Willoughby had deceived them all. But much had changed since that time, most especially she herself. She was no longer so easily deceived.

The musicians appeared ready to play. Margaret and Rose were led to the floor by James and a young man he had met recently who was down from Oxford. During this holiday and with a tentative arrangement to spend part of the season in London with Mr Creighton's sister, certainly Margaret would come to know a variety of gentlemen. With Rose as a confidante, Margaret had not much confided in her mother whilst in Sidmouth; although, truth be told, Margaret had never much confided in her mother at all. Did Margaret ever write to Elinor and Marianne? Were they her sources of wisdom?

Two men approached the ladies, one from each direction. Francine assumed a dance with Emmeline was their desire. Emmeline's posture tonight was not as high and elegant as usual, and her face held no smile, although her eyes darted about the room. Francine knew the quarry she sought. The first man to reach them asked herself to dance, not Emmeline. The other gentleman stopped short, and before walking off gave Francine a nod and a smile. How unexpected.

After several turns about the floor, Francine settled in a chair next to her sister, lemonade in hand. Emmeline was unusually quiet. Was this about the admiral? Francine's thoughts swirled in her head, like the miasma of candlelight and smoke that hovered over the dancers in the room. How could she best aid her sister? Assuredly the admiral was not the man for Emmeline, but her heart was set on him, and her sights focused on the life she dreamed of with him. A life that would doubtless be more nightmare than dream.

"Have you danced with anyone, Em?"

Her sister regarded her from the corner of her eye. "No, I have not. There is only one man I wish to dance with. These others do not compare, Fran. Oh, what am I to do? How am I to win him? Time grows short."

Fran pursed her lips. If he had gone off her sister, all the better. Would it help her sister to know how losing the admiral would instead be a stroke of luck?

The next dance was beginning. Where was Margaret? Ah,

there in the formation with Rose and ... Florrie? A quick appraisal of the room did not reveal her father. The young ladies looked flushed yet appeared to have energy to spare. Ah, those days when one's body could so easily keep up with one's dreams and desires.

Mr Creighton appeared in front of her and gave her a sidelong look.

"Ladies, might I persuade you to take a turn out of doors? The evening is very fine, the wind calm. It will be a respite from the somewhat smoky air indoors." He reached out a hand to each of them.

Emmeline shrugged. "What could it hurt? There is nothing to see here, no one of interest. Frankly, I don't know why I chose to attend with no assurance from Marcus." She rose with an air of resignation.

"Thank you, Mr Creighton, that is most thoughtful. I suppose the smokiness is due to the lack of breeze tonight." She reached for his offered hand and they locked eyes.

"We shall keep to the walkways so as not to ruin your dancing slippers."

There was a terrace of sorts, with levels reaching down towards the beach. A few benches were scattered about, along with some potted shrubs and small trees. Lanterns hung from elegant light posts that, together with the moonlight reflecting off the water, created the aura of a magical garden. Couples sat together, strolled arm in arm, stared at the moon and each other. A few stood in the lee of the topiary seeking privacy, and perhaps a stolen kiss.

The Creighton party ambled towards one particular couple, a tall well-built gentleman with his back to them, obviously pressing his suit and more with a woman far past girlhood. She tossed her raven curls and half-turned from him with a coy smile. Mr Creighton directed his party ever closer to the amorous couple but Emmeline paid no attention and instead stared at the sea with a forlorn look.

The raven-haired lady attempted to wriggle away from the man's partial embrace when Emmeline turned on her heel and made for the pavilion.

"Em, where are you going? Please don't leave yet," Francine pleaded.

"Such views of loving couples puts my heart in more wretched pain than ever. I cannot bear another moment." With that she flounced back up the stairways towards the terrace doors.

After she had entered the pavilion, Cecil Walford appeared, shaking his head.

"I should have anticipated your sister's willful refusal, knowing her fiery character as I do—or as I imagine I do."

The three conspirators looked helplessly at each other, with glances at the ardent couple.

"Soon enough my sister will see Florrie on the dance floor. I wonder if the admiral will show himself indoors, or rather continue his unseemly pursuits elsewhere?"

"His present partner holds no *tendre* for him. Indeed, he owes her money. She no doubt has her own agenda to get it back," Mr Walford confided.

"Good luck to her, I say."

"Well said, Mrs Dashwood." Mr Creighton exchanged a rueful smile with Mr Walford.

Francine's attention was drawn like a magnet to the couple as their affections became more obvious, with the admiral leaning in for a kiss. A heated flush rose within Francine's body and she turned to face the sea, welcoming the slight breeze.

"I hope her trap works better than ours did."

The gentlemen chuckled.

Francine gathered her skirts. "Let us return indoors. I wish to keep an eye on my sister, and see how Margaret and the girls are getting on. It is nearly time for the supper."

Mr Creighton offered his arm. Mr Walford followed them up the stairs and into the pavilion.

Margaret soon appeared. "Mama, did you see Florrie has arrived?"

Florrie dipped a curtsey and smiled.

"How nice to see you, dear. I am happy you were able to attend. There is nothing like a ball to liven up a young lady's life."

"I am very happy to be here, thank you."

"Mama, can Florrie stay with us tonight at Seaview?"

Francine turned her eyes on the girl.

"My father has taken rooms at the inn, but I would rather not ... well, with smoking, drinking and the company he ..."

"Of course you may, Florrie. I am sure you girls will have much to talk over."

Florrie's face lit up. Was it with relief at being spared her father's raucous antics after over-imbibing? Or sadness at being left alone? Florrie must often be alone, and Francine's heart was heavy at that realization.

Francine spied Emmeline in company with the Whittakers and Mrs Jennings, on their way to supper. Francine took Mr Walford's offered arm. He patted her hand. "Do not worry, my dear. That was only our first plan. We shall now carry on with the rest. After all, we have the water cruise yet to work on our quarry. And he does not yet know he is being hunted!"

Mr Walford's smile was reassuring.

A moment later, at seeing Florrie, Emmeline left her place in line and worked her way through the crowd to Francine and the girls.

"Florrie! I did not see you earlier! Where is your father?"

"It is nice to see you, Mrs Harrington," Florrie replied with a curtsey and an arched brow. "My father is here, somewhere.

He is of no interest to me at a ball. I regret I cannot tell you where to find him."

Emmeline scowled at the answer, but after a pause she found her manners. "Pardon my directness. It is nice to see you as well, Florrie. In my opinion young ladies should attend as many balls as possible, and I hope this one is ... productive ... and pleasant for you. Your gown is striking."

After the crowding in the supper rooms, it was a relief to enter the larger ballroom again. Fresh sea air now poured through the open doors, causing the candles to flicker. To Emmeline's great delight Admiral Tennant strode in through the terrace entrance and made directly for them.

"Mrs Harrington! I had hoped to find you here. Just as Florrie and I arrived a business associate commanded my attention and I am just now free. Has you evening been pleasant?" He looked around the group with a charming smile.

Francine dared not look at her comrades for fear of giving herself away.

Emmeline's eyes lit up with such delight it nearly broke Francine's heart. But her sister was not yet in possession of the knowledge she and the others shared. She would tell her tonight. Tell her everything. Surely that would open her eyes —and close her heart to such a scoundrel.

"You have made yourself scarce of late, Admiral Tennant. We were sure you had forgotten our party." Emmeline offered him her sweetest smile.

"Forgotten? How could I? My crew has been readying the *Windermere* for our pleasure cruise. But I must own that my business interests have kept me busy. Always something to attend to, is that not so, gentlemen?"

His smile was open but Mrs Whittaker was right—his eyes admitted no penetration and his gaze with each of them was momentary.

"Shall we cruise the waters on Friday then?" Sir John asked.

"Aye, as long as the weather holds, that is the plan. I look forward to sharing with you my love of commanding my ship —smaller though this one may be—and exploring the many coves and caves here on the south coast," he said, his deep voice commanding attention.

"Admiral, may I ask about seasickness? We have been discussing this, and possible preventives. Might you recommend something to bring with us, or take before departing?"

"Seasickness, bah," he scoffed. "That is for the weak-minded. I say keep your eye on the horizon and drink plenty of wine." He gave a hearty laugh but none of his listeners joined him. There was an awkward silence as they marveled at his rude disregard for Mrs Dashwood's sincere question.

"Sir," Mr Creighton said in his most level voice, "some of our ladies have never been aboard a vessel. They simply wish to be considerate of the others in our party by trying to prevent such an occurrence. It is a show of courtesy for us, and a sign of respect for your expertise at sea for her to ask you such a question."

The admiral appeared to feel the remonstrance implied. "I see. I have no remedy to offer, but perhaps some of the maids or apothecaries in Sidmouth might be more useful, madame." He gave Mrs Dashwood a perfunctory nod then turned his eye on Emmeline.

"Ah, the music begins. Mrs Harrington, might you honour me with the next dance?" He held out his hand and put on his most persuasive grin.

Emmeline rose. "Certainly, Admiral Tennant." But she turned and gave Francine a questioning look.

Perhaps her sister was not so lost as they feared?

CHAPTER TWENTY-THREE

*T*he second ball concluded with nothing swoon-worthy for Francine to write about in her holiday journal or to her daughters. The moon hung low over the seaside village as she sat, pen poised over paper, at the lady's desk in the room she shared with her sister at Seaview. The gowns were hung away, nightclothes donned, and Emmeline was brushing her hair.

"You are quiet tonight, Fran."

"Am I?"

"You know you are. I thought you might have an opinion about my dancing partner."

"Do you mean the only man you danced with?" She closed her journal. "You must be the one to choose the impression you leave on the residents of Sidmouth."

"Such old-fashioned pish-posh. Just because I danced only with him—"

"And spurned offers from other men—"

"Well, yes. Still, here at the seaside, it surely does not signify that we are engaged."

Francine paused a moment before speaking. "Do you wish

it did? Do you hope he might succumb to local opinion? I should think you know him better than that. He is not a man to care about anyone's opinion. Even yours."

"You think me wrong to have once again accepted his attentions?"

Francine shrugged. "Has he treated you with the thoughtfulness and consideration you know you deserve?"

Emmeline set her brush on the dressing table, then turned to her sister. "This is my last chance, Fran. If I cannot secure Marcus, then I must surrender to growing old alone. Once we leave Sidmouth, we neither of us are likely to meet any eligible men. You at the cottage, me at the dower house. Our children will be gone and we shall be alone. Alone and forgotten. That is a future I cannot face." She slumped onto the bed and a tear rolled down her cheek. "My dear Miss Burney is right. *To a heart formed for friendship and affection, the charms of solitude are very short-lived.*' No, Fran, I will not be able to bear such loneliness. He is my best possibility."

Francine walked over and sat next to her sister, grasping her hands. "Might you change your mind about him if you learned some ugly truths? Things that would preclude the kind of life you imagine with him?"

Emmeline looked hard at her sister. "What more do I need to know? He has been quite honest with me, with all of us. He has shown us the … less desirable side of himself, the one that emerges when he's in his cups. And that he can become preoccupied with business. He is not perfect, Fran. But any man will have his flaws. Marcus could have any woman, even young wealthy women. He seems to prefer me. Why is that a bad thing?"

"Does he prefer you? Or are you the only one willing to put up with his foibles?"

"That is unkind, Fran."

"But it is true. And there is much more that is true, and far more odious. He has a darker side than you are aware. I know not how to tell you these things, but you must know the truth. Once you do, it will be easier to return home and never think of him again."

"Odious? Please, do enlighten me as to what it is you find so abhorrent in him. You, with your vast knowledge of society, and of men. Go ahead, speak!"

"I shall, but only because of my love for you as my dear sister. I will begin with the lesser of the evils. He is a free-trader. He is part of a smuggling ring—liquor, tobacco, and silks mostly. That Mr Maher I had met is a comrade of his. They appear to run the operation."

Emmeline's jaw dropped. "But why? As a retired admiral, he must have plenty of investments and income. He talks of playing cards but I have not seen him gambling."

"And where have you been that gambling would be done openly?"

Her sister had no reply.

"As to the money—one of our friends had wondered the same, and so investigated with the Navy. Mr Tennant was once a captain, but was dishonourably discharged for his illegal activities on the high seas. He never was an admiral, and even the title of captain is not one he could now honourably claim."

Emmeline paled. "No, that cannot be. He had so many stories, so many heroic tales."

"Tales of others' heroism. Anyone can retell a story and place themselves in the role of hero."

"No, I cannot believe what you are saying. Even if some of it is true … perhaps he came here for a new start. To raise his daughter. At Bellevue." She clasped her hands. "Who is telling you these things? I suppose Mr Creighton has been snooping around. Or Mrs Jennings repeating gossip from the servants. I put no store in it."

"Mr Creighton did not elaborate on why Mr Maher was not the sort I should socialize with, not until he learned of the connection with Mr Tennant; then he became concerned enough to come to my rescue. As did you, if I may remind you."

Emmeline frowned. "Town gossip. That is all."

"Mr Walford's friend in the Navy confirmed Mr Tennant's status there. It is a fact. And Mr Walford's business in the North led him to the discovery of the most heinous crime of all—Tennant is not a widow. He is married, to a Spanish noblewoman who is Florrie's mother. He committed her to an asylum to gain full control of her fortune. The recent fire at the asylum shed light on the true condition of his wife—that she has no mental infirmity. She is perfectly capable, and saved several others from the flames. Even if he wanted to, Mr Tennant cannot marry you; not while she lives."

"And it is Mr Walford who is claiming these truths? Mr Walford, who everyone knows hopes to wed me himself. It is all a fabrication. He is a shrewd man. Why should we believe him? I do not. Wretched saboteur!" She rose and paced the room.

"Emmeline, it is not only Mr Walford. Someone else of eminence—Lord Manning, in fact—has first-hand knowledge about Mr Tennant's deception as well, and has known for longer than Mr Walford."

"Then he is in league with Mr Walford—and I doubt not there is payment involved." Her nostrils flared. "Trying to discredit the admiral. Fran, I cannot believe you would give credence to these Banbury tales." Emmeline's fists opened and closed repeatedly as she paced ever faster.

She spun around to face her sister. "Why do you wish to hurt me so? Are you jealous—because you have not found a husband, and I have? How can you say you care about me? Turn your attention to Margaret. Get her married and cease your trespass on my life!" With that, she burst out of the room.

Francine remained on the bed, still and silent, her heart aching for her sister. Would she come around after reflecting on the history with Mr Tennant? She walked to her own bedside, turned down the covers, snuffed her candle, and lay in the dark for she knew not how long.

CHAPTER TWENTY-FOUR

A crowing cock startled Francine awake. She bolted upright. Emmeline's nightclothes were strewn on the bed. At least she had returned to their room. But was that a good sign? Or had her sister delivered her own midnight missive this time?

Francine rang for the maid, who arrived shortly with tea. Once her toilette was complete, she descended the stairs, hoping to find a more rational Emmeline at the breakfast table. But the table was empty. Seaview was wrapped in a heavy curtain of fog, but already the sunlight poked its slender beams through here and there.

Whilst pouring a cup of tea from the sideboard Francine heard the muffled clatter of the girls, and soon they appeared in the dining room.

"Shall we sea bathe today, Mama?" Margaret asked as they crowded around, filling their cups and plates.

"You girls are awake early after such a late night. Surely you will need to nap like babies this afternoon."

They grinned, pulled up chairs, and settled in to break their fast.

Although she had no appetite, Francine took a plate of toast for herself and sat down. "Let us wait for the others to decide upon sea bathing, although we may have a long wait. We do not all have the energy of you young people."

That seemed agreeable and the girls chattered on about the events of the night before whilst Francine's thoughts wandered this way and that through the labyrinth of her mind.

A sleepy James stumbled into the breakfast room and heaped food on his plate, breaking into a grin at the sight of Florrie.

For a time, Francine listened to the anecdotes from the previous night—who danced with whom, how many times, who wore the most ravishing gown, the best headdress. James raved about the poached salmon and the sandwiches, but his eyes never left Florrie. Was he falling in love? Or growing to love Florrie? Francine knew not, but was sure his father was well apprised of the situation. Mr Creighton was a man of unusually deep understanding. She had never known a man like him.

When she had heard enough of gowns and dancers, Francine poured more tea and moved to the fireside in the parlour. The fog was lifting but the air was chilly. The birds had just begun their morning song when Mr Creighton entered the room, cup in hand.

"Mrs Dashwood, good morning. I am glad to see another adult has managed to rise before noon." His face melted into a smile and Francine was pleased to have his company. He gave her a sense of being protected, yet in his presence she also felt strong and composed—a most unusual combination, one she had never known before.

"Our hour of returning was late enough, but perhaps you did not sleep well?" he asked, concern etching his countenance.

"You have read my face. I am wretched at disguise. Lucky for me I am not an actress."

"No, you would not be successful there, I fear. What troubles you?"

Francine sighed. "My sister. Last night we talked. I told her the truth about Mr Tennant. She would have none of it. And finally fled the room. I did not hear her return, but she had changed out of her nightclothes. I have not seen her this morning."

He nodded thoughtfully. "I cannot say I am surprised. It was kind of you to try to inform her."

"I hope that, after some reflection, she will come to accept the situation."

"There is only so much you can do, Mrs Dashwood. She has the information, and now it is up to her."

They sat in silence for a time as the fire crackled in the hearth.

"Do you know of the plans for today, Mr Creighton?"

"Indeed I do. We gentlemen will be fishing in the afternoon—a new cove the guide recommends, the later timing dictated by the tide. I swear I could fish every cove and river in England and still not get my fill of the sport!"

She smiled at him looking so well and seeming so at peace.

"You also read me well," he said. "This holiday has done me the world of good. Getting away from familiar scenes, and being in the company of new and old friends has been just what I needed. I am sure waves of sorrow will inundate me here and there as time goes on, but for now it no longer feels like I am trapped at the bottom of a deep dark pit and sinking more still. I thank you for your part in that."

"Me? I've done nothing," she said with a smile.

"Perhaps it is just the pleasure of your company," he said, returning her smile.

Soon the household was bustling with activity as the

others awoke and the men made ready for their fishing excursion.

"You ladies will be left to your own devices today," Sir John said with a jolly laugh.

"I am sure we will find many sources of entertainment and pleasure that do not require the company of gentlemen," quipped Mrs Jennings.

As the men departed Seaview Place, Sir John called out, "Why Mrs Harrington, whatever are you doing in the garden at this hour? A little chilly for a lady, eh? Get yourself indoors now and warm up by the fire."

Francine peered out the parlour door into the entrance hall to see Emmeline hasten up the stairs, but it was not long until she descended again with her bonnet and reticule.

"And where are you off to so precipitately? And alone?" Mrs Jennings asked with a goading smile. "A secret rendezvous with a lover?" Her laughter trilled about the room.

Emmeline blushed furiously. "Nothing so enticing, Mrs Jennings, I hate to disappoint. I have some shopping to do and will see what the lending library has on offer. I shall leave the lovers' rendezvous to you!" She smiled and whisked out the door, leaving Mrs Jennings chortling.

The fog had dissipated and the day was unusually calm so Francine carried her small writing desk out to the garden and settled at the wooden table to write to her daughters. What news had they imparted in their most recent correspondence? She pulled out their letters to jog her memory. Each had been short, not much more than a note, with both daughters claiming they had nothing of interest to convey, and both admonishing her for keeping them in suspense about her holiday adventures.

July —

Dear Elinor,

I must beg your forgiveness at my tardy correspondence. The days fly by here, sometimes with many activities and sometimes with busy nothings. It is both exciting and relaxing—a pace very different from that at Barton. I must say the seaside has grown on me. I shall miss it.

The cliff ride was everything wonderful, with a little vexation thrown in. Margaret and her friends rode off on a lark but were reunited with us soon enough. Your aunt, however, rode off with the admiral and did not return for some time. She does wear on my nerves, especially when the admiral is involved. He calls to mind Willoughby. He left Emmeline alone in the woods! I still do not understand the whole situation, something about him feeling ill.

On our ride we met two gentlemen who were on a training exercise with their hawk. They live on the cliffside and invited us for tea. Imagine our surprise when their butler addressed one of them as "My Lord"! He does not yet claim the title of duke as his father still lives but is incapacitated by illness. Lord Manning invited us to a garden party. He gave a demonstration of flying his hawks, and called Margaret to assist as she had expressed such an interest. She was thrilled to be permitted to fly one of the hawks. We are invited to go hawking on horseback before we leave, and I confess I am as excited as Margaret!

Mr Walford joined us for the garden party after concluding his business in the North. He brought us shocking news about the admiral, who is not an admiral and is not a widower, having committed his wife to an asylum to get full control of her fortune! And all this time courting my sister! Mr Tennant also has connections with free-traders and smug-

glers. Yet he appears so gentlemanly. Mr Creighton and Mr Walford are assisting me in trying to detach my sister (she does not believe the allegations), and will try to also assist the wife and her daughter Florrie—who has become fast friends with Margaret and Rose—in resolving their dilemma. I am grateful for the presence of the gentlemen here. I wished for you to be apprised of this devilish situation, but please do not tell Marianne. We must not worry her, in her condition. I know you will agree. I shall tell her only of Lord Manning and the hawking.

We are to have a sailing excursion on Mr Tennant's ship. I know not if this will take place in light of these developments. For myself, I would be pleased to hear the scheme has been abandoned, but Mr Creighton and Mr Walford believe it necessary to act our parts until they can confront Mr Tennant with his misdeeds.

The night of the second ball saw the town flooded by a fierce storm so we stayed at Seaview Place whilst the storm raged. We attended our second ball last night. Margaret and her friends had another delightful time I believe, although she confides little in me these days. I hope she has written to you?

This morning Mr Creighton admitted that this holiday has been most helpful for him after losing his wife in January. And I must say that I feel quite transformed by our journey as well.

I look forward to seeing you and Edward again.

Much love to you both,

Mama

Francine was sure her decision to keep any upsetting information away from Marianne was for the best. Her second daughter took everything to heart so deeply. Shocking news could not be helpful in her condition. The truth would be shared once they were all reunited and everything resolved. Although at the present moment, Francine could not see how things might work out. She mended her pen and took another sheaf of paper from the writing desk.

. . .

July —

My dear Marianne and little one,

May I already write to the little one? I cannot wait to meet him or her. I hope you continue to be well. Yes, I deserve to be chastised for being tardy in writing. The days fly by here, sometimes with many activities and sometimes with much leisure. It is very different from Barton and I shall miss the seaside a great deal. I hope to someday return.

The cliff ride was everything exciting and the view from the top was spectacular. The sea goes on forever and seems to melt into the sky with no horizon discernable. I enjoy being in the saddle again, very much. Margaret and her friends rode off on a lark, vexing Mr Creighton and myself, but were soon reunited with us so all was well. And we met two gentlemen who were riding out, training a young hawk. They live thereabouts and invited us for tea. Imagine our surprise when his butler addressed him as My Lord! He does not yet claim the title of duke because his father still lives but is incapacitated by illness.

He later invited us to a garden party. His house, Atlas Hall, is very old. He said the Atlantic was once called the Atlas Ocean. His friend is very well-versed on architecture and they are doing many improvements, but in an informed and artistic manner. They have an amazing view of the sea, and a tower with a telescope! At the party we were given a demonstration of hawk flying, and Margaret assisted and even flew one of the hawks. She was thrilled! I hope she wrote to you about it. I must say I share her interest, and we are invited to go hawking on horseback before we depart Sidmouth.

We missed one of the balls due to a raging storm that flooded the streets for a few days. Our second ball was last night and Margaret and her friends had a lively time. This has been a wonderful experience for her and has prepared her for a sojourn in town during the season. Mr Creighton says his sister wishes to take a house in

London next year when her daughter comes out, and he will arrange for Margaret and myself to join them. He is so kind.

A sailing excursion is planned on the admiral's ship, weather permitting. Most mornings are foggy but the afternoon is usually fine and sunny. A fire is welcome mornings and evenings when the fog is present. I am enjoying the holiday a great deal and feel almost transformed.

Take care of yourself and the tiny life within.

Much love to you all,

Mama

After preparing the letters for the post, Francine was closing up her desk when she heard a rider approach in great haste. Emerging from the garden through the gate, she saw Florrie at the door knocking frantically, and a footman tending to her mare. She held a leather case in her arms. Whatever could this be?

CHAPTER TWENTY-FIVE

"Thank goodness you are here!" cried Florrie. "I did not know where to turn. We must act immediately!"

Francine ushered the girl into the parlour. "Please sit down. Shall I call for tea?"

"There is no time for tea, Mrs Dashwood."

After directing that the mare be tended to, the servant was dismissed and the door closed.

"There. We are private now. Whatever has happened? And what is this bundle you carry?"

"Is Mr Creighton here? I trust that he would know the best course of action."

Francine frowned. "No. He and the other gentlemen are out on a fishing boat at some cove or another. Whatever is to be done must be done by us. Now tell me of the situation."

"Oh, dear. It is everything horrid. It is beyond—"

"Florrie, you must stop and gather your thoughts. Now take a breath and start at the beginning."

The young lady made a successful effort. "This morning I awoke to the sounds of the carriage being readied and then departing. Most unusual, as my father rarely uses the carriage and never arises before noon. I dressed in haste and made for the breakfast room. My father was nowhere to be found. I opened the door to his study, where a candle was burning! He is only that careless when he is foxed. As I rushed in to snuff it, I hurt my foot, and found I had trodden on a set of keys. I knew not what to think. There was no fire in the hearth but a note was tossed there, unburned, which I retrieved. It said, "Yes! Let us leave at once. I am coming to you now at the church." It was signed 'All my love, E'."

Francine gasped. That could only be Emmeline.

"On his desk, papers were strewn about, as if he had been looking for something. The drawer was open in the map cabinet, and one of his maps was also missing from the wall. His desk is usually locked, but I tried the key I had recovered and it worked. I shuffled through the drawers, hoping to find something that would explain why he left in such haste. In the bottom drawer I found this leather pouch. And as I read the papers within ..." she burst into tears.

Oh, my—what am I to do? I must get to my sister, but ... Francine hurried over to Florrie and put an arm about the young lady's shoulders, which were racked by sobs. "Please, Florrie, try to continue. What did the papers say?"

The girl straightened and shook her head.

"Mrs Dashwood, my mother is not dead!" Tears poured down her stricken face. "These papers show he has committed her to an asylum. An asylum! How could he? I do not know where the place is, but I must go to her at once."

"Yes, you must go to her, but first we must determine where and how. And back to that note. I suspect it is from my sister?"

"That was my conclusion. They have eloped, have they not?"

Francine's mind raced. If they were making for Gretna Green …

"Where did the carriage tracks lead, Florrie? Did you notice?"

"I did. I was determined to catch the coach, but it was too far ahead of me by the time I was dressed and had my mare ready to ride. The carriage did not go north at the crossroads. It made for Sidmouth, but I lost the track near the church. I knew not what to do and could only think of seeking help at Seaview Place, from Mr Creighton."

"You did right by coming here. I must get to my sister, before … I must tell you what I know, quickly, and then I must ride." She rang for the servant, who appeared in a twinkling. "Please fetch a horse for me from the livery. I prefer to ride Lightning if he is available. It is of great urgency. And send my maid to help me make ready. Go!"

The footman's eyes widened and with a quick bow he sprinted away.

"What do you know, and how?"

"There is no time for all the details, but Mr Creighton and Mr Walford both know of these things. Mr Walford informed us at the garden party. What you have learned is true. Your father is not who he says he is. He is not your real father, neither is he an admiral. He is involved with some unsavory characters in illegal business and we are trying to stop him. Your mother is safe and in the protection of Mr Walford for now."

Florrie began to cry again at this hopeful news.

"Of immediate urgency is rescuing my sister, before she is ruined or ransomed! Lord Manning also knows of these affairs and will help us."

"He does?"

"Yes, he also uncovered some of your father's schemes. We are fortunate to have such allies amongst us."

Francine rose and paced the room. "Let me think. This could be dangerous, especially for you. If your father has you in his possession, that gives him great leverage against your mother. I believe you should stay here. Yes. You must tell Mrs Jennings and Mrs Whittaker what you have learned. Show them the papers. Tell them to keep everyone here today, indoors. And to inform the constable, and have him put an extra watch around Seaview. Oh! Would that we knew where my sister was taken! I must think. Ah, Lord Manning knows the area well. I shall ride for Atlas Hall and enlist his support. You and the ladies go over those papers for clues and information that might help convict Mr Tennant."

A knock at the door revealed the maid, who helped Francine into her cloak and boots.

"Do be careful, Mrs Dashwood." Florrie embraced her.

"Be on your guard here. Have the butler say the ladies are from home today. But to take any messages that may be offered. I shall return when I can."

The footman entered. "Lightning awaits you, ma'am." He assisted Francine in mounting the horse. She turned to Florrie and nodded.

"Godspeed, Mrs Dashwood."

CHAPTER TWENTY-SIX

*F*rancine's heart raced within her chest, but she knew better than to immediately ask Lightning to run at full speed. The horse needed to warm up. The weather was fair, but a bank of clouds hovered at a distance offshore. Would that drive the fishermen home early? Would it conceal those intent on doing her sister harm? With a stab it occurred to her—perhaps the sailing excursion was never meant to take place. Perhaps Mr Tennant had readied the *Windermere* to carry her sister away—and not on an elopement. Oh! An elopement would be terrible enough! But a bigamous marriage? Ransom? Slavery?

Some passersby stared at her, then averted their eyes. She *was* riding unaccompanied, and their questioning or shaming looks made her all the more eager to leave the village behind. When the cobblestones ended and the horse's hooves met with springier turf, he began to gather himself and she allowed him to move into a canter. He seemed to sense her urgency and stretched out, almost grasping at the hillside with his front legs. She liked this horse very much indeed.

Was Emmeline still under the false impression that Mr

Tennant wanted to elope with her? When would she realise the dreadful truth? Where was he taking her?

The horse's withers provided a resting place for her trembling hands whilst his powerful muscles propelled them up the winding road. He was moving steadily, and the rhythm was calming. She leaned forward to ease his load and breathed deeply of the salt air, alternately looking out to sea or up the hill as the path turned; but she saw only her sister's face. Could Lord Manning really help them? How?

Before long Francine trotted through the gates of Atlas Hall. Had the gatekeeper recognised her from the garden party? She doubted the gates were so easily opened to strangers. After dismounting, she gave Lightning a loving pat before the stable boy led the gelding off to cool down and rest. A footman led her to a small sitting room where she was soon joined by the butler. He bowed and did not scowl—did he also remember her?

"May I tell Lord Manning who—"

"I am Mrs Dashwood and my business is urgent. Thank you."

His brows lifted but he bowed again and strode off in a pressing manner while she removed her gloves.

The clatter of boots—several boots—met her ears before her eyes met the residents, Lord Manning and Mr Wheeler—and Mr Walford!

"Oh, how fortunate! I had thought you on the fishing outing today. I sought out Lord Manning in a desperate plea for help."

"My dear Mrs Dashwood," Mr Walford said, taking her arm. His eyes held a hint of alarm at seeing her state of distress.

Lord Manning reassured her. "I am always at your service, Mrs Dashwood. Here, come into my study and explain how we can assist."

She sank into the settee, took a breath, and gathered her thoughts.

"I do not know how you can assist. I can only tell you the situation and hope you may concoct an immediate remedy. It involves my sister," she said, giving Mr Walford a speaking look, "and more ... more of the shady business surrounding Mr Tennant."

Three heads nodded, and Lord Manning said, "Please, do go on. We were just discussing the ramifications and remedies of that situation."

"You may speak plainly," Mr Walford said. "I have confided all to these gentlemen, and they have provided further enlightenment."

"That is all well and good, but it is now much worse. It appears my sister has gone off with Mr Tennant, early this morning. By the note Florrie brought me I concluded that Emmeline believed she and the admiral were eloping. I know him too well to hope that to be true, and his marital status, well ..." Tears welled in her eyes. "I fear he will ransom her ... or worse. I may never see her again. Her poor children ..." She broke into sobs.

"This is an unexpected wrinkle," Mr Wheeler said with a frown. "Are you sure they are not gone north to Gretna?"

Francine took a deep breath to compose herself. "No, they are not. Florrie rode after them and no tracks led north from the crossroads. She then made for Seaview Place, with a leather case full of documents, one indicating her mother was still alive. I told her a little of what we know. My directions were for them all to remain in the house today, unseen, and for all callers to be refused, although notes should be taken in by the butler or the footman. A solicitor will be needed to explain the paperwork."

"Fortunately, Wheeler here is a man of law so he can

handle that when the time comes. As for the rest ..." Lord Manning rose and called down the hallway for a servant.

"Send a messenger to the harbour at once. Tennant's ship must not be allowed to leave its berth. If it has already departed, another ship must be sent in pursuit, with sturdy men—armed men."

"Geoffrey, I should go to the harbour also. As you approach by land, I should approach by sea so Tennant cannot escape." Mr Wheeler's look was resolute.

Lord Manning strode towards the window. "Yes, I believe you are right. Thank you for that viewpoint. Make haste—and Michael, do take care." They exchanged an intense look but Francine could not interpret the meaning.

"Oh, whilst at the harbour, inform the constable, and send the boy to find and retrieve our fishermen, wherever they might be. The fleet manager should know. Fetch them back to Seaview Place at once."

Mr Wheeler quitted the room, leaving the final arrangements to the others. The servant stood at the ready for the next command.

"Ready two horses. Walford and I shall make for a certain cove I know where smuggled goods are often landed and concealed, and from where it is rumoured captives are sometimes shipped out. There is a network of caves and tunnels. I explored it often in the past."

The servant bowed and turned on his heel but before he left the room Francine cried, "Wait! Ready my horse as well. I shall ride with the gentlemen."

The servant gave his master a quizzical look.

"Mrs Dashwood, it is far too dangerous—and the ride itself so treacherous, I cannot—"

Francine turned a steady gaze on Cecil Walford. "I *will* assist in the rescue of my sister, even if I must follow you on my own." Her eyes skewered him.

He cocked his head. "Creighton says she is a more-than-adequate horsewoman."

Lord Manning looked at her and when she did not waver said, "Then it is settled. Do as she requests." He ordered beverages and dried fruit and meat be readied. Boots and jackets were donned and the three were in the saddle in just over a quarter hour.

As they trotted along the lane to warm up the horses, Lord Manning said, "I also directed a maid to carry some hothouse fruits to Seaview Place. Within the basket is a note saying help is on the way from three directions, and that you are riding with us. I hope that will put the ladies there at ease, especially Miss Tennant. What a shock for her."

"It was indeed. She was quite distraught, and wished to go to her mother at once, but did not know where …"

Mr Walford said, "Rest assured, Mrs Dashwood, we will reunite them as soon as may be. What glorious happiness will be restored then, if we can remove Tennant from the picture."

"Remove him? Surely you will not—"

"A shot to the heart would be too easy," Lord Manning said with conviction. "We have settled on banishment as a fitting punishment, preferably to the wilds of New Holland or New South Wales. But first, we must rescue your sister." With that, he urged his mount on and led them along the clifftop lane at a gallop.

Once they reached the cart path, Francine conceded its difficulty had not been exaggerated. It had been trodden by many shod and booted feet and traversed by two-wheeled carts, but nothing wider. Mr Tennant's coach could not have negotiated this; he must have sent ahead for horses or brought them behind the coach, rendering this not an impulsive mistake but rather a thought-out strategy—which did not bode well for her sister.

Had Emmeline exaggerated her fortune to encourage a proposal? And instead encouraged a kidnapping?

They stopped at a point along the trail where activity could be seen on the rocky shoreline. Two skiffs were tied up and a finer ship anchored offshore. Waves surged and splashed around the cruel, jagged rocks. The approach by sea was equally treacherous.

"The *Windermere*, I wager," said Lord Manning. "Ready to sail for Calais. Fortunately, they have not yet departed; tracking them in France would be much more challenging, and the crossing can be arduous." He pulled out a spyglass. "We must accomplish our task here, now. Ah, another ship departs the harbour yonder. Wheeler is underway!" He chuckled to himself and returned his focus to the beach. "I do not see a woman, unless they have re-costumed her as a man. Not likely, and really no need. I have seen only two other men —oh, and there are two more. Now, are Tennant and your sister hidden in the caves? Or are they onboard the ship?"

The skiffs were making for the *Windermere*. The rescuers panicked for a moment, until they saw contraband being packed into the skiffs and ferried to shore. It was a fortuitous delay, repeated a few times, and allowed Wheeler's ship time to approach.

"Now, Walford, we must go down and give ground support." Lord Manning turned to Francine. "Mrs Dashwood, you must remain here with the horses. There do not appear to be more than a few men to contend with, and I wager a handful of bribes will turn them to our side. But in the event gunplay ensues, you must witness our progress ... or failure." His face turned grave. "If things go ill, ride to Sidmouth and report to the constable what has happened. Take both our horses with you. May we count on you?"

They stared at her. She was near to collapse, but then,

from somewhere inside, her courage rose. Her heart leapt and she said, "Of course. Give me the spyglass, and go. Godspeed."

The men made their way stealthily down the narrow twisting path. Francine tied the horses securely and situated herself so she could see the beach and the *Windermere*. The scene spread below her was like a living chessboard, and all the pieces were in motion. I really must learn to play chess.

CHAPTER TWENTY-SEVEN

Francine aimed the spyglass at the *Windermere*. Mr Tennant would not grovel in a cave when he could rest confidently on his ship. And her sister would complain loudly of damp and dirty accommodations—unless she had been drugged. Francine kept a keener eye on the ship, the better to see if her sister emerged from below deck.

Time crawled by as Wheeler's ship approached. The skiffs were still unloading contraband. She had heard of the free-traders, and at times had sympathy for them, getting food and goods to those who struggled and could not afford the high taxes being levied, but she had not given the issue deep thought. Having always lived inland, Francine never saw any free-traders that she was aware of. Then Mr Maher's face popped into her mind—not the type of free-trader she had pictured. Until now, she had gone through life quite unaware, of which she was now uncomfortably aware. Vowing to do more reading forthwith, she would become informed of the issues of the day so as to have more intelligent and thoughtful conversations with more intelligent and thoughtful people. Like Mr Creighton. His kind gift of the architecture book came to mind and her heart softened.

Cecil Walford and Lord Manning maneuvered along the rocky ledges leading to the caves. Then everything happened at once. Near the caves, Mr Walford and Lord Manning managed, with little struggle, to subdue the men who had been ferrying the goods ashore. In a trice, they were bound, hands and feet. Mr Wheeler's ship came alongside the *Windermere*. The admiral emerged from the cabin and doffed his hat in his most affable way, until Mr Wheeler drew a gun. Somehow two of Mr Wheeler's men had boarded the *Windermere* and taken up positions behind the admiral. Soon his hands were bound and he was taken below. Cecil Walford got the prisoners to the ship, and was soon at the helm himself. But there was no sign of Emmeline. Mr Walford hollered something to Lord Manning, who remained ashore. He then turned and began his ascent to where Francine waited. She looked through the spyglass again—still no Emmeline. Where was she? Was she safe?

Francine could do naught but stay with the horses until Lord Manning reached the cart path, breathing heavily after climbing the rocks. She offered him a drink which he took gratefully, but he waved away the food.

After he caught his breath, he spoke. "Well, Mrs Dashwood, the stars have smiled on us today. Wheeler will tow the *Windermere* into the harbour, where Tennant will be placed under arrest; and the list of charges is long indeed."

"My sister! Where is my sister?"

He patted her hand. "She is safe aboard the *Windermere*. Walford will attend her as they are towed in. No one could care more about her than he does. Yourself excepted, of course." He smiled and sat up straighter, his energy appearing to return. "She had been sedated but was coming about and appears to be unharmed. I recommended a physician examine her when she returns to Sidmouth. Walford will send for him when they reach the village."

He rose and untied his own horse, and Mr Walford's. "Here, let me assist you in mounting—"

"No need, my lord. These rocks make for handy mounting platforms." She was in the saddle in a twinkling.

He laughed. "Creighton was right. You certainly know what you are about with horses." He took his reins and the other horse's lead in hand and mounted, and they began the climb to the wider cliff-top lane. They made their way to Seaview Place under a sky streaked with gold and orange.

When they entered the house, a cheer went up. Mr Wheeler's party had just returned with the news that Mr Tennant was being held in a locked room at the hotel, a guard within and a guard without.

"Emmeline! Are you hurt?" Francine hastened to her sister who was sitting quietly on the chaise. Cecil Walford was seated next to her. Emmeline reached out and the sisters embraced.

"The doctor has pronounced her unharmed," Mr Walford said.

"How foolish I have been, Fran," Emmeline whispered.

"Now is not the time. Let us talk freely in the light of morning. For now, I am just happy to see you alive and well, and even smiling."

"We have Mr Walford to thank for much of that. He and Lord Manning—and Mr Wheeler—are heroes worthy of renown. I will tell you all in the morning."

Francine smiled to herself. *Emmeline has no idea that I was there too.*

Florrie approached her and Francine opened her arms to embrace her.

"Thank you for believing me, Mrs Dashwood. And comforting me. I am so grateful."

"You are a brave young lady and have a great adventure ahead of you," Francine said, placing her hands on Florrie's shoulders. "I shall continue to assist you however I can until you are united with your mother and these other issues are resolved." Their emotions overflowed through smiling tears.

"Smiling after such an ordeal?" Charles Creighton's voice came from behind her. "I believe there is a heroine here to thank as well—two heroines to be exact." The others turned at the sound of his voice. "Miss Tennant began the chase for Mrs Harrington, and Mrs Dashwood enlisted and accompanied the others along the way."

The party clapped and cheered again.

He reached surreptitiously for Francine's hand and squeezed it tightly. In a husky voice meant only for her ears he said, "You cannot know how relieved I am that you are returned in safety."

Francine faced him and their eyes each found a safe harbour. His admission emboldened her and she squeezed his hand in reply.

"I have you to thank for the adventure. Lord Manning would not have let me ride with them had you not given Mr Walford such a good account of my equestrienne skills," she whispered. They exchanged an affectionate look.

Sir John's voice rang above the others'. "We must have a full accounting of this adventure, tomorrow, here at Seaview, before the noontime. You too, gentlemen," he said, indicating Lord Manning and Mr Wheeler. "You are at the centre of this story it seems."

Lord Manning replied, "We shall join you then. Do not start without us!" With that they departed and the others made for their beds.

～

The next morning the sky held only a pale wash of pink. Emmeline and Francine rose early. After tea and toast, they made for the beach with some of the others. The Creightons and Mr Walford would swim, and the girls would sea bathe.

The sisters found a sunny spot and spread a blanket on the ground. Neither spoke for a time. The waves washed in and out with a regularity that was comforting.

Then Emmeline spoke. "Fran, can you forgive me all the trouble I've caused? I know I let you down. I did not guide you in society as I had promised. Indeed, I am the one in need of a guide. I am nothing but a fool."

"We came here to meet new people, Em. You met the admiral—rather, Mr Tennant—and I met Mr Maher. That does not say much for our socializing expertise, does it?" After a moment's silence, she said, "I think rather than meeting others who were new, we became renewed ourselves. Perhaps that is what draws people to the seaside after all? Renewal."

Emmeline nodded. "And I met someone who had been there all along, but I was too blind to see his true nature. Mr Walford is a heroic man. And not just to me. He explained the situation with Florrie's mother. Do you know all of what he is doing with his mills? He owns the town. He inherited it from his father but did not approve of how his father used those poor workers—even the children!—until they could give no more, just for the gain of personal wealth. Cecil has rebuilt the town, Fran. He built a hospital, an asylum, an orphanage, and a school, along with adequate and safe housing. Upgrading the mills and reducing danger were uppermost in his mind. The asylum is being rebuilt even now, and will be investigated and put under new management. He is a modest man with impeccable values. When we first met, I did not understand his somewhat direct manners. And I did not appreciate his sense of humour. They say love is blind, but I was too blind to see love."

They exchanged a long look of understanding.

"Did Mr Tennant convince you of an elopement? That is what we deduced from the note Florrie retrieved from the hearth."

"He did. At first. But when we did not take the road north, I asked questions. Then he said it would be quicker to elope to France as his ship was ready to sail. It was chilly in the carriage and he offered me brandy from a small flask. I believe it was something other than just brandy. I swooned. I did not fully pass out but I could not think clearly. I hardly remember riding with him on the horse or making my way down the rocks. The sea air revived me a little and then I was put aboard the ship, where the swaying of the waves lulled me into a deep slumber. When I awoke, Mr Walford was there. He gave me some coffee, which I usually don't care for, but this time the bitter taste was welcome and I began to feel energy in my limbs again. We talked all the way back to the harbour. Fran, what do you think will become of Mr Tennant? Will he go to trial?"

"They talked of banishment, if he would sign over all his finances to his wife and testify that he was abandoning her; only then could she be granted a divorce. That is their leverage. If he does not agree, he will be prosecuted. And who knows how that might turn out? He does have some high connections. Or he could hang."

"What a mess I have made," Emmeline said, dropping her head and dragging her hand in the sand.

"You did not make the mess, Em. You walked into it, and it nearly engulfed you."

"Yes, I suppose you are right."

"Fran, do not be annoyed, but it puts me in mind of a

passage I had never thought would apply to me. May I share it?"

"Certainly. From Miss Burney I assume?"

Emmeline smiled. "It says *'Imagination took the reins, and reason, slow-paced though sure-footed, was unequal to a race with so eccentric and flighty a companion.'* I have been so flighty, so blind. How can I ever thank all of you?"

"Our reward is that you were saved in time. And the joy to come for Florrie and her mother."

"Indeed. That poor girl."

After a few minutes of silence, Francine ventured to say, "So Mr Walford? You think differently of him now?"

"I do. I most certainly do. And what of you Fran? You and Mr Creighton appear to have grown close during this holiday. He seems more recovered from his loss."

Francine tried to hide her smile, but her sister knew her too well. "We have become close. I might venture to say good friends. He is kind. Thoughtful. A good father to his son, and a fair guardian and adviser to the girls, and to me. This holiday has shown me how dependent I was on others, and especially on Elinor—for years. Oh, I love my girls very well but I burdened her with duties that should not have been hers until now when she is running her own household. That was badly done on my part. I felt more like one of my girls than their mother. During our residence here, Mr Creighton consulted me on decisions for our young people, and that made me think."

Emmeline nodded thoughtfully.

"The horse riding—Em, I cannot imagine why I gave it up all these years. It has so renewed me. I hope Sir John might have a lady's mount he can lend me from time to time. I have also decided to follow my interest in architecture, an interest Mr Creighton shares. And whilst watching the rescue scene play out, I vowed to learn the game of chess."

"The rescue scene? You were there?"

"Yes, but I will explain later for the whole group. I am glad you and I had this chance to talk in confidence about these things that are not for others' ears."

"And here come the others!" Emmeline said with a laugh.

Soon after their return from the beach, Lord Manning and Mr Wheeler arrived. Francine arranged for refreshments to be served in the garden and the group gathered at the tables there.

After the situation had been explained and questions asked and answered, Mr Walford spoke to the subject on everyone's mind.

"What shall become of Mr Tennant, you may ask? Gentlemen, it is time we make for the hotel and conclude this business. Mr Tennant shall have his choice of two evils, and we shall drive him hard towards the choice we wish him to make, the choice we feel is in the best interest of Florrie and her mother."

"I must come with you," Florrie declared.

Mr Creighton's eyes softened. "Miss Tennant, I think that would be unwise. He should not set eyes on you again, nor you on him. The break is made. It will soon be time for you to bond with your mother instead. It is best to let Mr Tennant go. Can you do that?"

Florrie's eyes grew wide and filled with tears. Mrs Jennings put an arm around her shoulders. "My dear girl, I always say, *'keep such memories as bring you pleasure and discard the rest'*. You will reunite with your mother soon and have your whole life ahead of you. He does not deserve your farewell."

The gentlemen, in a show of unity, all made for the hotel, even James. They returned in a disturbingly short time.

"He did not escape from you, did he?" Mrs Jennings asked in alarm. Emmeline clutched Francine's hand.

Mr Walford looked at Emmeline and then at the group. "No, he did not. But he is smart enough to know when he is bested. He made the choice we had hoped for, and Wheeler has gone to draw up the papers even now. Wheeler is also reading through your papers, Miss Tennant, and will advise you on financial and property matters in the days to come. He and Lord Manning will join us for dinner tonight, at which time we shall begin arrangements for your mother to return to you. Do you wish her to come here?"

"Yes, I think that would be best, if Mr Wheeler agrees. She and I can live at Bellevue, or even at the London Inn if Bellevue has too many painful memories for her. She likely has worse memories from the asylum. I cannot bear to think of it. His utter cruelty. I must attend to the household in the meantime. There are changes to be made. How soon can we expect her?"

CHAPTER TWENTY-EIGHT

*T*he remaining days of their holiday passed just as desired. Promenades, sea bathing, another ball, lectures, and concerts filled the time pleasantly—as did fishing for the gentlemen, and painting for Mrs Whittaker. But two of the activities held a special place in the memories of some of the party.

Lord Manning kept his promise of hawking on horseback for those interested. The hawkers included himself, Margaret, Florrie, James, and Mrs Dashwood. The watchers, also on horses, were Mr Creighton, Mr Wheeler, Miss Rose, and Sir John. All rode through woods and meadows, along the cliffs and into the hills, stopping at various places to fly the hawks.

"Oh, Mama, might there be some way we could fly hawks at Barton?"

"I am as thrilled as you with this new activity, but we have neither horses nor hawks," Mrs Dashwood replied with a rueful smile.

"You shall always be welcome at Atlas Hall, ladies," Lord Manning assured them. "Is there another seaside holiday in your future?"

"I sincerely hope so," Mrs Dashwood answered. "I shall miss not only the hawking, but also the cliffs and the sky and the sea itself. And this wonderful horse. He is not sour, as so many get who are pressed into service for a variety of riders of dubious skills. What could be more odious for a horse?"

"He does seem a fine mount," Mr Creighton observed. "And unusually suited for you. It seems you move and think as one."

"We do," she replied, her eyes alight. "He is my perfect horse. My heart breaks to leave him."

Charles Creighton nodded thoughtfully.

After a splendid day of hawking and a fine dinner at Atlas Hall, there were a few more days of leisure, including one which took place aboard the sleek sailing vessel that Michael Wheeler had used during Emmeline's rescue. They had all been unaware at the time that he owned the craft, the *Vida Bella*, and was a master of sailing.

"Because circumstances conspired to deny you the pleasure of a cruise, you must accept my invitation to come aboard my ship, which shall soon call the *Windermere* her sister if my negotiations are successful." Mr Wheeler had said at the dinner.

Those interested in seeing Sidmouth from the sea boarded the *Vida Bella* one fine afternoon. They had been out of the harbour less than a quarter hour when a ghastly looking Margaret approached her mother.

"Mama, I do not think the ginger is helping. And the smell of the peppermint nearly made me wretch. Oh, what can I do? This is awful." She leaned over the rail and gave up the contents of her stomach, ginger and all.

"Poor girl," Mr Walford said in sympathy. "Look at the

horizon. Or look at the shore. See if that avails any relief, Miss Dashwood."

Margaret did her best but nothing improved; she fell to her knees and curled into a ball.

"Let me inform Wheeler," Mr Creighton said. "Perhaps she can be got back to shore. Fortunately we are not too far out yet."

And that is just what was done. A suffering Margaret, accompanied by her friends Florrie and Rose, was taken ashore in a skiff. Francine was hard-pressed to let her daughter go alone, being ill.

"The sooner she is ashore, the sooner she will recover," Mr Creighton said. "Your presence will have no effect either way. Look! There is Mrs Jennings waiting to take them all under her commodious wing. Do not give up this chance to see the south coast from the water, I beg you. Besides, your sister may have need of you. I have an inkling a surprise is afoot," he said with a sly grin.

"What are you up to?" she asked, not sure how to read that smile.

"It is not me who is up to something, but all shall be revealed shortly."

Francine did not suffer as her daughter did and enjoyed the sea and the spray as the *Vida Bella* made way along the coast when once again free of the harbour. Cutting through the waves or alternately riding them up and down was not unlike being on a horse, in her mind, and the view of the cliffs and the hills was glorious.

"Mr Creighton, I now see what you meant about being amongst the elements of water and sky and wind. It is most refreshing."

"So we are of one mind in this matter. I am pleased."

"On this, yes, and on other matters as well. Our shared

interest in architecture, and our love of horses, give us much to talk about, do they not?"

"I could talk to you for hours about nothing at all, Mrs Dashwood—and probably be the wiser for it!"

They laughed together, a deep and freeing laugh of the soul.

A ringing bell caused the passengers to turn and move to the center of the deck, where Emmeline sat next to Mr Walford, both enjoying the breeze in their faces.

He said to those aboard, "My lord, ladies, and gentlemen, I have called you together as my dear friends to witness a deed of derring-do." He paused for effect, and the onlookers exchanged puzzled expressions.

"I shall now perform a task fraught with risks, both physical and spiritual." Mr Walford was obviously delighted at having everyone's attention. Emmeline sat forward with interest as the others gathered around.

"In spite of many wishes coming true these past days, and wrongs being righted, I have still one dream that I now dare to pursue." He slipped from his chair onto one knee to face Emmeline, pulling a small pouch from his pocket.

"My dear, brave lady. When last I broached this topic, you assured me in no uncertain terms that you and I did not share the same vision of happiness. But now, in consideration of the last few days—especially our time spent on the water—I am taking a great gamble that your heart has taken a different turn. Emmeline Harrington, will you consent to be my wife?"

All on board fell silent. Emmeline's eyes grew wider than Francine had ever seen them, then a smile broke over her sister's face like welcome sunlight.

"I am speechless. I had not expected this. However can I answer … except to say yes! Yes, I will marry you, my patient, kind and heroic friend."

He reached for Emmeline's hand and placed upon her

heart finger a golden ring with an amethyst stone surrounded by diamonds—a ring so beautiful even a queen could not but treasure it. She gazed at the ring and then at Mr Walford. "Thank you for not giving up hope as I muddled my way to you."

He grasped both her hands and kissed them, and then kissed her lips as their well-wishers clapped and cheered.

"My courage has been rewarded," he said, with some astonishment. "Thank you, friends, for sharing in our happiness. We will inform you of arrangements as they are made by this woman who knows how things ought to be done and will do them all with finesse and beauty."

Emmeline blushed at his referral to that first dinner and her brusque dismissal of his professed romantic interest and his dinner manners. She exchanged a look of understanding with Francine, whose eyes sparkled with tears of joy.

July —

My dear Elinor,

My sensibilities have been tested both high and low. I can hardly believe my own daring and endurance. Emmeline thought she was eloping with the admiral, but his true intent was kidnapping! Lord Manning, Mr Walford, and I managed to rescue her before any harm was done. All is well that ends well, and this has ended very well indeed! Emmeline is engaged to Mr Wolford. He has proved himself to be a man everyone should esteem highly. He asked for her hand in front of all of us while cruising on Mr Wheeler's ship—all of us except Margaret (and Rose and Florrie) because Margaret quickly developed severe seasickness and had to be taken ashore. This does not bode well for her idea of becoming a sea captain's wife.

We did also go hawking on horseback and Margaret and I have both taken an immense liking to the sport. We have neither the equipment (horses and hawks) nor the means, but Lord Manning says we are always welcome at Atlas Hall. I also wish I had the means to bring home the horse I rode while here, Lightning. But of course we lack the funds to purchase him or to keep him. It breaks my heart but so it is.

This has been a most pleasant journey and I have filled my holiday journal with so many events and observations. We leave in a few days and I look forward to seeing you and Marianne again and telling you ever so much more about our adventures here. Please share this news with Marianne and let us make arrangements to meet as soon as may be. I hope you both might also manage to stay for a few days at Barton. There is much to tell.

Your loving mother

After a heartfelt farewell to their new friends—which for Francine included Lightning—the holiday party made for home. The young ladies had much to talk about—the adventures of their journey and their future plans—whilst the older sisters had much upon which to reflect.

The reunion of Florrie and Isabel had torn at the hearts of every mother and daughter who witnessed it, with tears for all the years lost, but joy at the reunion and the possibilities for the future. As Isabel had spent very little time at Bellevue and had no unpleasant memories attached to the place, she and Florrie—after having it stripped of anything that might remind them of the unscrupulous former owner—moved in and began the process of making it their own. But not before Lord Manning and Michael Wheeler witnessed that former owner boarding a southbound ship and sailing over the horizon.

Florrie made plans to visit Barton Cottage in the autumn. At Mr Creighton's suggestion, Francine invited Isabel and Florrie to join them in London during the next season for the young ladies' official coming out. The girls' excitement knew no bounds.

The day before the travelers departed, Lord Manning received word of his father's passing. He had called it a blessing, although it caused great sorrow—he was now alone in the world, with no brothers or sisters. His good friend Michael Wheeler remained steadfast.

~

As the carriages lurched their way northward, accompanied by their esteemed outriders Charles and James Creighton and Cecil Walford, the young ladies exhausted their topics of conversation and dozed contentedly.

"I am so grateful that Margaret was able to experience such a great adventure. Without the kindness of these friends and relations it would have been beyond my financial capabilities."

Emmeline nodded. "It was an opportunity for all of us, Fran. I believe you and I perhaps learned as much as the girls, yes?"

"You are right, Em. I feel … a changed woman. Not changed at my core; but perhaps I have rediscovered my core and found an inner strength I did not know I possessed. Returning to Barton Cottage will be like coming back to a home I shall now see in a very different light."

"Allow me to paraphrase Heraclitus," said Emmeline. "*A woman who has traveled cannot return to the same home, because she's not the same woman and it will not feel like the same home.*"

They were silent for a few minutes, then Francine asked, "What of your wedding, Em? Are you sure of going ahead with it?"

Emmeline looked surprised, and then laughed. "Of course I am sure. I have never been more sure in my life. Cecil not only offers kindness and affection and friendship—and financial security—but the opportunity for great adventure as we work together in the rebuilding of the mill town into a model for all manufacturing towns. He has great vision, which I share. I am most eager to join him in his work, and he welcomes me doing so. That is far more exciting than being twirled about a dance floor—or being left in the woods!" She laughed at those memories, and Francine could now join in her merriment.

"I am very happy for you. It sounds everything wonderful and you shall be busy indeed refreshing Southleigh *and* traveling to the Midlands. I foresee no boredom or loneliness in your future, and I hope for many invitations to Southleigh."

"You are always welcome, at any time. You need no invitation—you and your children; and might I venture to say I see you being accompanied also by Mr Creighton?"

Francine's cheeks warmed with pleasure at that thought. "Indeed, with no carriage I shall need to rely on him or Sir John. It is too far for a lady to journey alone on horseback, is it not?"

"Cecil has requested the license and we hope to marry by the end of the month. Our honeymoon will, of course, be to the North, and a time spent in the Midlands at Hawthorn Hall for my son's wedding. Oh, Fran, everything has turned out so well for all of us."

"It has indeed." They locked arms and each retreated into her own pleasant thoughts whilst the carriage made its way back to Barton Cottage.

Francine and Margaret were welcomed home by Elinor and Marianne, and their husbands. Several dinners at Barton Cottage and at Barton Park were needed to regale them and

Lady Middleton of all the seaside adventures. Elinor brought along some of her newer watercolour paintings, with a promise to paint one of the seaside. She and Edward hoped to visit Sidmouth before harvest. Marianne showed off the baby clothes they had all been making. Lady Middleton's needlework was far beyond insipid, and she generously shared her talent in teaching Elinor and Marianne. A warmth began to grow between them as they bonded over children and babies to come.

The license was approved in a timely manner and the wedding of Emmeline and Cecil took place one warm August morning in the chapel at Southleigh. Francine attended her sister and Charles Creighton attended his long-time friend. James Creighton, Elinor and Edward, Marianne and Colonel Brandon and Margaret witnessed the ceremony, as did the Whittakers, the Middletons, and Mrs Jennings. Emmeline's son traveled for the occasion, as did Cecil's daughter.

After the ceremony, they all sat in the shade of the arbour, looking out towards the lake, enjoying fruits and cured meats before the heat became overwhelming. The bride and groom walked along a garden pathway, hand in hand.

"Well, Lucretia, we did partially succeed in our mission to have both sisters married by Michaelmas."

"Even though it took a trip to the seaside for Emmeline to recognise that her true love was here all along," Mrs Jennings replied with a merry laugh.

"Oh, I think that recognition would have come even if none of us had journeyed south," Mrs Whittaker replied.

"Do you, Cecelia? I do not. Often it takes seeing a familiar person in a very different setting in order to see them—you know—in a more romantic light. Do you not agree, Mr Creighton?"

"A change of perspective can indeed be enlightening," he replied. "And of course, being rescued must certainly elevate that suitor in the eyes of his lady." With a smile he turned to Francine. "Might we test my theory, Mrs Dashwood, by gazing at the lake from a closer viewpoint—say from that handsome stone bench?"

Francine's new strength had not yet conquered her tendency to blush and her colour was high. "I would enjoy that, Mr Creighton." She rose and took his offered arm and they followed the curving path that led to the lakeside bench. The antics of the swans and ducks provided amusement and the swathes of reeds and lilies framed the setting with colour and texture. Since their return from the coast, Mr Creighton had shared other books on architecture and landscape design and Francine was taking in new terms and ideas.

"Your sister appears very happy," Mr. Creighton observed as they eyed the couple returning to the arbour.

"I believe she is. I am so grateful to everyone who made our journey possible, and to those who rescued her from the clutches of ... well, I shall not even say his name. Yes, Emmeline's dreams have come true and I believe she and Cecil will be great partners in his project in the North, do you not agree?"

"I do," he said. The words rang out and hung in the air, seeming to carry special significance. "And there is something I hope you might also agree to with those very words." He took her hand in his. "Mrs Dashwood ... Francine ... over the past weeks I have come to believe I cannot truly be happy without the pleasure of your company, each and every day." His face was earnest, his eyes beckoned. "May I dare to hope you feel the same way about me?"

She caught her breath but spoke forthrightly. "I do," she

said, overjoyed at a conclusion she had desired but not dared to hope for. "I do feel the same. I love you. You have demonstrated your fine character every day I have known you."

"I regret I can no longer ask this on bended knee, however it is no less heartfelt—Francine, will you do me the honour of becoming my wife?"

Her eyes filled with joyful tears. "Nothing could make me happier than to spend every day with you, Charles." He took her hands in his and kissed them.

"And what of Margaret?"

"I will raise her as my own. She will have a home with us for as long as she wishes."

"That is a great comfort, Charles. And James shall be with us as well?"

"Of course."

His eyes glinted. "Perhaps, on our seaside honeymoon, we might also look for a seaside cottage, to make frequent visits there a part of our new life?"

"Oh, Charles! I should like that very much!" He took one of his hands away, reached into his pocket, and brought out a ring.

"A small symbol of my eternal love." He placed a platinum ring on her finger. The aquamarine stone edged with peridot chips glinted in the light and reflected the very colours of the sea, and of her eyes.

"Oh, Charles, it is lovely."

He took her face in his hands and leaned in, kissing her in a way that was tender but with the urgency of a flame ignited.

They turned at the sound of clapping and cries of approbation from their friends.

Then, of a sudden, a beaming Margaret appeared from around the house, leading ... could it be?... Lightning? Francine rose from the bench.

"Is that ... is it really ...?"

"The very horse. Your perfect horse. Let him be a reminder of the beginning of our friendship and love, and a symbol of the ongoing adventure in our marriage."

She threw her arms around Charles and he picked her up, twirling her about in their joint happiness. They walked up to the group and Charles took the lead from Margaret. He handed it to Francine whilst he caressed her cheek with a kiss. She rubbed Lightning's withers and kissed his nose, and was rewarded with a nicker. Then she looked at her daughter.

"Margaret ... you knew?"

"We all knew. It was the most difficult secret to keep!" she exclaimed, laughing with Charles. "I was bursting to tell you. Like Mrs Jennings says, if we have secrets here in the country, we do not keep them for long."

"Cecelia, our work is complete. Both sisters shall be married by Michaelmas."

"Indeed. This has been one of our most successful ventures!" Mrs Whittaker winked at her longtime friend.

With that, they turned their eyes on Margaret. "Next!"

THE END

Thank you for reading this book.
Please consider leaving an honest review at online or physical stores
or at other reader/fan page sites. Your review can help others decide
if they, too, might enjoy this story about Mrs. Dashwood.

ACKNOWLEDGMENTS

So many people helped bring this book to publication.

Many thanks to my beta readers, editors, and consultants: Allie Cresswell, Heidi Herman-Kerr, Cheryl Krutzfeldt.

Much appreciation to members of James River Writers and Park Avenue Authors writers groups, and the many online writing and publishing and Jane Austen reader groups for their feedback and support.

I must of course also acknowledge Miss Jane Austen herself, who remains a powerful and timeless source of inspiration, comfort, and entertainment for us all.

ABOUT THE AUTHOR

SALLIANNE HINES is a fan of all things Austen, and is an advocate for animals, children, and simplicity. She writes fiction and nonfiction. Sallianne is a lifelong horsewoman, parent of three, grandparent of eight, and shares her home with a bossy cat and two dogs. They all live together in a little house on the prairie. Sallianne believes we must each be the hero or heroine of our own story, and trusts it is never too late.

Upcoming works include: Other Austenesque sequels and side stories will follow as part of Sallianne's *"Mothers/Sisters/Friends Collection."* Margaret Dashwood's story is next! Two other nonfiction books are also upcoming.

Other works by this author include: *Love & Stones*, the story of a contemporary Austen heroine (2020); *Her Summer at Pemberley*, the story of Kitty Bennet after *Pride and Prejudice* (2020); and *About Editing, an essential guide for authors* (2023). Sallianne is editor at www.quinnediting.com.

To learn about new releases and to sign up for a quarterly newsletter go to

www.salliannehines.com

Made in the USA
Monee, IL
12 August 2023

40916353R00146